THE LAND OF
A THOUSAND GODS

A ghostly tale of Vikings, retribution and an
epic journey across a world of strange beauty,
mystery and terrifying secrets to be unlocked.
An unknown world inhabited with gods who
existed before the time of memory!

BY

D. J. CALLISTER

This publication has been supported by

ISBN No. 978-1-5262-0671-8

Published by D J Callister Publications

Printed by The Copyshop, IOM

Foreword

Santon, Isle of Man. The year, 798A.D.

Beginning at sunset the first day of August until sunset the following day, Celtic people would celebrate the ancient festival of the Feast of the First Fruits which marked the onset of harvesting fields glowing with the warm, earthy colours of early-ripening grain.

It was the point of the end of summer and the coming of autumn, a forewarning the days would slowly become shorter as the darker daylight hours began to encroach.

It was a festival dedicated to the great Celtic sun-god Lugh and indicated the final decline of his diminishing powers before he surrendered himself to the moon-goddess Aine.

The sun-god was metaphorically cut down by gathering the crops at harvest and then reborn in bread made from harvest grains. The first sheaf of corn was ceremonially reaped, threshed, milled and baked into a loaf. Once the sun-god in the form of grain had been sacrificed, the loaf was proffered to other gods as a symbolic offering of his bounty.

On the Isle of Man a great fair at Santon Village was to take place on Sunday the second day of August. More than half the population of Mann would undertake the long journey to the village to combine buying and selling produce and livestock with a day of feasting, entertainment and laughter, and to witness the solemn ceremony of marriage contracts presented and accepted.

They also travelled to take part in one of the most important of all the four great Celtic Fire Festivals, one which defined the changing of the seasons: Lammas Day.

Chapter One

Friday 31st July 798

Just before noon the sun was unable to penetrate the heavy grey mist of rain lying across the rocky slate cliffs tops of Port Grenaugh or the thick sea-fog covering its sheltered bay.

Brief bursts of lightning cracked and flashed over the headland as the sky darkened still further with the imminent arrival of the storm that had been building hours earlier far out to sea. A jagged lightning bolt some two or three miles long flickered in the tall cumulonimbus clouds, then lit up the sky with a brilliant flash of blue as it struck and rendered into thousands of pieces a massive boulder lying on the beach below the coastal promontory fort of nearby Cronk ny Merriu.

Despite the mist and rain, the day had begun stifling hot and muggy. At this exposed, inhospitable location, where the wild landscape was diverse and overwhelmingly beautiful, a lookout from Santon Village was assigned to keep watch, day and night, summer and winter for danger in any form approaching the island from the seaward side of the promontory fort. But today the sentry's gaze was fixed uneasily not on the sea but on a Manx shearwater whose black and white body was gliding effortlessly over the rise and fall of the surf.

He watched the bird approach the swelling waves at speed, then fly low over the water before diving and riding on the white capped breakers. Then the bird soared into the air, and the sentry's mouth became dry with fear as he saw the curved shape of four individual eyes clearly outlined in the black feathers on its back. He knew then with certainty the shearwater was Cliodna of the fair hair, daughter of the great Manx sea-god Manannan-beg-mac-y-Lleir.

Cliodna, a capricious sea-goddess and shape-shifter who liked to assume the appearance of a seabird, controlled the rain, wind and fog, and to catch a glimpse of the weather deity was a known portent of death. As a few heavy drops of rain splattered the sentry's upturned face, he was afraid the goddess had invoked the incoming storm to punish his village for an unspecified wrongdoing.

At the precise moment the winds came shrieking over the rocky cliffs, a rainstorm erupted from the ragged storm clouds swirling overhead. Lightning split the sky and terror tore through the sentry's heart when he saw illuminated in a shaft of light, the shearwater staring intently at him before it made a sweeping descent over the fort.

As he turned and ran through the gate at the landward side of the building he thought he heard a taunting voice reverberating in the wind, a voice that mocked him mercilessly as he ran.

Even though it was not quite noon, the quickly fading light dancing briefly over the crouching shadows of small trees made the sentry shiver with fear. Moments later the gloomy sky enveloped him in almost total darkness.

As he sprinted along the coastal footpath to Santon, the frightened man was filled with an overwhelming sense of panic when he saw the dim shape of a hare crossing the path in front of him. Another unlucky portent!

An hour or so after he'd departed, winds of up to a hundred miles an hour gusted wildly around the unattended lookout post, winds that lashed the Irish Sea into fifteen to twenty foot high waves that pounded relentlessly around the coastline. *But the sentry was not there to observe the waves that thundered ferociously into Port Grenaugh Bay and he was not there to light the beacons that would alert the settlement at Santon of an approaching enemy.*

Chapter Two

The Beginning

Surrounded on three sides by thickly wooded sloping hills, the village of Santon sat in the heart of a fertile green valley that had changed very little since time began. In sharp contrast to the rest of the valley basin, the eastern side lay flat and open and had the crystal clear waters of the Crogga River flowing gently alongside the settlement.

Only moments after the early morning sun had appeared from behind hills capped with a thick mist, the air resounded with the bellowing of cattle waiting to be milked, crowing cockerels, barking dogs, crying babies, screaming children and harassed mothers shouting at fathers quickly leaving the uproar of the roundhouses for the sanctuary of outdoors.

The atmosphere, already oppressively warm and sticky, was laden with the overpowering scent of wild honeysuckle when Agneish with eyes still heavy with sleep stumbled out of her father's house, followed immediately by a large, rough-haired brown dog who stopped for a moment to scratch inside his ears.

She sat down on an old tree stump shaded by a huge tramman tree which partly protected their house from direct sunlight during the hot summer months. Her father refused to chop it down no matter how much the tree creaked in a strong wind, as he, like many islanders, believed in the magical powers of the tramman to act as a charm against the influence of witches.

Yawning and rubbing her eyes, Agneish irritably pulled her thin woollen shift away from her damp skin, then looked up as flashes of lightning seemed to leap through the mists lying on top of the hills. She could smell the rain waiting to fall as cracks of thunder began to rumble around the valley.

A few yards away, her Aunt Creena was inspecting racks of smoked fish, selecting the best to include in the wedding feast of her nephew Bradan and his-bride-to-be, Kikil, the marriage ceremony to take place during the great fair on Sunday. As she turned her attention to a cow-hide curing over a fire piled high with willow branches and wet leaves, Creena also noticed the flashes of lightning and Agneish could hear her shouting to her eldest son to check the lobster pots with his brothers in case the threatening storm set in for the day. Her aunt uttered a little prayer to any god who might be listening that all would go well for the Lammas Festival, her nephew's wedding and the Santon Fair.

Although she had started to cough as dense black smoke drifted towards her from her aunt's fire, Agneish had to laugh at the bad-tempered expression on her cousin's face as he kicked over a pot of water boiling on a stone-fire ring set out in front of Creena's house. Fogolt had made arrangements to meet a girl from another village this morning and had planned to ask if he could take her to Sunday's festival.

'You're a cross-patch today Fogolt,' Agneish called out as her cousin stomped angrily away.

As he turned round and scowled threateningly at Agneish, Gormand and Hamond dropped the fishing nets they were mending and rushed to catch up with their older brother. Eighteen year old Fogolt could be very quick with his fists if anyone annoyed him.

Although the sun had barely risen, the settlement rang with the sound of noisy, idle chatter as people gossiped about their plans to celebrate the festival.

Women from the community had decorated the interior of the village *keeill* with bundles of bound sheaves of ripened harvest grains and wild flowers in the vibrant colours of the sun-god of gold, yellow and the deepest orange. The stone altar had been left empty in readiness for Sunday morning when a freshly baked loaf from the first sheaf of corn would be placed upon it as an offering to the gods.

The addition of several baskets containing generous varieties of fruit and vegetables laid on the rough stone floor in front of the altar were further contributions they hoped would please the deities.

Engus, Agneish's father was both chieftain and spiritual advisor of the village: however he and the community of Santon, like many Manx people while nodding their heads towards Christianity, unobtrusively carried on the old Manx way of life and worshipped the Celtic gods. Even so, on Sunday a hermit Irish priest living in the tiny cell adjoining the small *keeill* of Malew would arrive at Santon to give a blessing to the marriage of his son.

Bradan and Kikil had made a public announcement of their betrothal a year and a day ago and at Lammas they would seal their marriage contract with their cross and swap their silver betrothal rings, each engraved with two hearts and their initials, from right hand to left, as was the tradition.

At the sound of noisy, high-spirited laughter Agneish looked over her shoulder and giggled when she saw Cane whispering in her brother's ear. She knew he would be teasing Bradan about his wedding night. As the two men's laughter filled the air she hoped her brother's best friend from childhood, would be able to keep him sober and sensible until the ceremony.

Kikil was a quiet, pretty girl and Bradan had been in love with her for as long as he could remember. The day he'd asked her to be his wife Bradan had told his sister that Kikil was so beautiful that just to look at her made his heart sing.

Agneish knew their mother Voirrey, was delighted that tomorrow the moon would be at its fullest, which was a good portent for Sunday's wedding, as the added light from the moon would cast aside the shadows and repel evil spirits.

Behind her, her mother stepped out of the large entrance to their roundhouse and pointed silently in the direction of the herd of bellowing cows. Agneish didn't need a reminder from Voirrey's sharp tongue that milking them was one of her chores.

Her father appeared in the doorway and together they looked at their daughter. At seventeen she was a tall, slender young woman with eyes the colour of green agate and bright, silky red hair which hung to just below her waist.

As they watched her cut across the common land adjacent to their roundhouse with her dog, Catat, hard on her heels, Engus leaned slightly towards his wife and slowly inhaled the fragrant scent of the herbs and oils she used on her hair. Although it was still very early in the day, Voirrey had already fastened yellow glass beads to the ends of her long, reddish-brown curls, darkened her eyebrows and lips with berry juice and drawn a line of charcoal around her gold-flecked green eyes.

Voirrey looked up at her husband and smiled with contentment. With his shoulder-length black hair and drooping moustache streaked with grey, lively eyes and thick, full dark beard plaited into thin braids, she judged Engus to be still a very handsome man.

Like numerous people of Manx nationality, Engus was small in stature but powerfully built and there were many in the village who could remember that in his prime he could fell a man with just one blow from his massive fist.

Engus was not only Santon's chieftain and spiritual advisor, but also law-maker and war-leader and his final verdict on all matters was absolute.

He insisted lookouts were on watch on the nearby headlands at all times for sightings of unfamiliar ships and, as most of the settlement was united by a strong blood-bond, he felt the villagers had a moral obligation to help each other in times of sickness, famine and acts of aggression from another village. Engus had urged them to have pick-handles, axes or wooden staffs at the ready in case they would have to defend this year's crops from opportunists thieves during Sunday's fair.

As he absentmindedly rubbed his legs where the coarse weave of his woollen trousers was scratching his skin, Voirrey reached up and slightly adjusted the positioning of the bronze brooch he's pinned to the shawl hung over his left shoulder and felt a small glow of satisfaction when she saw he was wearing the necklace of amber beads she'd given him to honour his birthdate.

Engus was quick-thinking and hard-working and the village had prospered under his leadership. In the same way as the rest of the community, he worshipped the fertile soil of the valley, honoured the sun, the source of light and was troubled by the darkness which he associated with danger and death.

Santon had an industrious population of farmers, craftsmen and coastal fishermen. The close proximity of the sea gave them access to seaweed to add nutrients to the soil and fish to eat, while the rivers supplied trout and, occasionally, salmon.

They grew vegetables and fruit, and if times were good they ate well on pork, beef, mutton and chicken.

Cattle and sheep were put out to pasture on common grazing ground and their pigs fed in woods within reach of the village. Before the cold, bleak gloomy nights of winter set in, spare animals would be slaughtered so breeding stock could survive on what little grazing ground remained.

Surplus meat and fish would be wood-smoked or preserved in salt. Peas and beans would be dried and meal stored for grinding to make into flat unleavened bread. Each family would make sure their hearth was stacked high with enough peat and wood to see them through the long, winter months.

Suddenly Engus noticed a crowd had gathered near the Crogga River and without a word he left Voirrey and ran towards the growing numbers of villagers staring up at the sky. If the coming rains were as heavy as the murky clouds overhead threatened and the Crogga overflowed, many of the ripened ears of corn and rows of oats and barley planted near the river for undemanding simple irrigation would be destroyed.

Life was always a harsh struggle but this year the gods had been generous. The crops had flourished and although the summer had been exceptionally hot, the dreaded scourges of smallpox, typhus and cholera hadn't appeared.

Voirrey had followed Engus and listened for a moment to the raised voices of the men trying to resolve the best way to appease the gods if appalling weather meant they couldn't gather-in the crops in time to honour the Lammas Festival. Then shaking her head, she decided to return to the roundhouse.

Their home, like all the others in the village was entirely enclosed by a wide, shallow ditch and, as she re-crossed the walkway over the water, she noticed part of the timber fence erected around the perimeter of the ditch was in urgent need of repair. Flying hooves from Santon's milling herd of cattle repeatedly striking against the wooden posts, had recently caused considerable damage. She must mention it to her husband.

The threshold of the south-facing door was solidly paved with large stepping stones and Voirrey took care not to slip on the lichen growing on the damp stonework.

Inside the roundhouse was a series of circular corridors, the first one set aside for stabling livestock and storing grain. She halted here for several seconds, listening for rustling noises in the mounds of stored cereals, smiling when she was unable to hear anything. Engus must have disposed of the nests of field mice as she had asked.

She continued on through a doorway which led to passageways of various widths with each corridor having a different function. Bedrooms, larders and, despite the only light inside the house being created by rush-lights or the glow from a fire, areas had been set aside for spinning and weaving. She paused in the weaving room to pull a blanket out of a wooden storage chest, one of four lovingly-spun, woven and dyed as a wedding gift for Bradan and Kikil. She pressed it to her cheek before placing it back in the chest.

At the bottom of the chest were two thick brown sheepskin rugs, the dark fleece the natural colour of the Manx long-horned Loghtyn sheep. She knew Kikil would be delighted with them.

She moved onto the spacious inner room, its ample proportions and blazing open fire providing the main social area of their home.

The fire, formed by a bed of flat stones set into a shallow depression in the middle of the room, gave the family both heat and light and was kept burning twenty four hours a day. The smoke it emitted seeped into, then out of the thatched roof.

A suckling pig being roasted on a spit for the wedding feast left a stream of grease hissing and spluttering over the two iron firedogs placed at either side of the fire. The tantalising aroma wafting up from the sizzling crackling was making her mouth water.

Meat and fish were hung in the pitched roof where they would preserve and gain flavour from the warmth and smoke. Hanging alongside them were twisted lengths of drying herbs used for flavouring food and medicine.

Voirrey checked the contents of various willow baskets, making sure the leather drinking horns and the polished oak-wood cups, plates and spoons which she had thoroughly cleaned, were still unused. Some were hers, many lent by neighbours to cater for wedding guests, relatives and strangers who would travel for several hours, perhaps walking twenty to thirty miles to attend the triple celebration of a wedding, the Lammas Festival and the Santon Fair.

Mentally Voirrey ticked off the list of people she had asked to provide entertainment. There was the *benaaishnee,* a female fortune-teller, *cailleach groarnagh,* the old woman of spells and the *seanachadh,* a teller of tales who would keep the guests amused when darkness fell. Musicians included a group of four men with bone whistles who assured her they would get the younger visitors dancing and the older ones tapping their feet; a small child who played a set of woodwind pipes and had a sweet singing voice, bell ringers with bronze hand bells fashioned in the shape of a blackbird, the sight of which always drew cries of delight, and a man who played a Celtic horn.

She knew her sister Creena would be busy selling her herbal medicines at the *chibbyr,* a holy well outside the *keeill.* The *chibbyr* was where the sick and dying came to ask the gods to restore their health, others to cure infertility, lameness, or to relieve the pain of toothache. The blind asked to see, the crippled to walk; some appealed for a plentiful harvest the following year and many would offer what payment they could as an incentive to the sun-god who dwelt in the holy well during the night.

At the fair there would be men trading sturdy Manx ponies, vendors selling fruit and vegetables, woodcarvers offering objects carved from an assortment of woods and a crier employed by pedlars to loudly praise their skilful handiwork in creating beautiful brooches, buckles, beaded necklaces, earrings, pins and combs. Eventually the number of marketers trying to sell their wares to the crowds who would begin to assemble in the open space made available for use by the villagers of Santon to hold their market, would fill it with a confusing babble of noise.

The people attending the fair would be in high spirits as they danced, laughed and sang in gratitude for the bountiful harvest and, as Lammas was also a fire festival, in the evening they would wait excitedly for Engus to light a huge bonfire to reinforce the sun-god's strength before the deity had to defer to the supreme powers of the advancing darkness.

Voirrey had made a corn dolly from a number of dried stalks of corn, oats and barley and intended to lay it in her hearth on Lammas Day.

During the next Lammas Festival she would dig it back into a field so the spirit of the sun-god could pass from harvest to harvest. Now, if only the storm-god would wave his arms and scatter the storm clouds in a different direction, Sunday would be a perfect day.

She moved back through the house to count again the assorted joints of meat, flat cakes enriched with chopped apple and juicy damsons, rounds of cheese, oatmeal biscuits, smoked fish, wooden casks of ale and her special homemade mead made from fermented honey and stream water. She must ask Creena if she had boiled the two pigs' heads and feet she needed for savoury jelly.

Voirrey was determined the wedding feast was going to be a lavish celebration, one the villagers would be talking about for years to come. She was unable to resist taking a slice from a huge joint of beef with the short-bladed knife always hanging from her belt and then biting hungrily into a raw onion.

Finishing her beef, she walked quickly through the corridors until she reached the bedroom. She took off her shift and laid it on the mattress of hay and feathers lying on the raised oak-framed bed. Walking over to a wooden trunk, she opened the lid and removed the clothes she had made to wear at Bradan's wedding.

Carefully she pulled over her head an ankle-length, woollen under-dress with long billowing sleeves in a shade of light apple green. The fine soft wool of the under-dress was pleated and gathered at the neck with a brooch decorated with a dozen seed pearls.

Over this she placed a pale yellow, strapped over-dress made from the same fine wool which fell in smooth soft folds down to her calves.

As a final touch she had spent hours embroidering a decorative border on the over-dress, finishing it off with a fringe to which she had sewn little amber bells as a guard against witchcraft.

She had a new silver bangle set with four pieces of red garnet, new leather slippers with shaped wooden heels and a long length of green ribbon to wind in and around her hair.

Humming happily, Voirrey took off the dresses and put them along with her slippers, bangle and ribbon carefully back into the trunk. Tomorrow she would ask the village children to pick masses of meadowsweet so she could scatter the herb amongst the fresh rushes that would be laid down for the feast. When the guests trod on the carpet of cream-coloured flowers they would release their heady, aromatic scent. She smiled as she remembered the herb was also known as 'bride of the meadow.'

She looked up as a tremendous clap of thunder reverberated directly over the roundhouse.

Rushing outside, Voirrey saw lightning ripping through the sky. The heat had become almost unbearable.

The sun had disappeared and the waning light was casting shadows over the deep, variegated purples and greens of heather and wild bilberries cloaking the hillsides, giving the impression it was dusk instead of early morning. Voirrey gasped with horror seeing the wooded hills hit by flares of lightning, setting fire to a thicket of trees.

She watched as a mass of twittering song-birds left the shelter of a canopy of mountain ash and with their departure the air was filled with a menacing silence.

An intense, intuition of danger clutched at her heart as strange, incoherent thoughts raced through her mind leaving her leaving her feeling dizzy and disoriented. Unbidden, her memory recalled a night two winters ago when the *seanachadh* had visited the settlement. The villagers had crowded into the *keeill,* the moderately sized chapel also serving that night as a meeting house to listen to the storyteller. Those that couldn't squeeze inside had gathered at the chapel door. She remembered women scurrying around, lighting dozens of rush-lights so everyone could see him and she could still recollect the rancid odours from the spluttering, smoking, animal fat the rush-lights had been dipped in; but somehow she couldn't remember a word the storyteller had uttered.

As if through a thick fog, she heard screaming and unfamiliar harsh foreign voices and then felt a rush of cool air as if men had actually sped past her. She started to tremble as she clearly heard her own voice filled with anguish, muttering her husband's name over and over again.

Back in the present, drained and confused, Voirrey's emotions were chaotic as she ran through the village searching for Engus. As she ran, she saw flocks of seagulls flying inland and she knew then the storm-god was creating a devastation that had yet to happen.

The noise from the villagers was deafening as they helped each other to secure livestock before the approaching storm broke over their heads. Children shouting with excitement, chased dozens of cackling hens into shelter. As soon as the hens were safely inside the ground was filled with scores of small birds searching for any grain the hens had left behind.

Then Voirrey caught sight of Engus still standing with the same group of men who earlier had been concerned about the river overflowing. Each man was looking skyward at a huge formation of threatening black clouds.

Because of the developing weather conditions the men realised there might not be a celebration at sunset tomorrow to honour Lammas, so all spoke in favour of offering the fattest ears of corn to Easel, the God of Prosperity. They hoped the corn would establish a bond between themselves and the Divinity, so he would intervene if necessary to stop the river from bursting its banks. If you asked the gods for help you must give them something in return.

Shudders swept through her body and she found it difficult to breathe as she waited for them to finish discussing their proposed bequest to the deity.

Voirrey had been born at dusk on All Souls' Day, a day dedicated to prayers for the dead. The date also marked one of the most important Celtic festivals, Samhain, the doorway of the Celtic new year and the season of shadows and darkness. Important, because in the darkness below the ground came the whispers of hibernating seeds as they awakened from their sleep to reappear as new growth in the spring.

This was the night of the Feast of the Dead when the 'veil' between the worlds of the living and the dead was at its thinnest, as on this night the pathway connecting the two worlds was freely travelled by spirits whose soft murmured messages to the living was carried to them by the wind.

It was widely believed that a child born at Samhain had the gift of 'two sights.'

Steadying her breath, Voirrey walked over to Engus's side and said quietly, 'I have a bad feeling about today and tomorrow Engus. I know when the winds descend on us and begin to howl over the village we shall all be in great danger, but from what I cannot tell.' She pressed his arm urgently, her expression trying to convey the importance of her words.

'Listen, the air is already full of leaves the wind has ripped from the trees and there are shadows close to the roundhouses I cannot explain, but there is one thing of which I *am* certain: when the moonlighter appears we must all be in our homes!'

To Engus's dismay his wife spoke with an air of shocking finality and there was a look of unmitigated sadness in her eyes.

After staring intently at Voirrey's troubled face, Engus exercised his authority and began shouting orders for everyone to lead their animals inside as quickly as possible and every last one of them was to make sure the large quantities of hay stacked in ricks ready for the winter was securely covered and tied down before the thunderstorm broke over their heads. He further instructed that no-one was to leave their home until he told them.

People barely had time to collect their children, animals, pet dogs and hunting hawks before the winds began to gather momentum and in the swiftly fading light the sky quickly filled with flocks of crows returning to the treetops.

It was eerily dark now over the village except for sporadic flashes of lightning as Voirrey hurried towards her house. Dry leaves torn from creaking branches of trees caught in her hair as she turned round to catch a glimpse of the silhouette of Santon's three hills against the skyline. She had a strange and frightening feeling she would never see their outline touching the heavens again.

The power and strength of the south-westerly winds accompanied by torrential rain came in the early afternoon. As the storm's fury intensified, the waters of the Irish Sea were whipped into freak waves of such wild and savage ferocity the entire coastline became littered with huge banks of dirt and debris.

After a period of time the following two days entered into the chronicles of Manx history as a testimony to the terrible events that had yet to take place during the first and second of August of the year 798 A.D.

Chapter Three

Nightfall, Friday 31st July 798

As darkness approached, the small raiding party of five *snekkes* hugging the shoreline of the eastern coast of the Isle of Man were desperately seeking refuge from gale force winds, thunderstorms, high seas and a deluge of heavy rain that was making their longships uncontrollable.

Ulfr had ordered the lowering of the *snekkes'* large, red square sails to prevent them being ripped to pieces by the gusting coastal storm, but lowering the sails had made the longships unstable and completely at the mercy of wind and sea. The Norsemen were now using every ounce of strength remaining in their aching backs, stomachs and arms to manoeuvre their vessels as near to the coastline as possible, grimly aware that the height of the waves had increased within the last hour.

The strong turbulence and poor visibility caused by blinding sea-spray was making their task almost unachievable when the men realised Ulfr was shouting and pointing towards a shallow-sloping beach tucked away between two rocky headlands.

Demonstrating their tremendous physical endurance and skill, the Norsemen redoubled their efforts until they reached the sheltered harbour of Port Grenaugh Bay.

The steersmen and twenty four oarsmen in each ship navigated the vessels into the bay's low waters and, once there, each man jumped quickly into the sea. Then moving swiftly, the lightness of the wooden crafts enabled them to pull the ships a considerable distance along the beach and out of reach of the surging waves.

Within the bay the sharp angles of rocky cliffs had altered the direction of the wind and lowered the height of the waves, providing the exhausted men with immediate relief from rough seas and the full force of the gales.

'We'll stay here tonight,' Ulfr shouted to Geirr. 'Rest, then send out a scouting party at first light'.

'I'll let the men know,' Geirr shouted back, his reply almost carried away by sudden rushes of blustery winds.

As his younger brother hurried away to relay his decision to the one hundred and twenty three crew, Ulfr took a moment to listen to several loud rumbles of thunder and realised as Thor, the Norse God of Thunder and Seafarers raced his horse and chariot across the skies, he must be wielding his magical hammer *Mjollnir*, to instigate the displays of lightning that were now tearing apart the heavens. Hanging from a leather strap around Ulfr's neck was a silver replica of *Mjollnir*. He raised it to his lips in an expression of gratitude to this most revered of Norse deities for their safe deliverance to dry land.

Ulfr was the third born son of a prosperous farmer and property owner in the town of Tonsberg, a major trading port at the head of the Tonsbergfjorden Fjord in south-eastern Norway. In the manner of most Viking boys of good family, he had been sent away at the age of five to be raised by a relative, in Ulfr's case an uncle who had taught him the essential skills of a Viking warrior and successful agriculturalist.

He returned to his home many years later an unpredictable, quick-tempered colossus of a man who had been trained adeptly in the use of sword, spear, battle-axe, javelin, bow and arrow and if need be, to fight to the death in hand to hand combat.

He had been taught how to build and repair ships, how to navigate using the stars and coastal landmarks and had become proficient in planting and caring for crops. He recognised herbs which might save his life, could raise goats, cattle and sheep and over a period of time had become an accomplished negotiator when bartering for goods.

He had also returned with a strong hunger to own his own lands.

Geirr, his father's fourth son and one year younger then Ulfr had also been sent to a foster home at the age of five and had returned to his father's house similarly trained in the art of warfare and profoundly impatient to put into practise the knowledge he'd acquired.

Traditionally, the first born son inherited the family farm situated near the top of the long, steep-sided Tonsbergfjorden Fjord and the second son, when he married, would be allocated a substantial stretch of land large enough to grow crops, rear animals and build his own farmhouse. There wasn't enough arable land to support four sons so their father decided Ulfr and Geirr would each be given a generous amount of money which would allow them to decide on a trade or profession that would provide them with an acceptable income.

Ulfr knew exactly what he wanted to do!

He persuaded Geirr to add his inheritance to his own, then he convinced their father to lend them both a further considerably larger amount of money as a loan, promising to repay the full value, plus interest.

With the money the brothers bought five small fast crafts known as *snekkes*. They were warships, strong, lightweight and shaped to skim through the water. The shallow draught of the ships enabled them to travel far into the interior of any region by river or stream without the need for harbours, making it possible for them to be brought ashore almost anywhere.

They paid woodcarvers to cut and shape five intimidating figureheads, four of them with the distinctive features of dragon-heads for the prows and carved dragon-tails for the sterns, the dragon-heads would look downwards at the sea to scare away any sea-monsters or threatening sea-demons. The figureheads could be easily removed as the ships approached land in case they frightened the sea-nymphs who inhabited the deep waters near many of the shorelines.

The brothers would each command his own ship and while Geirr was content to have a dragon-head jutting forward at the prow of his and chose to name his craft 'Sea-Serpent from the Long Fjord', as the meaning of Ulfr's name was wolf, for his own he had them carve an immense head of this predatory animal and named his ship 'Skoll'.

Norwegian folklore depicted 'Skoll' as a savage wolf destined from birth to relentlessly pursue two horses pulling the enormous chariot carrying the sun across the heavens. Like the wolf, Ulfr wanted to put all his energies into relentlessly pursuing (in his case) his fortune as soon as possible, and like the wolf he would snap at the heels of anyone who stood in his way.

Every ship's gunwale was pierced with holes for oars and each ship had a single large sail made from a double thickness of wool dyed bright red. Ulfr knew a glimpse of red sails and dragon-heads appearing out of the mists of the northern seas would strike terror into the bravest of hearts. In bad weather the sails could be lowered over the ships and fastened down like a tent to protect the men from the wind and rain.

The brothers chose their crew carefully, all hand-picked freemen who would thrive on the exhilaration of making hit-and-run raids along foreign coastlines. Many of them were young farm boys lured by the promise of a year or two of lucrative plunder and trade.

As a cheaper alternative to metal armour, Ulfr ordered the men to use leather jackets soaked in hot beeswax, then to thoroughly dry out each coat over a period of several days. This made the leather sufficiently hard enough to deflect a forceful blow from most weapons.

Then Ulfr and Geirr placed thin slivers of iolite into the pouches hanging from their belts.

Ulfr's uncle had taught him how to use the dark, violet-blue gemstone mined from deposits in Norway and Greenland, as a polarising filter to help navigate the open seas. When a seaman looked through the shifting colours in an iolite lens he could determine the exact position of the sun as the 'sunstone' marginally changed colour when it was turned in the light. Sailors soon learnt to identify which tint marked the accurate position of the sun through both fog and cloud cover. It was an invaluable compass to the crew.

Ulfr had proved to be a natural leader and under his guidance the farm boys also learned to steer by the sun and stars. Despite their limited diet of dried or salted meat, water, beer or sour milk to drink when sailing on the open seas, as the months went by they developed into superbly fit, strong men with awe-inspiring stamina. They also became a group of barbaric, merciless individuals who did not hesitate to loot and kill.

They made profitable raids upon the Orkney and Shetland Isles, the Outer and Inner Hebrides, Skye, Mull, Arran and the Irish coastline, returning home time and time again with a prolific supply of gold and silver coins, wine and their most important commodity *thralls*, who were slaves owned by all the crewmen to be bought, sold or exchanged.

The brothers sailed their ships over wide-ranging distances to encompass an extensive area of Europe, including Germany, The Netherlands, Spain, and Portugal. Nearer to home in Scandinavia, commerce was beginning to flourish in small market trading towns which had sprung up along several coasts nearby to natural harbours or fjords. Ulfr and his crew could now sail their *snekkes* close to the trading centres where they exchanged *thralls* for silver, spices, pottery, glass and jewellery. In addition to slaves, they sold and traded furs, iron, wood and carved animals made from the ivory of walrus tusks and whale teeth.

Silver was the most common currency for trade and as each and every trader carried a small set of scales and weights, the amount of silver required to complete a transaction could be accurately established. When the traders weighed the silver presented for payment by the brothers and calculated a little more was necessary, Ulfr would simply hack a further piece from another coin or trinket, the weight and purity of the metal being more important than its appearance. Once their debt to their father had been repaid, the brothers buried their hordes of jewels, coins and religious artefacts along with a large amount of hack-silver, in a pit near their father's home.

Hoarding his wealth instead of squandering it was not difficult for Ulfr as he had met the girl he intended to marry, Ragnhilda, a cousin of his uncle's wife, but he realised he would first have to impress her father with an extensive display of wealth.

The sound of a heated argument between Geirr and another man made Ulfr spin round.

Ulfr was a big, muscular man, but for all his size he moved quickly and was in time to hear the crewman, Hrolf question his decision to sail to this small, unknown island when everyone knew of men who had become wealthy by repeatedly raiding the coastal towns of Scotland and Ireland.

He heard Geirr sharply tell Hrolf. 'Where my brother leads, you follow without question.'

Of all the crew Hrolf had proved the most difficult. He was sulky, irritable and hot-tempered and his constant boasting about his superior physical strength aroused anger amongst the others.

By employing a great deal of brute force with a smattering of diplomacy and common sense, Ulfr had kept these battle-hardened, sadistic men under control, but not by openly allowing them to challenge his leadership. Hrolf turned round, but before he could react to Ulfr standing behind him, a huge clenched fist smashed into the side of his head.

Ulfr stood over the Norseman's prostrate body, the violence in his pale-blue eyes unmistakable as his hand hovered over the sheath-knife dangling from his belt.

Breathing heavily, Hrolf struggled to his feet, his sneering feral expression causing Ulfr's features to tighten with rage, the tightness puckering a white scar running from under his left eye to the corner of his mouth. The eyes of the Vikings glistened with anticipation as they watched Hrolf stealthily remove his own sheath-knife. Ulfr kicked it away and moments later the two men were joined in combat.

Ulfr had a height advantage and his heavier body had many times overwhelmed more seasoned opponents. As their heads and fists clashed, both men seemed eager to fight to their last breath, as the tension and ill-feeling that had been brewing between them erupted into a savage hostility which engulfed them both.

Like a pack of dangerous dogs the crew surrounded the fighting men, their ferocious shouts goading the two combatants into further savagery.

Both men were drenched with sweat as they rained blow after blow on each other, then Ulfr brought his knee up hard into Hrolf's face and feeling the Norseman's nose break, he brought an end to the fight by kicking Hrolf viciously again and again in the ribs.

With blood streaming down his face and his head throbbing relentlessly Hrolf stared up at Ulfr. Then his eyes began to glaze and he was unconscious before his body hit the ground.

Ulfr stood over him clenching and unclenching his massive fists, not uttering a word as he waited for Hrolf to regain his senses. He glanced down as he heard groans escaping from his opponent's badly swollen lips.

As weak moonlight highlighted the blood flowing freely from Ulfr's mouth into his thick full moustache and matted blonde beard, Hrolf tried to focus his gaze on the angry face glaring down at him, both men equally bruised and battered from the blows they'd exchanged.

He watched through half-closed inflamed eyes as Ulfr slowly unsheathed his short hunting knife and bent over him, pressing the tip painfully into his throat. Hrolf stared straight ahead. He wouldn't dishonour himself by pleading for his life.

Ulfr hesitated for a moment then made his decision. He pressed in the point of his knife until it drew blood. It was only a flesh wound, a warning, the next time Hrolf spoke against him he would be merciless.

Struggling to his feet, his face smeared with blood from Ulfr's blows, the expression on Hrolf's features was both hostile and vindictive as he staggered away to slump dejectedly against the side of one of the ships.

The rest of the crew clambered back on board the *snekkes* to remove possessions stored in the sea-chests they'd used as seats during the voyage.

They withdrew from the chests the long, warm, woollen cloaks which had the appearance of large, shaggy fur fleeces, a characteristic attributed to a weaving technique developed by Viking women. The cloaks would keep out some of the piercing winds stabbing their stiff aching limbs like needles. They collected their weapons and unfastened the shields tied to the sides of the ships next to the oars.

It was the weapons that even the most courageous of men defending their homes and families had reason to fear. Each raider owned a spear, knife, battle-axe, shield and double-edged sword, and from a young age most Viking males in every village had been taught to use them skilfully.

The majority of the men had beards, moustaches and long, sun-bleached hair over which they pulled snugly fitting, conical shaped leather helmets. Some of the helmets had a reinforcing strip of metal running down the central seam which extended along their nose for extra protection.

Their clothing, chosen for practicality and warmth, was the thigh-length, belted leather jackets which Ulfr had demanded were first soaked in hot beeswax. Under these they wore woollen tunics, long woollen trousers, socks and knee-high leather boots.

Jumping back on the beach the Norsemen gathered around Ulfr as he issued orders for guard duty. Fifteen men to keep watch while others slept, sentries to change every hour.

The incoming waves crashed loudly on rocks near the water's edge as the men wrapped their cloaks tightly around their bodies, then huddled together for warmth to wait out the night.

Ulfr found his mind occupied with thoughts of Ragnhilda, unsettling thoughts about her beautiful face and knee-length flaxen hair which was the exact colour of golden barley as it rippled in the wind. He pictured the longhouse he would build for her with the interior wall of the large room covered in the thickest of bear skins and wolf pelts. They would help to keep out the biting cold. He and Ragnhilda wouldn't sleep on a wooden bench fitted to the wall as other couples did, instead he would make her a free standing bed with a carved headboard.

Ulfr had long coveted a magnificent tapestry hanging in his uncle's wide hallway. It portrayed a dramatic interpretation of Odin, the powerful Norse warrior-god standing in the Great Hall of Valhalla where the souls of the bravest warriors slain in battle spent eternity. Odin had his two ravens, Hugin and Munin perched on his shoulders. Ulfr made up his mind he would barter with his uncle to own it. The tapestry hanging in his newly built longhouse would surely impress Ragnhilda's father.

He smiled as he thought of her expression when she saw his wedding gift to her, an incredible armlet. It had been fashioned in filigree gold and both curved ends had a stylised wolf's head with inlaid gleaming rubies for eyes. He had plundered it from a great monastery on the west coast of Ireland and as soon as he saw it he knew he had to keep it for himself.

He was smiling as sleep eventually claimed his exhausted mind and there were no more thoughts of Ragnhilda.

Chapter Four

Saturday 1st August 798

The new day came quickly and after a hurried breakfast of dried fish and cold beer, Geirr, a smaller man then Ulfr but with the same broad shoulders, fronted a scouting party of three men up the steep uneven slope leading out from Port Grenaugh. As they ran they were bombarded on all sides by screeching gannets leaving the security of cliffside crevices.

Frayed remnants of storm clouds still swirled weakly above the sheer rock face but the torrential downpours had ended just after midnight; then later, when the sky was tinged with the pink streaks of a new dawn, the wind dropped to a soft sighing sound barely strong enough to rustle the tall sea-grasses growing along the coastal footpath leading to the promontory fort at Cronk ny Merriu.

Once on the footpath, Geirr had to quickly decide which direction to explore first. He focused his gaze on the ground searching for tracks which revealed signs of recent movement. His eyes narrowed as he went down on one knee to make a closer examination of the waterlogged pathway. Although the path was flooded from the heavy rainfall, Geirr could see it was sunken and well used, indicating an established line of travel. He gave a low whistle to his men and the small scouting party started to run through the ankle-deep mud.

Some way in, the path broadened and banks thick with high gorse bushes and tall, yellow flowering cushag provided the Norsemen with cover as they ran.

They entered wide fields of yellow-green grass where the landscape changed to gently rolling hills. They continued their running pace, moving swiftly over ground sodden with rain, then climbing higher over hillsides covered with purple heather and laden with wet, slippery leaves, the gentle slopes of the green hills bringing the Norsemen nearer to the valley enclosing the village of Santon.

In minutes, their rapid strides brought them to the brow of a hill overlooking the settlement.

Geirr made a guttural sound as he stared at the roundhouses crowded together below him, then gestured to his men to step back into the shadows of trees still smouldering from being struck from lightning the night before.

Their eyes glinting with excitement, the men dropped to their knees and crawled slowly forward, making sure they kept within the long shadows cast by the trees, their muscles tensing as a dog, sensing the intruders, began to bark.

Geirr silently counted the roundhouses, thirty two of them in total, all built near a shallow, pebble-bottomed river that flowed from the east. Strong gusts of wind had blown dust and countless leaves across the top of the water, its crinkled surface now resembled the shrivelled skin of an old crab-apple.

Cautiously scrutinising the timber-framed circular houses (which he guessed were about eighteen meters in diameter), Geirr realised many of the buildings had suffered storm damage. Three had their roofs completely torn off.

The men's eyes gleamed as they stared greedily at the tended crops of cereals and vegetables. Although many of the rows of produce had been flattened by wind and rain, the Norsemen recognised this was rich, fertile soil suitable for producing yields that would support the entire settlement. They heard grunting pigs, clucking hens, bleating sheep, the whinnying of ponies and the deep drawn-out lowing of cattle.

They looked at each other with smug satisfaction. The gods had looked favourably upon Ulfr when he had decided to sail to this island; the voyage bore the signs of being a successful venture for them all.

Completely unaware of the danger they were in, the villagers searched through the scattered debris for anything that might be salvaged before releasing livestock onto common land as Geirr, his mouth twisted into a contemptuous sneer, watched a group of men immersed in an agitated discussion.

He grinned to himself: once he got back here with his crew, all those men's worries would be over.

Then he saw a young woman with waist-length red hair leave one of the roundhouses and walk in the opposite direction to where they were hiding. A brown dog was running beside her.

He watched her trudge along, often slipping on the soaking wet grass. Had she looked round and looked up, Agneish might have seen them.

Geirr signalled to the men to edge cautiously backwards. In moments, with their blood pounding through their veins with excitement, they were on their feet and racing back to Port Grenaugh.

Chapter Five

The Raid

Agneish began plodding her way through the thick mud and boggy grassland at the base of the hills surrounding the village, occasionally having to stop and rescue Catat when he sank down to his belly in the thickest part of the sludge, Catat rewarding her each time with a wet, rapturous lick. She was making her way north towards a wooded glade at the top of the valley basin where a deep pool rumoured to be bottomless, was constantly fed by a waterfall rushing down a gaping chasm in the hillside. It was said it was here the River Goddess, Murigen, dwelt.

Agneish wanted to thank the goddess for holding back the rising waters of the Crogga River, as she believed both Murigen and the God of Prosperity, Easel, had played their parts in subduing the river.

She shivered as a cool breeze tangled her hair, then found its way inside her brown woollen cloak. Ruefully she glanced down at the once bright colours on the hem of her loose shift, now soiled with mud and water.

As she wrapped her cloak securely around herself, Agneish noticed the blackberry bushes growing at the side of the hills were already sprouting the bitter-green berries that in just a few weeks would change into the luscious black fruits she adored.

Silently she tip-toed past an unembellished slate cross. No one knew its origins, as it had been on this spot longer than living memory but it was widely believed it had been placed there by the only surviving member of a family decimated by cholera.The cross was guarded by a mountain ash, as the spirit dwelling in the ash tree, also known as the *cuirn* tree, was especially venerated by islanders.

For the first time since early the previous evening, Agneish relaxed as she breathed-in the scent of wild roses entwined around the trunk of the tree. There had been an unsettling atmosphere at home last night, mainly stemming from her mother as Voirrey's air of nervous tension rapidly spread through the whole house. Agneish assumed her mother's mood was due to the possible cancellation of Bradan's wedding.

She walked on, eventually arriving at the outskirts of the village. Without paying much attention to either, she splashed her way through the deep mud lying on the communal burial grounds, then past the *keeill* set in the midst of a large number of stone-lined lintel graves and small, bluish-grey slate crosses, moving on from there as quickly as she could towards the top of the valley.

When she reached the pool, Agneish sank to her knees and uttered heartfelt thanks to the goddess, while, behind her, Catat gazed longingly at the brown trout lurking in the shadowy depths of the green water. Rising to her feet, Agneish beckoned Catat to follow her.

The wet and slippery surface she had trudged along to reach the pool and the self-same walk home, struggling to keep her footing, was exhausting, so much so that when she arrived at the *keeill* she hesitated for only a moment before pushing open the chapel door. She needed to rest before returning home.

The *keeill's* thatched roof had undergone just a slight amount of storm damage and the thick slate walls were, thankfully, untouched. The familiar faint smell of oil emanating from the hollow in the cresset stone on top of the altar, the unspoiled sheaves of ripened grains and wild flowers, the masses of fruit and vegetables laid out on the floor to celebrate Lammas, made her feel safe and secure.

Sheltered from the chill of the early morning, within moments of Catat's warm body snuggling up against her as she laid down on one of the benches, Agneish fell asleep.

She had only been sleeping for a few short minutes when low, grumbling noises rumbling from Catat's throat had her awake in an instant. Raising her head she heard what had disturbed her dog. Muffled voices being carried on the morning breeze and the faint sound of running feet.

Motioning Catat to be quiet, Agneish peered warily through the small window above the altar then nearly screamed out loud with fear as she caught sight of a long column of men beginning to ascend the northern section of the hills. She saw the glint of metal and realised they were armed. They were also out of sight of the main settlement.

Her mind worked feverishly as she tried to explore every possibility for the appearance of these men. Then she remembered a frightening story told by the *seanachadh* two winters' ago at the meeting house, about Norsemen raiding the island.

That had to be the explanation! Men from out of the north had come again to raid and plunder.

She wasn't under any illusions as to what the Norsemen would do.

Legendary for their looting and killing, they would take the settlement by force and ransack the village by stripping the houses and people of their possessions; then, when all had their share of the spoils, they would massacre the settlers and burn the village to the ground.

With the sunlight still glinting on their weapons, the Norsemen dropped out of sight. She knew they would be running now, just behind the crests of the hills, until they were overlooking the roundhouses.

There wasn't time to warn her father!

………………………………………………………………………………..

Except for the open eastern side of the valley basin, the outline of the triple chain of hills was of a curved crescent shape which gradually merged into one around the village and outlying buildings.

While many of the roundhouses had been built at the foot of the southern hill, some, including her parents' house had been erected towards the midpoint of the central section with the *keeill* and burial grounds further along at the outer boundary of the village nearer the northern area, as were the huts used by shepherds and herdsmen for shelter and storage.

Signalling to Catat to keep near to her side she raced towards the *keeill*.

Staying close to any large mass of shrub, she frantically splashed her way through countless muddy puddles and found the still water slowed her down unbearably as she ran towards the roundhouses leaving behind her a visible trail of waist-high trampled grass.

Agneish didn't realise she was sobbing as she tried to catch her breath. She had suddenly recognised there wasn't any need to rush, it would accomplish nothing, she was already too late! Then she remembered something. About a hundred feet above her father's house was a long shelf of slate which jutted out over the roundhouses below. An overhang on top of the slate of thick, prickly brushwood concealed a hollow space which gave a clear unobstructed view of the entire settlement. As children, she and Bradan had often used this cavity to hide from their mother.

She forgot about the need for caution as she struggled up the wet slope, groping wildly with fingertips splitting and tearing in her efforts to find clumps of moss and grass strong enough to clutch onto. She was now high enough up the gradient of the hill to check the length of the gap between herself and the slate shelf which was still some distance away, as well as hear the faint, indistinct murmur of the voices of villagers beneath her. She wasn't sure, but she thought one of them was her father's. Keeping her eyes focused on the slate, she moved slowly forward on her hands and knees, Catat digging-in frenziedly with his claws as he tried to keep pace with her.

Agneish reached the shelf and didn't feel the scratches as she thrust herself and her dog through the prickly bush. Catat stayed silent as he lay down beside his mistress.

Breathless, she looked up and was in time to see the Norsemen edge forward from beneath the tree cover on the edge of the southern hilltop. The raiders were now dangerously close to Agneish as the rim of the southern hill was only a little higher than the slate ledge. The men remained motionless as they waited to hear Ulfr give the signal to attack.

In the few seconds before they launched their assault, Agneish's heart tightened in her chest as below her she recognised the bent figure of her father splitting wood.

As she screamed Engus's name again and again, in the partial darkness underneath the canopy of the trees, Ulfr and Geirr grinned at each other.

'Now', Ulfr said softly.

She saw the running figures of the Norsemen burst out of the shadows and descend on the village, their eyes filled with a kind of madness as they shouted their battle cries.

Engus was the first to react. Spinning round in the direction of the shouting he saw Geirr thrust his spear deep into the chest of a young woman. She fell to the ground without a sound.

'Vikings!' Engus roared, 'Vikings! Arm yourselves! Vikings!'

In the ensuing confusion, Agneish firmly grasping Catat, managed to slide further down the hillside into a mass of yellow cushag.

In seconds the Norsemen were inside the settlement, their swords hacking ruthlessly at the fleeing villagers as Agneish, powerless to help, watched people she had known all her life mown down in front of her eyes.

Bradan and Cane were only armed with their fists and quickness of mind. It wasn't enough.

A tiny sound, almost animal-like, escaped Agneish's lips as she saw them both very nearly half-dead from brutal blows to the back of their heads being dragged along the ground, then flung face down to lie in a crumpled heap alongside Creena's three sons.

She saw Kikil running away from a thick-set Viking towards where Bradan lay. Her long brown hair which she always wore plaited into a huge number of beaded braids were coming undone, the loose beads flying through the air as she ran for her life. Hrolf caught up with her, his stare cruel and heartless as he plunged his knife into her back. Kikil gave one loud agonised scream, then called out Bradan's name before she died.

Although barely conscious, Bradan raised his head and saw Hrolf tearing a pair of jet earrings from the lobes of her ears. He lost consciousness, but not before Hrolf's face was clearly imprinted on his mind.

Although Agneish was watching with complete horror the terrifying scenes of carnage being played out on the ground below, her eyes were drawn again and again to a Viking with a white scar running from eye to mouth. He was a giant of a man, powerfully built, with very light-blonde hair falling to his wide shoulders, his face drenched with sweat as he continuously shouted orders to his men.

Agneish could see his pale-blue eyes crazed with blood-lust, staring out from beneath his leather helmet.

She had a terrible sense of foreboding about this man.

Everything seemed to be in slow motion as she watched her father use his axe to bring down a Norseman with a slashing cut to the side of the raiders head. Then she saw the scar-faced Viking move towards Engus.

Keeping a tight hold on his axe, Engus slowly turned to face Ulfr.

Firmly gripping his heavy, double-edged sword Ulfr glanced contemptuously at Engus's inferior weapon.

Engus didn't flinch as he met the callous gaze of the Norseman.

Her father's long beard and tunic top were splattered with blood where he'd stood and fought to keep his life, but Agneish knew he didn't stand a chance against the raider. He was smaller than the huge Viking and perhaps fifteen years older.

His face distorted with hatred, Engus lunged at Ulfr. The Viking stepped aside and holding his sword in an underhand grip grunted, as with an upward thrust he pushed it up and deep into Engus's stomach.

Although her heart was beating almost unbearably too fast, Agneish was silent as she watched the bearded Viking slice open her father's belly, her hate-filled eyes carefully noting every aspect of his appearance in case the gods decreed she saw him again.

Fighting for breath her father coughed and choked as blood gushed from his mouth as he fell to the ground.

She saw the Viking rip the necklace of amber beads from Engus's neck, then wrench the bronze brooch from his shawl.

Voirrey was crawling on her hands and knees to reach her husband's side. Ulfr barely glanced at her. He knew she was dying from the amount of blood staining the front of her shift. Voirrey wouldn't let the man she loved pass over to the secret shadowy Otherworld on his own. They would go together.

Tears scalded Agneish's eyes as she watched her mother grasp Engus's hand. In moments, both her parents were dead.

After he's roughly torn Voirrey's jewellery from the clothes on her dead body and ripped out the combs and glass beads she loved to wear in her hair, Agneish watched Ulfr stride away.

She knew this was a man of darkness, a killer who moved with ease amongst the shades of people he's murdered, shades who crept behind him as he walked.

The raiders began moving across the settlement. Wading swiftly through the shallow ditches around the roundhouses, they kicked open doors, slaughtering everyone they found until the walkways were littered with dead bodies.

Creena tried to escape on one of the ponies, then crumpled to the ground with a Viking's axe protruding from her back. The long wooden handle of the axe was capped with the carved head of a wolf.

Agneish saw two Vikings cross the threshold of her father's house. One was the scar-faced leader and the other she guessed was his brother. Although the second raider was shorter, the similarity of their features was unmistakable.

As befitting his high standing as chieftain, Engus's roundhouse was larger than the rest and as Ulfr and Geirr walked through the circular corridors ringing the interior they were jubilant to find room after room disclosing plunder worth carrying back to the longships.

They found large amounts of stored grain, brightly coloured bolts of woollen cloth, hanks of wool set aside for dyeing and quickly came across the larders housing the provisions for Bradan's wedding feast, both of them laughing as they reached for their knives to cut off a thick slice of pork which was still slightly warm.

After a thorough search of Engus's and Voirrey's bedroom they shouted with triumph when they found her casket of cherished jewellery and inside a pair of Engus's old boots, three full bags of copper and silver coins.

Agneish trembled with rage when she recognised the chest the smaller of the brothers was carrying out of the house. It was the one containing Bradan's and Kikil's wedding gifts of blankets and Loghtyn rugs.

The raiders roamed through the village in search of plunder, ransacking dwellings, stripping bodies of their valuables, unearthing hidden hordes of money, placing food, grain, cloth, ale, ornaments and jewellery into any container they could find.

High above the roundhouses the breeze carried to Agneish an odour she'd never encountered before, but she recognised it instantly for what it was: the stench of fear. Her senses were now so ravaged she found the distressed bellowing of a wounded cow as unbearable as the petrified screams of men, women and children as they fell victim to the raider's weapons.

They killed the livestock, then set fire to the houses and as thick black smoke began to swirl over dead or dying bodies, Agneish wept soundlessly for them all.

The raiders made one last sweep of the village leaving only, Bradan, Cane and Agneish's three male cousins alive.

Ulfr watched closely as Geirr bound the men's arms then ordered them to get to their feet, stressing his authority by booting them viciously in their backs. Prowling slowly up and down in front of the young Manx men, Ulfr's voice was harsh and menacing. They didn't understand a word he'd said but his meaning was clear. Obey or be killed.

A livid bruise on Bradan's cheekbone stood out starkly on his ashen face and his head was pounding with pain when a sixth sense made him look up towards the slate shelf. The next moment he was crashing to the ground as Ulfr, who thought Bradan was showing him a lack of respect, savagely smashed his battle-axe against the back of his head. Bradan collapsed without a sound.

Geirr watched in silence as Ulfr withdrew his sword from its scabbard and stared at this valued gift from his father. Made of tempered steel, the double-edged blade was honed to a fine cutting edge on both sides, enabling him to deal a lethal blow however it was wielded. The weapon's elaborately decorated hilt of runic characters in gold, silver and copper made the sword Ulfr's most valued possession as he believed these mysterious inscriptions had secret powers which would both protect and bring him good fortune.

Replacing the sword in its scabbard Ulfr turned to Geirr and said, 'do you remember what our father claimed he told everyone the night I was born?'

Geirr nodded as his brother continued. 'He said I have named my son Ulfr which means the wolf and I have beseeched Odin the most wise and powerful of gods that he will inherit a wolf's stealth and cunning so he may prosper, become wealthy and one day find the means to possess his own land.'

Geirr replied softly, 'aye, and my name means 'the spear', which indicates to me I must stand next to your side for you to use as your right hand.'

Ulfr deliberated for a moment before reaching a decision. 'We will return here as soon as possible, perhaps as early as next year and when we do we will strike swiftly to seize this island and govern it together. The soil here is good and the hillsides are covered with thick woodlands of oak and pine which will provide timber to build new longhouses and, reminiscent of our home, we will be close to the sea; but now it is time to return to the ships.'

The Norsemen had rounded up several ponies and flung over their backs as much of the looted goods the animals could bear, the raiders carrying the rest. Grouping together to form a long column, they set a fast pace back to Port Grenaugh.

The pain in Bradan's arms had become intolerable from having them so tightly bound. His body was raw with bruises where he had been callously kicked when he stumbled trying to keep up with their rapid strides, but all the time he had been covertly watching Hrolf running alongside the column, stopping here and there to provoke the other prisoners and laughing as he tripped them up, giving him an excuse to strike out as they struggled to their feet.

Sensing the presence of danger, Bradan raised his head and saw Hrolf standing at the side of him.

As he stared at Hrolf, Bradan could hear Kikil's screams of anguish ringing in his ears as he clearly recalled watching the Viking plunging his knife into her back. The memory aroused a feeling of hatred so compelling, it demanded he make an immediate attack. He gave a ferocious roar of pent-up fury and despair as he lowered his head and ran full tilt at Hrolf and rammed him savagely in the stomach, the violence of his charge sending them both spinning over the edge of the cliff.

The gods had been kind after all, as even under these grim, unimaginable circumstances, Bradan had been able to exact his revenge for the murder of the woman he loved.

Ulfr looked for a moment at the two crumpled bodies lying on the rocks below, then shrugging his shoulders regained his lead at the head of the column of men running swiftly towards the beach.

The raiders distributed the stolen loot between the longships, then made room for the prisoners, one only to a vessel so they couldn't communicate with each other.

Cain's face was streaming with blood and his jaw had been broken, but he was unaware of the pain. Like Bradan's three cousins he was in a state of shock, not able to comprehend the horror of the past few hours.

As the sighing sound of a south-westerly wind rippled white-capped waves and billowed the sails of the five *snekkes*, an exceptionally strong smell of salt filled the air, then out of a twisting swirl of water the figure of Aegir, the Norse God of the Sea appeared in front of the longships.

The terrifying sight of Aegir's gigantic body and the malevolence emanating from the glint in his icy-blue eyes petrified the Norsemen. They knew at once he was demanding a sacrifice before he would let them sail.

Without a moment's hesitation Geirr picked up the bound body of Fogolt and threw him into the salt water.

Smiling, Aegir submerged beneath the surface hunting the passage of Fogolt's soul as Agneish's cousin sank below the waves.

In minutes the longships were afloat accompanied by the screams of gulls as the current quickly took them out to sea.

As the ships gathered speed Cane, Gormand and Hamond revived enough to lift their heads, their gaze fixed on the island rapidly receding into the distance. They knew they would never see it again.

Chapter Six

Govannin

Agneish having sat motionless for over two hours watching her friends and family being slaughtered and the village of Santon razed to the ground, was now so traumatised by what she had witnessed, it took all her strength, both mental and physical, to get to her feet and follow the trail left by the Norsemen, until Catat whimpering with pain held up his right paw for inspection. After pulling out a large thorn lodged in his pad she stood up and urged him to hurry. Still whimpering, Catat chased after her as she followed the raiders, the imprints of their feet instantly recognisable on the flattened wet grass.

When he reached the exact place where Bradan and Hrolf had gone over the cliff, Catat stopped and began howling loud, mournful, plaintive sounds which made Agneish backtrack to where he was standing. Shudders were shaking his body and he didn't respond to Agneish's voice as his gaze fastened on the shingled strip of beach below.

Agneish walked to the edge of the rock-face and looked intently at the boulders directly beneath her and despite the unnatural outline of his bent broken body she recognised Bradan immediately.

Fighting to keep her suddenly ragged breathing under control, Agneish carried on running towards the headland overlooking Port Grenaugh Bay as she quickly realised this was where the trail left by the raiders was leading. She managed to reach the cliff top facing the bay before a peculiar numbness spread throughout her body and her legs buckled beneath her.

She lay there safely hidden amongst a mass of tall sea-grass and watched the longships putting out to sea. Very soon the fading light from an overcast sky swiftly swallowed them up and then they were gone.

Banging the ground with her clenched fists Agneish began to scream. Piercing, pain-filled screams of unbearable torment as she asked the gods how could they let this happen. Nearly demented with grief she pleaded for vengeance for her father, mother, brother and then for all the villagers the Norsemen had killed today.

There was no sign from the heavens to indicate the gods had heard.

Alone now with only her dog for company, Agneish trudged wearily back to the silent village. As she drew closer, the stench of scorched flesh and thick smoke from slow burning wood irritated her lungs, setting off a wheezing cough. Catat whined softly; he was afraid of the new smells and stayed a step behind his mistress.

Taking a deep breath, Agneish walked slowly into the settlement, stumbling past the burnt corpses of friends and neighbours as she moved towards the smouldering remains of her father's house. Tears seared her eyes as she stared down at the bodies of Engus and Voirrey, their hands entwined in death as they had been in life.

She looked at her father, his dark eyes although now lifeless and unseeing, seemed to be gazing up at her from his blackened and blistered face, but the kindness and strength that had made her love him she knew was gone forever. She bent down and gently closed his eyes.

Mindlessly Agneish reached out and stroked what remained of her mother's burnt hair as she began to hum over and over again a lullaby Voirrey had sung to her as a child.

An hour passed and Agneish's mouth and throat became dry with thirst. As she walked towards the Crogga River all about her the charred grass was littered with dead bodies and she suddenly found herself struggling for breath when she recognised the contorted features of her Aunt Creena. Catat stayed close behind her, desperately wanting to leave this place with its strange smells of burnt-out wood and singed flesh.

Kneeling down and scooping water up to her mouth with her hands, the coldness of the liquid made her gulp for air. Her throat was now so swollen from the stinging acrid smoke she had to force down each mouthful.

As night closed in, Agneish saw long-eared bats flying soundlessly through the tainted smell of slaughter and wood smoke now carried on the evening breeze, and then the white, heart-shaped face of a barn owl as it hooted twice before embarking on its hunt for food.

Prowling restlessly around the dying embers of what remained of her village with Catat always following one step after her, Agneish, trembling with exhaustion, eventually laid down beside her dead parents and curling herself into a ball, fell asleep. A low warning growl from her dog awoke her a short while later.

Her senses fully alert, she slowly turned her head in every direction till she saw outlined in the flare from a slow burning thatch a shadowy outline standing a few yards away.

Her scream of terror brought Catat instantly to his feet and rush headlong at the shadow. Agneish saw an outstretched hand grip hold of her dog, then heard a stern voice uttering a sharp command and a trembling Catat crept back to her side.

'So,' the voice said, 'at last you awake.'

As the shadow moved towards her Agneish leapt to her feet and found herself facing a man about five foot tall his face shaded by the pulled up hood of a floor-length deep-blue cloak secured at the neck by two shiny clasps fashioned in the shape of crescent moons.

Before lowering her eyes in panic at the appearance of this stranger Agneish saw as he threw back his hood the skin tone of his long thin face and narrow nose had an unnatural pallor, almost ethereal in its ghostly whiteness which served to highlight the glittering brightness of his deep-set dark eyes. He had a narrow short black beard trimmed to a sharp point and his straight black hair reached almost to his shoulders.

'Who are you?' She asked shakily.

'I am Govannin, a member of an esteemed family of goldsmiths and metal forgers to the gods and the only ones entitled to wear their award of distinction, a ring which bears the crest of a master craftsman.' He held out his left hand and on his middle finger was a large stone which glowed with such a deep rich green brilliance it seemed to be on fire. Cut into the surface of the stone was an ornate design of a set of scales etched in glistening gold.

With eyes wide open with shock, Agneish stared at the slight figure leaning heavily on a silver staff and as he moved a little to one side she noticed his spine seemed to be somewhat crooked.

'What do you want from me?' she asked bleakly. Surely someone like this could only have come from the Otherworld.

Govannin was silent as he looked searchingly at Agneish, then abruptly he tapped his staff on the ground and immediately a sudden indefinite shape of flames sprang up in front of her, but curiously flames without heat. She flinched as he reached out to stroke her mass of bright red-hair.

'The gods heard your pleas and listened favourably to your petition, but it is the colour of your hair which swayed two Celtic war-goddesses to offer their aid and support.

'Your hair is the exact colour of blood and therefore worshipped by the goddesses. Two of the most powerful, Agrona and Cathubodia, both goddesses of war and slaughter have pledged to help you in punishing those responsible for the deaths of the people you loved.'

Her face ashen with fear, Agneish whispered, 'you *must* be from the Otherworld.'

'I am *not* from that abyss of unfathomable misery,' Govannin replied harshly. 'My family live in the foothills of a mountain entirely encircled by a great river which for countless centuries we have used to pan for gold. The supplies of gold dust and nuggets never diminished and we were able to maintain the high standard of our profession. As a result, the gods' found us reliable and trustworthy and that is why Agrona and Cathubodia have sent me to escort you to their world, the Land of a Thousand Gods.'

Agneish blinked rapidly, her expression strained and frightened at hearing Govannin's strange words. He carried on. 'Long before mortals existed, my family which now sadly compromises of only my grandfather, father and myself, managed to survive by making ourselves invaluable to the deities.

'Today it is impossible to calculate our value to them, as some of the pieces we have forged are beyond price, in particular one individual piece of mine which I will reveal to you in due time.

'When we arrive at the Land of a Thousand Gods, it will be my responsibility to guide you to the deities from whom you may beg for help. Those that hold the highest position of authority are four supreme beings known as the Watchers. Their power, influence and decisions play an indispensable role in the fabric of the immortals society. They also individually guard the portals between the worlds.

'The goddesses will send one other to join us on our journey, as make no mistake, it will be a very dangerous expedition we embark on as we seek the right to gain access and travel to the gods' mountain kingdom. On the way we must seek permission from several deities to enter their realm and, as the Eternal Guardian of Mann, the first one to grant his consent must be Mannanan-beg-mac-y-Lleir.'

Agneish stared at this peculiar person for a long time before she began to tremble, then shuddering uncontrollably from head to foot she fell to her knees knowing that what was happening now was a result of all she had witnessed, a terrible dream, a nightmare to be repressed before her mind became permanently unhinged; yet she felt as if it *was* an encounter that was actually taking place at this moment, as she felt Catat's wet tongue repeatedly licking her hand in an effort to gain her attention in the only way he knew.

Govannin strode quickly towards her and lightly placed his hands upon her head before gently pressing her temples. In seconds she felt peaceful and relaxed as renewed strength coursed through her body. He tapped the ground again with his staff and the mysterious fire without heat which had almost died away to nothing, sprang back to life, the flames illuminating a grimace of pain on his face as he slowly eased his crooked spine into sitting in a cross-legged position in front of the fire.

As he slipped off a worn, black moleskin haversack from his back, Govannin motioned Agneish to sit facing him and in the following silence, as she waited for him to speak, the sound of dying fragments of a burning roof falling to the ground made her cry out with fear. Catat gave a warning growl, to whom or what, he didn't really know.

Govannin nodded to himself, then hesitantly as if unwilling to tell his story, noisily sniffed the air before he began to speak, giving Agneish time to notice his scuffed dusty boots and the wide sleeves of his cloak heavily spattered with candle grease.

Govannin started to talk. 'The scent of death here is strong and it would be prudent to leave this place as quickly as possible, but first I must tell you the complete story as to why I was chosen by the goddesses to accompany you through their land, but to do this I must start near the beginning of earthly time.

'My family's home is a subterranean world set deep in the foothills of the Purple Mountain. On the summit of the same mountain lies the Kingdom of the Gods. This hidden world is where we lived and worked, a secretive, creative family unseen by the deities, but nevertheless known to them. We were legendary for our metal work in gold, silver, magical weapons, magnificent armour and more importantly for our knowledge of alchemy.

'My grandfather is the greatest practitioner of alchemy our world has ever known as he alone discovered the secret sought by all alchemists, *how to transform base metals into gold!* The forty leaves of papyrus on which my grandfather wrote down his formula for extracting this precious metal from a molten solution of lead, iron, copper, tin and zinc, and creating a glittering gold liquid, were tightly rolled together and stored in an air-tight container. The secret of its whereabouts is known only to us.'

Agneish saw him smile for the first time as he went on to describe the workroom his grandfather used when he was working on a specific formula. 'As a young boy he allowed me to wander freely around the room on the condition I never touched anything, a promise I gave unreservedly. Entering this room was an awe-inspiring experience.'

Govannin recounted in great detail the shelves bowed with the weight of jars, phials, containers and bottles of all sizes bearing labels marked with the ingredients stored inside. Calcined gold, lapis lazuli, oil of vitriol, quicksilver, brimstone, burned hawthorn and many, many more, and then went on to say: 'Over a long period of time my family had gathered together a treasure house of rare and valuable metals, gemstones and basic elements essential to our work which we carefully concealed from the rest of our kind, dwarves like ourselves.'

Agneish shook her head in bewilderment to hear Govannin describe himself as a dwarf. Traditional village stories passed down through the years portrayed dwarves as being small like very young children, not tall as he was.

'Possessing this myriad of precious metals was a source of great anxiety to my family as unfortunately many of our race are envious of another's good fortune and would have stolen them if they could.'

He cut short his story as he noticed Agneish's confused expression. 'Well that's enough about our property,' he said sharply, 'I will now try to explain how I came to be here today. I *asked* the goddesses if I could accompany you through their land.

'How this came to be begins with the sun-god Bladud. With his orange-red hair Bladud was easily recognisable as he drove his chariot through the heavens, but his vanity was so great he yearned for more and more attention. This desire became so compelling that he commissioned my grandfather to create a spectacular shoulder cape made from beaten gold, which would gleam so brightly everyone would have to cover their eyes when he appeared in the sky.

'When the finished cape was placed around his shoulders, grandfather gave him a solution to drink. It was gold trinkbar, a liquid containing gold-dust. This would ensure Bladud's radiance would never fade.

'Bladud was euphoric and insisted he must choose a reward.

'Grandfather asked for time to think about his decision but in his heart he already knew what he wanted.

'We were dwarves, a race that shared one distinctive characteristic. We were all of miniature stature and his secret wish was to look like the people who lived above the ground.

'Long, long ago he's spent some years panning for gold in the mortal world and when circumstances permitted he had taken time to observe the men and women who lived there. He decided they were all he wanted to be, blessed by good fortune by being tall and strong and with the sun beating down upon their faces instead of living in a world of darkness. So upon my grandfather's request Bladud elevated our family's height to the size of mortals. This proved to be not a blessing but a curse, particularly in my case as the transition from dwarf to mortal form didn't go smoothly.' Govannin gestured towards his crooked spine. 'Then our own people became jealous of the sun-god's high regard and began to avoid us. But fortunately no one could take away our inherent creative abilities and *that was our true measure of good fortune!*

'Our family moved from beneath the earth to live in a vast cavernous chamber in the side of the mountain, spacious enough for us to live and work there quite comfortably. Thereafter my grandfather was often to be found sitting outside with his face turned towards the sun.

'One morning we had a visitor, Barinthus, the charioteer who transports the dead to the Otherworld.

'The charioteer had an image in his mind of a very special sword, a unique concept he would only entrust to the most celebrated swordsmith to bring into being. My father!

'Grandfather and myself left him alone with the charioteer to discuss the god's requirements.

'We heard them talking all through the day and continuing on long after night had fallen, now and again hearing father say forcefully. 'Impossible,' or, 'that could *not* be achieved,' or shouting at the top of his voice, 'out of the question.'

'Finally Barinthus rose to his feet saying he would return in one month by which time he hoped my father would have something to show him. This was said in an almost threatening manner.

'We found father sitting with his head in his hands bemoaning his fate at being chosen for such a preposterous assignment which he claimed was beyond his powers to fulfil and that a month would not be nearly enough to even come close to achieving what Barinthus had in mind. With a hopeless sigh he muttered it was absurd, unrealistic but from now on he must be left alone to accomplish what he could, as the charioteer was a ruthless god who would wreak retribution on all three of us if he couldn't design something near to his demands.

'He told us Barinthus coveted a sword which would be his unmistakable symbol of power. My father must match the hue of the blade to the colour of the darkest night and like the night it must have secret depths to enable the blade to burn stealthily without revealing smoke or flame. It must be forged from the finest, sharpest steel and the blade had to be of a great length with a curved back-edge which bore the words *Bringer of Fate.*

'When unsheathed from its scabbard, the sword must emit a thin sliver of light to show a cadaver the way to the Otherworld and set into the surface of the crosspiece there had to be a prostrate figure of a skeleton. When Barinthus approached the death-gate, the doorway between the living and the dead, the skeleton would sit up and beckon the charioteer's passenger to step down from the chariot and walk alone through the door.

'When Barinthus touched the cadaver lightly with the *Bringer of Fate* as he or she passed through the death-gate, the cadaver's image must stay visible to all the gods till the morning sun rose in the east.

'***This*** was the task demanded by Barinthus from my father.

Govannin continued: 'He retired to the workroom, spending hours rummaging through raw materials in his search for any likely component which might solve the enigma of the required composition of the charioteer's sword. During the second day of my father isolating himself in the workroom I made a chilling discovery.

'I had waded into the river to pan for gold as usual when the water rose up and swept me away, the swell of the river carrying me on and on until I found myself outside the gateway to the Realm of the Dead.

'It was a warning from the charioteer.

'When I eventually arrived home I managed to stutter out my story, shivering uncontrollably as I tried to describe the gatekeepers to the Otherworld and the foul, rotting smell emitting from the hideous, misshapen creatures standing guard outside the entrance.

'From then on the three of us worked together on the construction of the sword.

'Day after day we laboured tirelessly, each of us showing a single-minded determination to find a solution to the arithmetical problem of infusing conventional steel with an alchemical preparation. We hoped by using our combined knowledge and range of creative skills we would produce a sword permeated with the dark powers demanded by Barinthus.

'We experimented with many new methods of incorporating the sinister dark magic into the metal, undertaking so many trials and tests we were completely exhausted.

'One night I was awakened by grandfather shouting in his sleep as, even deep in slumber, he was endeavouring to resolve our situation. 'We need to try copper acetate mixed with an ounce of verdigris and an equal amount of gold saffron,' then his voice faded as he dozed off again before shouting. 'Torrefaction of silver might do it!'   Eventually he went to sleep.

'The next day grandfather noticed that parts of a slim sheet of black steel we had forged, then hammered into shape two days earlier, had begun to generate a soft glow. The three of us looked at each other, unable to quite believe we had created a previously unknown process. *The steel was no longer passive but had become an active malleable energy.*

'There and then we shaped the blade from the sheet of steel.

'We were jubilant until I reminded them we had only three days left to fashion the complete sword.

'My father immediately responded by reminding us about a hidden trapdoor in the floor of the workroom which led deeper and deeper into the heart of the mountain. An escape route from the charioteer if we needed one.

'Far back in time grandfather had explored a large underground cave and with a great sense of elation realised he had discovered rocks formed under conditions of intense heat. The molten rock near the surface had solidified near the soft crust of the surface and using a technique known to our family he was able to change it back into red-hot flowing liquid.

'On his instructions, we used minute particles of the magma to introduce stealthily burning heat into the blade. Again under grandfather's instructions we placed the powdered grains of a rare bright yellow gemstone into the magma. When the blade was heated the brightness of the powdered grains would give enough light to the steel to show a cadaver the way to the Otherworld.

'We made the skeleton for the crosspiece from the bones of a dead banshee, a female spirit who, when she was alive, would give an ear-splitting cry of devastating sorrow when she sensed an imminent death. When the skeleton sat up to beckon the cadaver through death's doorway it would still give the same ear-splitting cry. My father then undertook to carefully etch the words *Bringer of Fate* along the sharp curved edge. Then finally as a spectacular offering to the charioteer he decorated the scabbard which he'd richly plated in gleaming silver, with a miniature gold death mask of the Norse god Odin, in readiness for the day, he Barinthus, heard Odin, whom my father knew the charioteer hated beyond reason, had finally been transported to his final resting place of Valhalla.

'The sword was ready for the charioteer's return visit.

'Barinthus listened intently to my father as he explained about the properties placed within the weapon and roared with laughter when he heard about the skeleton's cry of sorrow. After testing the blade's fine cutting edge and running his finger's slowly over Odin's death mask, the charioteer was exuberant. Barinthus recognised instantly the sword was a masterpiece.

'The three of us were now completely drained of energy. Finding a way to introduce these underlying dark powers into the metal had been problematical and gruelling, but it was my grandfather's health which had suffered the most. The only reward my father requested as he formally presented the *Bringer of Fate* to Barinthus was that the river be returned to its normal manner of functioning.

'The request was granted immediately.

'When Barinthus had taken his departure, grandfather was silent for a long, long time. When he eventually spoke we were surprised to hear him say he realised we were in the wrong world. He wanted to return to below the ground.

'Once back in our normal domain of darkness and shadow our energy and strength was restored to us and grandfather never looked at the sun again.'

Rising to his feet Govannin sighed as he said. 'There is much more to tell you but I will leave that for tomorrow. Now we must rest.'

The following morning the sun hadn't yet emerged from behind the chain of hills when Agneish began to search through the remains of the village for a long-handled spade, the need to lay her father and mother to rest was overwhelming.

Govannin sat alone, seemingly lost in thought. Suddenly he stood up and called out to her to abandon what she was doing as they must leave at once for the shoreline near Calf-Island or they would be too late. Agneish's eyes widened, her look conveying complete bewilderment as to what he was talking about.

Noticing her expression Govannin opened his haversack and took out a small leather pouch. Inside the pouch was a tiny green phial. Before removing its stopper Govannin told her the phial contained a solution of powdered harts-horn and crystals infused with aromatic oils. The solution was an old family remedy and could be used as both stimulant and restorative. The dwarf took his time as he sought for the right words before he began to speak. 'One quick inhalation of the mixture will clear your mind for several minutes of all that happened yesterday, this will enable you to grasp the significance of what I am about to tell you, so please inhale the solution and listen carefully.'

As she held the phial under her nose Agneish became aware of a potent scent and its effect upon her was instantaneous. She couldn't remember anything before this moment when only Govannin's words seemed to matter.

'Many in the Land of a Thousand Gods and beyond, which includes myself, heard of your plea for vengeance. I was quickly made aware of the war goddesses' desire to help you and it took just one or two seconds for me to realise what consequences your anger and grief could have for me.

'Without further delay I sent word to Agrona and Cathubodia to ask if I would be allowed to accompany you to their mountain kingdom. I will freely admit this was for purely selfish reasons.

'My grandfather and father have achieved far reaching success and recognition by each creating their own individual pieces of outstanding artistry. I too wish to obtain the same famed excellence as an artisan who fashions exquisite designs of beauty and delicacy.

'I have created a specific object especially shaped and designed as a gift for the Watchers. If they consent to wear it, my personal status as a skilled craftsman and goldsmith to the gods will have been attained, but first we must meet Manannan-beg-mac-y-Lleir.

'Submerged beneath the Irish Sea, just south-west of Calf island lies an island nearly as large as Mann itself. Some Manx people call it a lost island, others say it's a ghost island, but in reality it is neither. It is the home of Manannan, the great Manx sea-god who has brought into existence an Island of Dreams and Shadows.

'He has given his pledge to Agrona and Cathubodia that today, just before sunrise, his island will rise once more from the sea, but only for one hour. It is there we will meet him.

'We must make haste as when the first rays of the morning sun strike the summit of its highest hill, Manannan's isle will sink back below the waves. The Guardian of Mann will wear his magical cloak of mist which reflects and mirrors the colours of the sea and throw the cloak around the island to render it invisible as it rises above the swell of the tide.

'I have been informed he will send his coracle the Wave Sweeper to collect us.

'Manannan is a great master of magic, trickery and illusion and if he agrees to allow you to travel through the Land of the Gods, I am sure he will supervise your safe passage to the gateway between your world and his.'

Govannin's expression was sympathetic as he looked closely at Agneish. 'I must insist your dog remains here in the village. I fear the dangers of travelling to that far distant land to petition help from the gods and goddesses could expose us to unknown and unpredictable risks. Catat in particular would be in danger from the Morrigan's exceptionally aggressive guard dog if they should so decide.'

'The Morrigan?', Agneish queried wearily, feeling incapable of making her own decisions even though the mind-numbing effect from inhaling Govannin's solution seemed to have worn off.

Govannin put his finger to his lips. 'There is no more time to talk. I will send your dog to sleep and he will remain in this quiet state of rest until we return.' Seeing Agneish's look of panic he said soothingly. 'Don't worry, I give my word he will be perfectly safe until then.' Catat began to whine mournfully, he seemed to understand he was going to be left behind.

Govannin placed his hand on Catat's head and in a very soft voice uttered an unfamiliar command. Catat instantly fell asleep.

Looking at her dog, his head resting on his front paws and his eyes now tightly closed, Agneish felt a lump in her throat so large she could barely swallow. 'Promise me,' she said desperately, 'Catat will be safe. He's all I have left.'

Govannin held out his hand. 'Take the green phial and keep it out of harm's way. When we return open it and hold it under his nose. It will act as a restorative and your dog will awaken instantly none the worse for his enforced slumber.'

'Soon it will be close to sunrise. From this moment Agneish you must do exactly as I tell you.

'First I must separate you from the world you normally inhabit. To do this I must free your mind from your body, so breathe deeply, close your eyes and I will take you to a place which is the time before the present and where you will accept everything I tell you. 'Now hold out your hand.'

Hesitantly Agneish closed her eyes and held out her hand. Govannin grasped it tightly and began whispering in a soft melodious tone, the timbre of his voice so soothing and gentle it was like listening to a pleasing melody. Agneish felt the strongest sensation of happiness and well-being flooding into her mind. She was now detached from her surroundings but not entirely oblivious to the fact she seemed to be moving through the air.

'Open your eyes Agneish.'

There wasn't an element of surprise in Agneish's expression when she saw she was standing on the shoreline close to Calf Island.

As thin beams of pink light touched an eerily silent Irish Sea, within a short distance from the small adjacent island a heavy mist and fog bank began to build up over the stretch of water near to it, then a coracle emerged from the mist and came to rest on the beach directly in front of them. Once they were seated, Wave Sweeper moved off to where Manannan's Isle of Dreams and Shadows would rise above the waves. As it sailed through the low cloud and thick mist Agneish thought she glimpsed an indistinct shape lying within them.

Suddenly the coracle began to rock violently from side to side and she screamed with terror as an enormous white-capped breaker formed a straight line in front of the boat. The breaker rose higher and higher and she saw the curved crest of the heavy wave was now a gigantic head with a mouth spewing white foam. Agneish smelt an overpowering stench of salt as she felt its icy breath on her face.

Govannin called out and the wave disappeared.

'It was a Water Elemental,' he explained, 'a basic primitive force created by Manannan to guard his island from intruders.'

As she tried to stop her hands from shaking Agneish became aware they had sailed through the fog bank into bright sunlight and as warm soft winds blew gently around them and grey seals slipped off low lying rocks to swim alongside the coracle, Agneish saw the clear outline of an island.

Wave Sweeper beached smoothly on the sandy shore in front of a rocky inlet and Govannin, who apart from explaining about the Water Elemental had remained silent throughout the short journey, now asked her to step out of the boat. As she stepped ashore on Manannan's isle a rainbow appeared in the sky.

Agneish stared in amazement at trees with black leaves and tightly closed pink buds which looked like mother of pearl shells, then whirled round to gape at bushes with masses of violet-tinted blossoms with five spiny arms that reminded her of the small sea-creatures her father had called sea-stars.

Noticing shrubbery with blue branches and icy-white flowers, Agneish bent over them and recoiled with shock when instead of the sweet smell she expected their perfume smelt strongly of the sea, then gasped with delight when she saw partly hidden amongst tall yellow grasses with seed pods which seemed about to burst, a hind with her fawn. Standing close to them was an enormous stag.

'Don't look at them,' Govannin urged sharply. 'Nothing will be as it seems on this island. They may be the woodland-goddesses Flidais and her daughter Fland. The stag may be Keevan, God of the Woodlands and Hunting. If they are deities it would be perilous to stare at them until we are sure we have Manannan's protection.

Agneish turned and walked quickly back to the beach.

She caught her breath in wonder as she gazed at the colour of the sea surrounding the island. It was a brilliant blue-green and so crystal clear she quickly glimpsed the world of dreams and shadows Govannin had told her about.

Shifting light patterns like ghostly apparitions moved, blended and changed into images that floated then dispersed beneath the seawater like a phantom watery land of colour.

Govannin stood waiting quietly beside her, his eyes continually searching for a sign to indicate the presence of another. Then he saw it! The rainbow was leaving the sky.

As it moved towards them it resembled drops of coloured mist and Govannin's heart began to pound wildly as he recognised Manannan's cloak.

Fand, Manannan's wife, the fairy Irish sea-goddess known as the Pearl of Beauty was wearing it.

She was small, delicately made, with a beautiful face and luminous dark-blue eyes. Her golden hair reached to her ankles and around her head was a garland of yellow cushag. The neck and hemline of her dress of misty greens and blues was enhanced with the sheen of lustrous unblemished pearls.

Fand smiled and her voice was soft as she told them her husband had sent her to judge whether Agneish's cause was one worthy of being chosen by the gods, despite his being harassed by Agrona and Cathubodia to do so.

Govannin nodded at Agneish. 'Begin,' he said quietly, 'tell your story in your own words.'

And so Agneish told her story, dry eyed but with a voice filled with such intense rage and sadness Fand winced with pity. When she had finished Agneish stared stonily ahead as Govannin and Manannan's wife glanced silently at each other.

Finally Fand spoke. 'I have been authorised by my husband to give you permission to enter the Land of a Thousand Gods if I felt the ordeals you have undergone were deserving of such a special consideration. I do, and so I grant you on his behalf the right of passage through our land.

'I will send a guide who will be riding Enbarr, Manannan's horse. Once you have been joined by your escort my husband will allow all three of you to cross the seas astride his back. Do not be afraid of wherever Enbarr may take you as he can gallop along water at astounding speeds as if he was on land. No one has come to harm whilst riding him either on land or sea.

'My husband is the Guardian of the Gates between this world and the Otherworld's Land of Youth and Promise as well as the Blessed Isles far out to sea where the soul travels to spend eternity.

'Enbarr will avoid the perils of travelling too close to the doorways of the one or two remaining Otherworld's not under my husband's authority. But beware if you hear a soft musical sound which is pleasing to the ears as it will be a silver branch laden with golden quivering fruit and is part of Manannan's apple tree. The sound opens the doorway to the Blessed Isles, but I am sure Manannan will ensure you pass them without fear.

'You may see him travelling across the sea in a chariot drawn by 'horses' formed from the waves. He is as mysterious as the mists which cover the sea in their endeavour to withhold its hidden dark secrets from view. These are the same mists from which it is said he made his magical cloak.'

Fand turned to face Govannin and held out a golden ring. 'Take this. Manannan has sent you his signet ring inscribed with the Three Legs of Mann. Show this to anyone who doubts you.'

Govannin passed the ring to Agneish so she could look at the three armoured legs etched on the ring in gold and silver. Pain pierced her heart like a dagger as she whispered. 'Whichever way you throw me I shall stand.' A defiant phrase her father had been proud to repeat over and over again.

Manannan has asked me to tell you he may decide to join you on a section of your journey, where or when he has yet to decide.'

Fand gazed gravely at Agneish before continuing. 'The seeds of the Norseman's future have been placed in the wind by Agrona and Cathubodia, but only you can sow them.'

Agneish shivered as a tingle ran down her spine at Fand's words but Govannin smiled with evident satisfaction.

Fand spoke again. 'Wait here and your guide will be with you shortly,' adding grimly, 'as soon as you pass through the gates to the Land of a Thousand Gods you must search for where the first light will make its appearance above the eastern horizon on the day after tomorrow. You must know exactly where to find it, for this is the measure of hours you will be allowed to stay in our land. If you fail to do this you will be trapped there for time without end.'

Govannin nodded. 'I'll find it,' his tone grateful at being given this warning.

'I'm sure Manannan will make sure no harm befalls you,' Fand said smiling kindly at Agneish. 'In the meantime I will send word to the Morrigan that you will need their help. Goodbye and good fortune.' Then she was gone, leaving behind her a trail of coloured vapour, but not before she cast a severe glance at the three motionless deer.

When Govannin turned round the deer had vanished. He took a deep relieved breath, they *had* been deities as he had suspected.

'You have mentioned the Morrigan to me, but you didn't tell me who they were,' said Agneish.

There was a brief silence as Govannin searched for the words to explain to this naïve young woman who until yesterday had little understanding of the world outside her village.

'As you know someone is being sent to guide us to the gates of the Land of a Thousand Gods and I must warn you these gates are guarded day and night by the Morrigan's watch dog. He is never allowed to sleep!

'The Morrigan is the supreme Celtic goddess and a powerful shape-shifter who can transform herself into separate forms. She will present herself to us in the guise of one goddess or three.'

Agneish's brows drew together, wrinkling her forehead as she tried to concentrate on the information Govannin had just given her. But she didn't, couldn't, understand what he meant. Govannin carried on. 'Collectively they are known as the Morrigan and individually by many different names. The Crone, the Dark Goddess, the Phantom Queen, the Queen of the Otherworld and many others.

'She is both fate and death, warrior and protector and her symbol is the carrion crow.

'If she appears in her triple aspect, two of her sisters could be Badb and Macha. Badb is known as 'Fury' and could emerge as a crone wrapped in a black cape made from crows' feathers. Wearing this cape Badb is in her favourite disguise of a carrion crow, a corpse goddess who can be found flying over the carnage of a battlefield screaming raucous wild cries as she heralds the death of a warrior. In this manifestation she delights to feast on the decaying flesh of the dead.

'Macha is renowned as 'Battle', so called because she encourages fighters into combat madness and as the spirit of a dead warrior resides in his head she captures their spirits by feeding on that part of their bodies. She is savage, war loving and will pursue any who *leave* the field of battle, but in the guise of the Dark Goddess she will drive men *towards* the ecstasy and thrill of conflict.

'As the Phantom Queen she is a fearful figure who leads spirits *out* of the Otherworld.

She presides unopposed over death and destruction and is the bringer of eternal darkness.

'In every guise they are all choosers of the combatants to be slaughtered. Once a fighting-man's head has been severed from his body and given as a gift to Macha by an enemy of the dead warrior, the goddesses guide the spirits of the fallen to the world beyond reality. They can be seen galloping through the sky in the form of a black horse carrying its rider towards the death-gate. Beyond this doorway is the Otherworld.

'They are the Keepers of the Keys which open the gates to the Land of a Thousand Gods and each of the trinity holds a separate key. Only the

Morrigan can decide who will pass through them, so all three keys are required to unlock the gates. If they decide to help you, you will have gained a formidable ally.

'But for now we must wait for our guide.'

Govannin instructed Agneish to keep quiet and calm no matter what happened. 'I know what these gods can get up to,' he said ominously.

About ten minutes passed then the sky erupted with flashes of forked lightning. Govannin looked up to the heavens and Agneish heard him take a sharp intake of breath. Following his glance her heart began to thump as she saw outlined in the flashes of light a rider astride a huge white horse, clearly urging the creature to jump across one fork of lightning and land on another. His head was thrown back as if he was roaring with laughter.

'It's Taliesin. So, a fool has been sent to guide us,' spoke Govannin.

'Who is Taliesin?' asked Agneish.

'Only a minor god,' Govannin said with a dismissive sniff, 'one who has never previously been invited to visit the mountain kingdom, but I have heard he has very useful assets. Wit, cunning and music. Taliesin is a bard, a Prince of Song who is skilled in the art of arranging melodies or verse suitable for setting to music. Perhaps Manannan anticipates he will write a dramatic composition celebrating your journey, possibly something for the great sea-god to listen to on a winter's evening.'

Govannin turned his head, then put his fingers to his lips and said. 'Listen.'

Hauntingly beautiful music that made Agneish shiver was resounding through the air. She closed her eyes for a moment and when she opened them a stunningly handsome young man with thick, shoulder-length blond hair, pulled back and held in place with a thin cord of twisted leather was galloping downwards towards them. Agneish saw he was running his fingers lightly over the strings of a golden lyre.

Her mouth dried with fear. For despite all that had happened these last twenty four hours, violence and death were commonplace in her world.

This was not!

'Greetings,' Taliesin said softly, his eyes meeting Agneish's as he jumped off his horse. She saw he was beardless and had eyes of the brightest blue she had ever seen, eyes that seemed to gleam with amusement as he looked at Govannin's disdainful expression.

Her mouth was too dry to reply but Govannin gave a brusque nod as he acknowledged the Prince of Song's politeness.

'I am Taliesin,' he said bowing to Agneish, 'a god commanded by a higher one to stand between three worlds. Yours, mine and Manannan's.'

Agneish was lost in wonder as she gazed at this tall young god, the sight of him arousing awe and excitement. She noticed that the wide sleeves of his pale-blue shirt were slit down the centre revealing a generous inset lavishly embroidered with thread of the brightest gold. Fastened to the belt of his silvery-grey trousers was a short sheathed dagger. He wore thigh-high, light-blue leather boots and the gleaming gold armlet fashioned in the shape of a miniature lyre on his upper left arm made Agneish's eyes widen with admiration.

Taliesin looked at Govannin. 'We must leave here without delay, the first rays of the morning sun are almost ready to strike the highest point of Manannan's isle.'

The dwarf stared anxiously at the sun. 'Tell us what you want us to do.' He had no intention of spending the rest of his life below the sea.

Laughter lines crinkled the corners of Taliesin's eyes as he smilingly patted the neck of the white horse. 'This is Enbarr, the great sea-god's horse who will carry all three of us safely to my world. He will ride in a direct path across the sea till we reach a golden bridge. Once on the other side of the bridge, we will be in the Land of a Thousand Gods. You must trust me and do exactly as I say.'

Govannin inclined his head hurriedly in agreement.

'Enbarr will take a hidden pathway through the mists that only he can see. Fand has assured you that no one has met their death whilst astride his back, that was not just a speech, but reality. Come we must leave here at once.'

A feeling of terror began to overwhelm Agneish leaving her incapable of speech.

'Look up at the skies,' Govannin told her quickly. 'The angry spirits of the dead from your village are demanding revenge.'

As the early morning light brightened the sky she saw scuttling across the wide expanse of the heavens the faces of her parents, Bradan, Kikil and many, many more. They were being carried along by a wind that was rapidly gaining momentum. As its speed increased in power and force, it seemed to Agneish the wind was trying to speak.

Strangely the glimpse of her parents' faces calmed her.

'I put my trust in the gods who sent you to me and I will follow wherever you lead,' she said.

'Then we must go,' Taliesin said firmly.

They mounted Enbarr, Agneish in front of Taliesin and Govannin behind him, the dwarf uncomfortably pressed against the lyre now resting across the Prince of Songs' back.

Taliesin whispered in Enbarr's ear and the huge white horse turned his head and looked at the riders. His intelligent dark eyes seemed to be trying to convey a message that all would be well. Agneish felt surprisingly comforted.

Enbarr galloped towards the shoreline of the Irish Sea surrounding Manannan's isle, rearing up once before he plunged into the sparkling waves.

Winding spirals of coloured mists sprang up in front of them, clouds of mists in shades of the deep-blues and greens of the sea by day and then changing to the midnight-blue and purple hues of the swell of rolling breakers at nightfall.

Govannin's cloak billowed out far behind him as they rode through freshening winds and breaking waves and as Enbarr galloped on through the mists Agneish found the extraordinary silence all around them both peaceful and strange.

Far out in the distance Taliesin pointed out the Blessed Isles, some small, some large, and Agneish heard Govannin heaving a great sigh of relief when the isles were safely behind them. Mindful of Fand's warning he thought he heard the tinkling of bells. The dwarf was the first to see the golden bridge as it came into view, the only sanctioned approach to the gods.

The creamy-white of spurting sea-foam spilled over them as Enbarr jumped out of the sea, cantered across the bridge, and leapt onto a small sandy shore. Looming in front of them was a huge wall with two enormous black gates chained firmly together and secured with three gold deadlocks.

As Agneish stared at the carved ebony crows sitting on top of the round fluted columns positioned at each side of the gates, Taliesin strode forward and plucked out of the air the gilded horn of a white hart, a revered mystical deer held sacred by the deities.

He said, 'When a god waits outside the gates he must blow the horn to announce his arrival.'

A minute or so passed before they heard the rustle of material slithering along the ground, then an old crone wrapped in a cape of crows feathers stepped out of the shadows, accompanied by a large, powerful, deep-chested dog with a long, thick black coat. It was a breed of ancient lineage used exclusively as a guard dog by the deities and this one had been a gift from Arawn, one of several co-rulers of the Kingdom of the Dead. In this rare species of dog their eyes were always sightless, endowing them with an exceptional sense of smell.

His powerful muscles rippled with tension as the crone gathered up long invisible fetters forged by her commands.

She asked in a cracked, rasping tone. 'Whom do you seek here?'

Although she was shaking with fear Agneish managed to whisper. 'The Keepers of the Keys.'

At the sound of Agneish's voice the black dog began shuddering uncontrollably and a sulphurous yellow-drool dripped from his jaws. His frenzied, high-pitched howls as he strained against the restraints of the unseen fetters, quickly motivated Govannin and Agneish to step back from the entrance. Taliesin remained where he was.

'I am the Morrigan, Keeper of the Keys. Only I can unlock the gates. Who sent you to me?'

'Fand, the wife of Manannan-beg-mac-y-Lleir,' Agneish answered shakily.

The old woman was silent for a moment, then queried. 'You are here to plead for help from the gods within the gates.?'

'Yes.'

Agneish held her breath as Govannin said loudly. 'I am Govannin, goldsmith and metal forger to the gods, sent by Agrona and Cathubodia to escort this mortal through your land. Fand has also sent Tallesin, Prince of Song to lead the way. I have on my person the great sea-gods signet ring inscribed with the Three Legs of Mann. I was instructed by Fand to show this ring to anyone who might doubt my word.'

The crone's eyes widened with surprise, then she asked quietly. 'May I see it?'

Govannin nodded and withdrew the gleaming ring from a deep spacious pocket on the inside of his cloak.

The crone stared at the ring for only an instant, then immediately said. 'You may enter the gates.'

As if he had understood the words the Morrigan had uttered, Enbarr turned round and cantered back along the golden bridge, then leaped into the sea. In seconds a sea-mist shrouded him from view.

As she looked at the old woman the hairs on the back of Agneish's neck began to stand on end as the feathered cape the crone wore changed into a gathering of dark shadows. Agneish cried out in fear as the shadows materialised into a tall, black-haired goddess dressed completely in red.

A shiver ran down Agneish's spine as the goddess slipped a scarlet cloak from around her shoulders revealing a chain around her neck strung with one beating heart.

The goddess smiled as she sensed the fear Agneish couldn't hide.

Another shadow materialised as storm clouds blazing with flickering lights, before changing into a goddess holding the head of a slain warrior. A third emerging shadow, Govannin realised with horror, was the Queen of the Otherworld. He became mesmerised by the large vessel held by the first goddess which contained tiny glittering red crystals. He recognised it instantly as a time-tracker!

The time-tracker had been fashioned from two individual chalices linked vertically together to form a union of spectacular style and detail with both chalices continuously overflowing with twisting wisps of pale-pink to dark-red smoke. The lower chalice held the crystals and, when turned over, the bowl-shaped cup released a cloud of red gemstones that sparked and flashed as a trickle of the tiny stones flowed from the top cup into the bottom.

Around the side of each goblet were the coiled bodies of two golden miniature fire salamanders. Their open mouths discharged sudden flashes of dancing flames together with the minute blood-red crystals that had been forged in the fires of a volcanic crater.

Govannin's face lost colour when he heard what he thought was a masterpiece of creative art give an audible hiss.

The tall goddess looked intently at Agneish before saying. 'Remember, as soon as you enter these gates you have to search for the day after tomorrow. You *must* know exactly where to find it. From the moment the entrance closes behind you I will turn the chalice over and the time-tracker will begin tracking the hours you spend in our land. You must return to the gateway before the last crystal has dropped into the cup.

'When the sun-god rises twice more you must knock forcefully on the gates. I will answer and allow you to depart. Be vigilant, if you are late your past will not matter nor your future, as you will remain here throughout eternity.

'You will find this is a place unlike any other, so I caution you to be alert for any indistinct shapes that move furtively away from you. It may be an indication that some malevolent beings are present.'

The Morrigan walked to the gates and turned the keys in the deadlocks. Agneish held her breath as the entrance to the Land of a Thousand Gods swung slowly open.

Chapter Seven

The Day After Tomorrow

The sound of the gates banging firmly behind them struck terror into Agneish's pounding heart and at first she found it impossible to concentrate on what Taliesin was saying.

'Before we venture further into my world we must look for the day after tomorrow. To do this we must travel in the direction the sun-god will rise, which is, of course, facing east.'

Govannin agreed, but Agneish's voice shook as she asked Taliesin how could they possibly find something that didn't yet exist.

Taliesin laughed. 'Now we are behind these gates anything is possible.'

The three of them began walking towards the faint red glow still just in evidence in the early morning sky.

They stopped to read a signpost with the marker pointing towards the east which bore a basic unadorned inscription: *Seeress.*

'Ah yes,' Taliesin said thoughtfully, 'she is a goddess without a name. Originally she was from another world and I understand her planet and all things on it were lost. I was informed that from its creation the concept of her world was doomed to failure. Our gods heard her cries of, 'Somewhere amongst the stars there must be a planet like mine,' resounding through the heavens and took pity on her. She has been called upon by the ancients to sit beside the stream of Moments Past and Future to provide guidance to travellers as she has the gift of prophecy. I think we should seek her advice.'

Immediately Taliesin felt a light touch on his arm.

A grey-cloaked woman of greater than ordinary height was beckoning them to follow her.

She led them to a broad stream with gloomy shallow waters which were just beginning to lighten with hazy sunlight. Her expression was distressingly sad and although her cloak was wrapped tightly around her, the seeress's body seemed extremely thin.

'How can I help you?' she asked in such a quiet gentle tone they strained to hear her.

As she pulled off her hood they saw her hair was short, thick, spiky and a glittering metallic silver in colour. Her face was oval with high cheekbones and her pale skin had a translucent sheen, but it was her tilted, almond-shaped silver eyes which caught their attention.

They were colourless and uniquely different from all others because the light shone completely through them. Govannin knew at once that the seeress had the capacity for great insight into the centre of thought of any individual.

Taliesin stepped forward and quickly explained they were in pursuit of the moment in time when the first appearance of the sun-god would become apparent on the day after tomorrow. It was imperative they knew where to find it.

The seeress sat down beside the stream of Moments Past and Future and let her head fall onto her bent knees. After a minute or two she reached out and dabbled her right hand in the stream and allowed the water to flow leisurely through her outstretched fingers. Immediately the large, polished stone ring she wore on her hand became clouded with mist. The seeress noticed Govannin staring at the stone and told him it now contained images of the past. She looked at Agneish and smiled compassionately as she said. 'Before I provide the answer to your question I would first like to speak about you. Time events occur in irreversible finality. For you, the past, present and future are bound unalterably together. Ahead there are mysteries you will solve and some you will leave unsolved. There are problems that will be resolved and some will remain unresolved. Stand resolute against your enemy and your courage will be rewarded. That is my advice to you.'

She gazed curiously at Govannin before saying enigmatically. 'Beware, in this land the soul can be lost or stolen.' She didn't offer an explanation for her warning.

Turning to Taliesin she said 'Ahead of the first light turning night into day a songbird called the Time Messenger sings throughout the hour *before* the sun-god rises. He sings a rising crescendo of low, high and full notes as he heralds in the new day. When you hear him and I promise you, you will, this should be taken as a sign of impending danger to yourselves. That is all I can tell you except now you must seek the crossroads between the worlds.'

They thanked her and as they walked away from the stream Govannin turned his head for one last glimpse of the seeress. He saw she was weeping and knew it was from hopelessness at being unable to explain the inexplicable mystery of the disappearance of her world.

They had left the stream far behind when a voice carried by a light wind drifted towards them. Taliesin thought it was the voice of the seeress. It instructed Govannin to tap his staff twice on the ground and a trail would appear, to lead them to the crossroads they sought.

Govannin tapped the ground with his silver staff and Agneish saw the flames without heat spring out of the earth in the same way they had appeared in the scorched remains of her village. The flames moved ahead of them in the form of a thin line.

As they followed the trail of fire which constantly sprang up in front of them and then extinguished itself once they had walked past, Agneish looked at Taliesin and said wearily, 'I'm very tired. How long now before we reach the crossroads? And how will we know them?'

Taliesin replied, 'Long, long ago, a Celtic cross was erected just beyond the crossroads we seek, at a position chosen by the deities because it is precisely aligned between all four corners of your world and mine. The goddess Almha will be waiting there. She is a wise and knowledgeable gatekeeper who will guide those who search for the most favourable direction to travel.'

As they trudged along a seemingly unending road, no one noticed a white owl silently flying far above the ground ahead of them.

Turning a bend in the road they saw the crossroads, then morning rays of sunlight singling out a huge stone Celtic cross.

Govannin and Agneish were astounded to see a large, white owl perched on top of the stone, but Taliesin knew Almha had modified her appearance and shape-shifted into a bird of prey.

Taliesin was aware that when Almha appeared in the form of the white owl she was regarded with reverence by the other deities, as in those moments she had the capability to see into the corners of theirs' and Agneish's world in four different directions at the same time. In a hushed voice Taliesin told them that when she assumed this shape, the other deities called Almha 'the Phantom Owl.'

The bird stared unblinkingly at all three, then focused its complete attention on Agneish who found she was unable to move as the bird seemed to be staring into the depths of her soul.

Govannin had realised the owl was a shape-shifter and, like Taliesin, remained perfectly still. They knew the goddess was assessing Agneish's chances of success in the Land of a Thousand Gods.

The black-billed bird made a series of clicks, brief sharp sounds, before it opened and stretched out its enormous wings. In front of their eyes its thick plumage and heavily feathered taloned feet began to change in one fluid motion into the form of the goddess Almha.

Agneish had never seen anyone so beautiful.

The goddess was impressively tall, slim, narrow-waisted with an abundance of heavy golden-hair which spread out around her shoulders.

She wore a simple white dress which fastened at one shoulder with a brooch cut from delicate twisted gold, set with moonstones, a stone as ancient as the moon itself. But it was her thickly lashed eyes that fascinated Govannin and Agneish. The irises had the identical yellow tint of an owl's, while the pupils were formed as a vertical black straight line.

Almha inclined her head graciously as she greeted the travellers. Taliesin she had met before and had been delighted with a charming verse he had written describing her exceptional beauty.

Govannin and his creatively-gifted family she had heard about, and the details relating to Agneish's quest for vengeance was already being circulated throughout the land. Some of the deities found the account interesting, others more mean spirited, did not.

Looking closely at Agneish the goddess explained what she must achieve.

'You need to search for the four divine beings who protect the gateways between the worlds. You will only know them as the Watchers as their names cannot be revealed to you. They dwell on the summit of the Mountain Kingdom of the Gods.

' The most powerful Watcher is the Guardian of the North and Earth. He acts as sentinel over the time when the hours of daylight are at their shortest and the sun-god appears to stand still. As this day has the most darkness he must take particular care not to allow any of the malignant spirits who wait just outside the gateways to move unseen into an unsullied world.

'The Watcher of the South is the Guardian of Fire and he acts as sentinel over the time when the hours of daylight are at their longest. As this day has the most light the Guardian of Fire has to be prepared for when the chariot carrying the sun-god stops, turns, and changes direction from north to south. This is the moment when the sun-god is at his greatest distance from the earth and it is the specific duty of the Guardian of Fire to protect the temporary empty space between our world and yours.

'The Watcher of the West is the Guardian of Water and he is the sentinel who watches over one of two points in time when day and night are of equal length. He cares for the season of growth and renewal.

'The Watcher of the East is the Guardian of the Air. He is the sentinel of the other point in time when day and night are of equal duration. He understands the voices of the bitter winds which marks the season of dull skies and leaves dropping freely to the ground.

'Before you will be permitted to meet these four divine beings you will make the acquaintance of the war-goddesses, Agrona and Cathubodia. They will want to observe the mortal they have pledged to help. If your conduct and manner earn their esteem they will ask the Watchers to intervene against the Norseman on your behalf.

'The Watchers will listen to every detail, every point and aspect of your story with great courtesy and if you can gain their respect they *will* help you!

'To reach their kingdom, at nightfall you must use the only access to the summit. A winding footpath at the side of the mountain. When you reach the summit you must wait there 'til the sun-god rises, when three gateways will be revealed to you. But I now give a grave warning: you must enter the kingdom through the gateway known as the Realm of the Morning. You must decide for yourselves which is the correct gateway, but if you reflect about what I have just said, it is instantly recognisable.

'Enter through the second gateway and you will cease to exist. The reason for the third gateway is unknown.

'This information is the maximum amount of assistance I am allowed to offer in support of your right to enter our mountain kingdom.

'At every stage of your journey leading to the Watchers, Agrona and Cathubodia will note how you face adversity. Courageously, I am sure,' Almha said with a warm smile.

The threat of danger heightened Agneish's abilities to respond bravely to the goddess. 'I have experienced hardships all my life,' she said slowly. 'Death and disease are part of my everyday existence and, but for my father, so would have been lawlessness. In honour of his memory I must be as fearless in this land as he was in his.'

Almha nodded in approval at her spirited reply.

She turned to Taliesin. 'The next step for you all will be to walk along the Path of Trepidation.' Taliesin and Govannin both took a sharp intake of breath.

The risks and dangers of this pathway were well known to both of them. Apprehension was written all over Govannin's face, his expression caused by the imminence of danger to Agneish who had been entrusted into his care by two merciless war-goddesses who took immense pleasure in ferocious savagery and bloodshed.

Taliesin spoke next, deliberately taking more time than usual in uttering his choice of words to add extra weight to the importance of his comments.

'The Pathway of Trepidation was created solely as a playground for all the gods and many of them will be testing and watching you carefully. As a god myself, and entirely for my own amusement, I have walked along the path many times, but the trials and rules are changed every day. Be aware,' he said sternly, 'what lies ahead of you is a contest, a demonstration of their skills and your judgement in assessing how to play their games. You must be brave, show no fear and if you amuse them they will allow you to continue.'

'You must listen to Taliesin and do exactly as he tells you, his knowledge of this land and those who dwell in it is why Fand sent him to serve as your guide,' Almha said softly.

She pointed to the stone cross. 'The centre of the Celtic cross represents the gathering place where all the forces of life meet; it also marks the position midway between here and the River of Eternal Rest. I will advise you how to avoid it.'

Govannin shuddered at the mention of this dreaded river. He knew it was a place where spirits haunted the riverbanks to meet and entice their victims to jump into the waters and seek the final oblivion of everlasting sleep.

The goddess then spoke directly to Govannin. 'As a gift from Fand, from this moment your silver staff has been endowed with two unique features. If asked, it will always blaze a trail in the direction you need to travel. Just tap it twice on the ground as before and follow the flames. To quench your thirst or satisfy your hunger, tap it five times on the ground.

'The Path of Trepidation is that way,' she said gesturing towards the north, 'this direction also avoids the River of Eternal Rest.

'Your soul has a shadow,' Almha added to no-one in particular.

Govannin had the strangest suspicion she meant him, but the goddess avoided his shocked gaze.

'After you leave the Path of Trepidation there may be another trial,' Almha warned as they walked away.

Chapter Eight

The Path of Trepidation

Softly strumming his lyre, Taliesin acted on the goddess's instructions and led them in a northerly direction until they reached a post bearing the sign, Path of Trepidation.

He stopped beside the post and looked closely at Agneish's tangled hair, soiled cloak and grimy hands and then at Govannin's twisted crooked spine and at his countenance now deeply etched with pain. Conscious of the fact the gods liked to gaze at nothing less than physical perfection, the Prince of Song hoped they were in a charitable mood.

Shrugging his shoulders he turned onto the path.

As they walked along, the track became narrower, darker and partly obscured by the shadowy silhouettes of stunted shrubs. Incredulously, in the midst of the low, scrubby thorn bushes whose vague shadows seemed to lack any convincing substance, there grew sizable trees bearing apples of the deepest crimson.

'Can I eat one?' Agneish asked Taliesin.

'No', he replied.

Agneish grimaced with annoyance, she was hungry.

Govannin remembered what Almha had said. To quench their thirst or to satisfy their hunger, tap his staff five times on the ground. Tentatively he struck the ground with five light blows and immediately a narrow stream of fresh sparkling water ran alongside the pathway. Placed next to it was a large bowl of fresh fruit.

Savouring the sweet smell, Agneish gazed in wonderment at the ripe, fleshy, unfamiliar fruit. There were large purple youngberries, aromatic green muskmelons, large knobbly yellow jackfruit, ripe guava, round, juicy, orange mangosteen and the sweet red fruit of the heart-shaped cherry. Sitting on top of the bowl and dripping with amber liquid, was the most enormous honeycomb she had ever seen.

Their thirst quenched and having gorged on enough fruit to satisfy their appetite, the group walked on, Govannin and Taliesin constantly glancing warily around them.

As they passed another tree bearing the deep crimson apples, Agneish stopped to listen to the mesmerising song of a bird perched on a branch near the top. The melody sounded so full of sorrow it made Agneish want to cry.

'I thought I saw something move just ahead of us,' Govannin said.

Taliesin quickly identified what Govannin had seen.

'Throughout our land there is *no-one* so loathed, *no-one* who arouses such revulsion as the abomination known as the Seller of Souls,' Taliesin said angrily at the sight of an old woman lurking beneath a clustered mass of deformed trees.

'I must insist, do **not** step of this path as beyond those trees lies a burial ground littered with the bones of those lacking in caution. I can smell the rotting flesh from here' Taliesin said.

Taliesin tightly gripped Agneish's shoulder. 'Whatever you see in the moments ahead will not be real,' he said fiercely. 'Remember, the old woman will try to trick you.'

Agneish's stomach churned with fear as the Seller of Souls stepped in front of her and looked directly into her eyes.

She began to speak, her voice soft and beguiling: 'I can sell you the soul of your brother,' she said gently, 'but I will want something in return.'

She waved her hand and behind her a fire sprang into life. A shadow walked slowly out of the flames and although his pallor and disjointed movement rendered him almost beyond recognition, as his sunken eyes flickered weakly in her direction Agneish's face drained of colour. She knew it was Bradan.

Excitedly she called out his name as she stepped off the path.

Both Taliesin and Govannin felt a pressing sense of danger as the songbird fell silent and then inexplicably a crimson apple gave a chilling cry as it plummeted to the ground.

Taliesin pulled Agneish back onto the pathway so violently he wrenched her arm.

'By stepping off the path you have unleashed all the destructive forces the gods placed here for their own amusement. There are life forms present along this pathway you could never imagine. Spectres who will walk next to you with soundless footsteps as they move unobserved at the side of other desolate tormented souls, each spectre with a malicious desire to cause you harm. Worst of all, horrific, depraved wraiths with a strong need to exist after death, travel constantly back and forth along this pathway. You must hope we don't meet them.'

Taliesin was very angry. 'Where is your brother now?', he demanded scathingly.

Agneish looked around. The Seller of Souls had vanished and the only sign Bradan could have been there were a few drops of blood-red tears lying on the grass verge.

'Showing you a shadow you thought was your brother was just a cruel game played by the gods. They wanted to see if your wits were sharp and you were capable of reasoned thought. Eventually they will test your sense of survival.'

As Taliesin was speaking, Govannin realised they were now completely enclosed by a dark silent forest as the weak sunlight which had previously filtered through the tops of the trees had now disappeared.

A carrion crow shrieked overhead as Govannin picked up the crimson fruit from the ground. It crumpled to dust in his hand. Immediately he spun round as a sudden shrill wind rustled the tree tops, even though the rest of the forest remained quiet and still. Govannin began to tremble as the air resounded with the long mournful howls of hunting dogs.

Taliesin and Govannin stared at each other in disbelief as the dwarf said despairingly. 'The gods have summoned the Wild Hunt.'

Agneish looked bewildered, unable to grasp the enormity of what Govannin had said.

Taliesin explained. 'On the eve of the Festival of Lammas, the Lord of the Wild Hunt, known on this night as the Gatherer of the Dead, abandons the Otherworld for two days and nights to lead a procession of hounds and riders across skies or through silent forests to relentlessly pursue a chosen quarry. The hunt is always accompanied by powerful winds.'

Taliesin's eyes searched in every direction as the air became filled with the whinnying of horses and the drawn-out-baying of hounds.

Suddenly, the trees bent under the force of dry, dust-laden winds summoned by the gods from the four cardinal points of the earth, winds that roared and screamed as they rushed through the dense woodland with a sweeping, destructive energy.

The winds quickly diminished, then came the sound of crunching leaves moments before Cernunnos, Lord of the Wild Hunt and a principal god of the Otherworld appeared before them.

Govannin gazed with a mixture of awe and fear at this deity from the domain of the dead, keenly aware he was the most ancient of all the gods.

On his head Cernunnos wore a circlet of stags' antlers, heavily laden with loose trailing ivy, and around his neck, a wide gold torque. His straight black hair reached his shoulders and at the sides of his mouth drooped a thick, dark moustache. He wore a short black cloak embellished with detailed images of former successful wild hunts, and on his right index finger was a large gold ring engraved with skulls, mouths open as if they were screaming.

Sitting astride a huge, sweating black horse, Cernunnos with eyes the colour of the deepest jet, stared at Agneish.

'So, this must be the quarry the gods promised me.'

Taliesin's response was immediate. 'This mortal is not only under the protection of Agrona and Cathubodia, two of the fiercest slaughter-goddesses, she is also protected by the great sea-god Manannan-beg-mac-y-Lleir and his wife Fand.'

Cernunnos pretended to ponder before giving his answer.

'I was specifically directed to the Path of Trepidation by the gods, as here I was promised an excellent chase with a worthy quarry.'

'This cannot be allowed to happen,' Govannin said, his voice quivering slightly as he dared to question the time-honoured privileges of the Wild Hunt.

Cernunnos ignored him and spoke directly to Agneish 'If you are caught I will take you to the concealed entrance which opens upon my Kingdom of Shadows, the Otherworld.' His voice held the most sinister undertones Agneish had ever heard.

Paralysed with fear, her gaze became fixed on the phantom gathering of huntsmen sitting on horses hovering just above the ground, then on the massive heads, powerful jaws and strongly muscled limbs of the snarling hounds, their stealthy movement and obvious strength practically guaranteeing Cernunnos a successful hunt. Including his huntsmen and hounds there must have been about forty of these ghostly predators who hunted in packs to instil terror into the minds of their prey.

Govannin's astute mind was working quickly. He knew the watching gods would become increasingly bored and irritable if Agneish couldn't find a way to play their game. She must show some spirited tactical skills or they would despatch her to the Otherworld with Cernunnos without a second thought. Putting his hand in his pocket he carefully withdrew the gift from Fand, Manannan's signet ring.

Tightly curling Agneish's fingers around it, he whispered, 'I urgently recommend when you need to, you must use this ring to plead for help.'

He heard muffled sounds of talking, laughter, then a jaded voice declaring, 'This is much too tedious, let's get rid of her.'

Frantically, Govannin shouted, 'You must do something *now!*'

Agneish's heart was racing with blind panic as she stared at the primordial Celtic god who Agneish knew had existed since the beginning of time. Even on the remote island of Mann they had heard of Cernunnos.

She knew he wouldn't show her any compassion and if seized she would have to cross the threshold of the World of the Dead.

She tried to think but no useful ideas surfaced to the front of her mind, then instinctively she lifted up her tattered skirt and as fleet-footed as a deer fled into the heart of the forest. Behind her she heard loud exuberant laughter rumbling from the throat of the Lord of the Wild Hunt, then came an excited uproar from the ghostly procession as they began to give chase.

She ran along pathways swarming with twisted misshapen shadows endlessly crossing back and forth over each other and the air was alive with the hissing sounds escaping from these tormented spirits.

As she ran deeper and deeper into the forest, she became aware that the clamour of the hunt had become indistinct, almost muted, and the previously turbulent winds had dropped to a faint soughing sound. Soon, the only audible noise was the crackle of fallen leaves being trampled underfoot as she raced along thick, springy layers of leaf litter.

Somehow she had to keep ahead of the hunt.

She looked behind her and was exhilarated to see the paths she had trodden, which would clearly reveal the direction she had sprinted, were disappearing from sight.

Someone was helping her!

As she ran past ancient trees with cracked trunks and fissured bark, she realised the gods had created a forest similar to the ones at home.

She jumped over thick, decomposing branches covered with lichen; then, as she trod heavily on a puff-ball mushroom and a cloud of spores burst from its open top, she noticed, out of the corner of her eye, a cluster of red-spotted toadstools. Seeing them, tears began to run down her face as she remembered when still only a small child her father showing her toadstools like these and warning her not to touch them as they were extremely poisonous. She wiped the tears away with the back of her hand, she had no time for this.

Out of breath, Agneish leaned against the broad trunk of a tree overlaid with oak-moss and tried to remove the goose-grass clinging to her hair and torn shift.

A wild sow with grunting piglets expressed her disapproval at Agneish's presence by making a quick charge in her direction before retreating with her young litter further back into the central part of the forest.

Then in the stillness came the high-pitched yelp of baying hounds.

Terror-stricken at the realisation that the phantom hunt was closing in, Agneish succumbed to despair.

Heavy-legged she tried to run, stumbling repeatedly as she caught her feet in clumps of loose moss, slipped on damp, crust-like, patches of fungi and tripped over bulky tree-roots.

Then she heard the whoosh of wings as a bird flew just over her head. A crow!

With loud harsh cries it flew higher and higher as if urging her to look up. Raising her head she saw the pack was hunting her from the sky.

In this heavily forested area Agneish was able to move quickly into the enveloping shadows of tall trees, but had no idea what to do next except wait for darkness.

She hid in the trunk of a mouldering oak tree, listening to the baying hounds careering through the air, sometimes too far away to worry her unduly and sometimes so close she almost stopped breathing.

A sudden emergence of sunlight flooding through the treetops revealed another pathway and Agneish ran towards it, but she had been seen!

Cernunnos and his pack of spectral horses, hounds and huntsmen began to descend with lightning speed from the sky.

They formed two lines, then split up. One line remained stationary, lingering in the air just above the forest floor behind her, the other facing her on ground level, hoping to drive her towards the line hovering threateningly at the rear.

The hounds had caught sight of her running figure and were now so close they began growling and snapping at her heels.

Having nowhere else to run Agneish bowed her head in despair as the pack raced towards her, exhausted, she turned to face her pursuers when Govannin's urgent instructions about Manannan's signet ring rushed into her mind. Groping in the pocket of her shift she made a frantic search for the ring. It wasn't there! Then she became aware throughout all the trauma of her flight she was still clutching it tightly in her hand.

Triumphantly holding it aloft, she loudly called out Manannan's name.

Cernunnos, who had reined in his black stallion directly in front of her, narrowed his eyes as she cried out to the great sea-god.

She saw the figure of a man, his face shaded by the dense foliage of the trees, move out of the partial darkness provided by the leafy upper branches and into the sunlight. Bright rays of sunshine dancing on his long shadow served to highlight the shimmering colours of the cloak he wore around his shoulders.

The man advanced without haste towards the Lord of the Wild Hunt. He was very tall, powerfully built with thick white hair, a lengthy white beard and eyes of a deep blue-green, the exact shade of the open sea.

The gloating smile on Cernunnos's face vanished at the appearance of the commanding presence of Manannan-beg-mac-y-Lleir.

The Lord of the Wild Hunt took his time scrutinising the Lord of the Ocean. He looked at Manannan's strong, noble countenance and recognised immediately the Guardian of Mann was a warrior. He also knew the deity standing before him was the Protector of the Blessed Isles, an alternative gateway to where the spirit travels after death.

Here and there over the passing millions of years Cernunnos had seen Manannan travelling towards the isles, and, like himself, knew the sea-god had an influential role in the cycle of life and death.

Manannan turned to Agneish. 'So other deities would know you travelled with my approval through this land, I gave you my blessing and my ring.'

He gave Cernunnos a searching glance before he spoke to him. 'This time your quarry must escape the hunt. It is time for her to journey to the summit of the Mountain Kingdom of the Gods where the Watchers await her arrival.'

Cernunnos gave Manannan a disgruntled stare before saying angrily. 'And if I don't agree?'

Manannan said quietly: 'You have no choice, the gods honour my blessing. Look up.'

As Cernunnos glanced skyward he saw the heavens were becoming darker and the decreasing daylight was rapidly giving way to the approach of nightfall. Very soon the skies were covered with purple shadows and the soft illumination of starlight. The gods had turned day into night.

Cernunnos hesitated, uncertain of the outcome if he didn't accept his peer's decision. He glanced towards the sky again and saw every single light from the thousands of stars overhead was being extinguished, a reproving sign the chase was over. Agneish was to be allowed to continue her journey.

Then one lone star appeared in the darkness, Sirius, the brightest star in the night sky. The gods were waiting.

Manannan said sternly. 'You must sign the hunt's recalling horn.'

Cernunnos showed no sign of capitulation.

Suddenly lightning split the dusky sky, a warning to the Lord of the Wild Hunt that Tannus, the God of Thunder and Storms was making visible his disapproval. The blessing of the Guardian of Mann must be honoured.

As the thunder-god discharged flashes of lightning the deities reversed their decision to change day into night and in moments the heavens were blue again.

Manannan gathered Agneish close to him then wrapped her inside his magical cloak. As the forest faded from view she heard the enraged commotion from the phantom huntsmen and hounds as they realised she was getting away.

In seconds she was standing before Govannin and Taliesin on the Path of Trepidation.

Seeing the relief on their faces that she was alive and well, Agneish burst into tears.

Trying to comfort her, Govannin patted her awkwardly on her shoulder, while Taliesin's heartfelt relief at not having to explain her disappearance to Agrona and Cathubodia was palpable.

Manannan gave her a few moments to gather her composure. 'Well', he said, the tone of his voice gentle and sympathetic, 'we have looked favourably upon you Agneish and permitted you to emerge safely from your trial. But let me warn you, there will be more trials in the hours ahead and if you successfully complete them, tonight you must climb to the peak of our mountain. That will be your final trial and will use the remainder of your first day in our land. From sunrise until noon of your second day you will find deities on the summit who may wish to speak to you. The Four Supreme Beings who watch over all of us will meet with you from noon until sunset.

'At nightfall you must leave the mountain and make your way east to where the Time Messenger will herald in the new day. When you hear him you must journey without delay to the gates of the Land of a Thousand Gods. The Morrigan will open them at once to allow you to leave. Enbarr will be waiting for you and once you are astride his back Taliesin will escort you and Govannin back to your village.

His outline became hazy and his voice weaker as he began to fade from their view. Just before he vanished Agneish heard him say softly. 'Good fortune Agneish.'

Chapter Nine

The Swamplands

In his anxiety to leave the Path of Trepidation Govannin struck the ground with his staff with such tremendous force it jarred his spine. He hardly felt the pain as he watched a thin line of fire begin to mark out the trail they would need to follow. As they hurried in pursuit of the flames Taliesin noticed a thick cloudy vapour was stalking them stealthily from behind.

Govannin also noticed the vapour and paid close attention to Taliesin as he withdrew from a small casing fastened to his ankle a gleaming gold dagger.

Immediately he saw the dagger, Govannin knew instinctively it concealed extraordinary powers and could only have been cast by one of his own race.

The Prince of Song told Govannin it had been a gift from Segomo, a handsome but arrogant god of war who was never seen without his hawk sitting on his shoulder.

Segomo had been ecstatic about three works Taliesin had set to music as a tribute to the war-god's courage. The combination and quality of Taliesin's words describing Segomo's high social position as one of the foremost war-gods had been deliberately calculated to evoke images of Segomo's valour in the heat of battle.

The war-god had told Taliesin the dagger had been forged from the dying rays of the setting sun and as long as the god who owned it used the weapon in good faith and with honour it would render him incapable of being harmed.

Holding the blade tightly in his hand Taliesin urged them to follow the flames as quickly as they could.

They walked on, the mysterious vapour keeping pace with them until they reached a forbidding, inhospitable section previously unrevealed to travellers leaving the Path of Trepidation. Having heard the widely circulated rumours about a location resembling what lay in front of them, Taliesin realised this must be the Swamplands.

At once the vapour left the track and drifted to where a thick miasma reeking of death and decay hung over an extensive quagmire of slow moving water.

An uneasy silence fell upon the small group as they looked apprehensively at the bleak, swampy expanse of waterlogged ground.

There was very little natural light breaking over this silent, desolate place, making Agneish more and more nervous as she thought she saw something moving on the far side of the boggy terrain. Then, close to where they were standing, two lanterns blazing with light appeared on the surface of the water, illuminating the numerous rotting stumps of ancient trees jutting above the saturated ground.

Taliesin thought the lanterns must have been placed there, perhaps by Fand, as a concession to Agneish's and Govannin's frayed nerves as they stared at what had to be the grimmest, most unpleasant region of the Kingdom of the Gods.

Picking up the hem of her shift Agneish held it over her mouth, the putrid stench of decomposing matter rising from the swampy ground was making her feel ill.

Taliesin's expression was sombre as his gaze wandered over the trees growing in and around the soft, muddy, almost motionless surface of low-lying ground.

He looked steadily for some time at a dense prickly thicket of giant rag-web trees whose spiny growths were hung with unsightly webs. Covering the webs were masses of large, hideous, black-headed larvae. The enormous numbers of these newly-hatched, wingless, worm-like creatures made it impossible to establish the existence of any presence that might be hiding in the undergrowth.

Trying to shake off his fears, Taliesin walked to the edge of the quagmire and looked at the cloud of thick vapour hanging over the water.

'I have heard of this place,' he said despondently. 'It is an almost forgotten portal to the Otherworld. We have obviously been sent here as a test, another trial to determine our abilition. I myself know of no better conclusion to our journey than being able to present you Agneish, unharmed to Agrona and Cathubodia.'

Taliesin raised his arm and holding the short tapered blade by its hilt tossed the golden dagger up in the air. The dagger rotated rapidly around and around and as it spun it sent shards of light over the silent quagmire and at once a host of moving shadows became visible in the pure radiance contained within a blade forged by the rays of the setting sun.

Taliesin said very quietly: 'This section of the Otherworld is the home of countless souls who still retain the faculty of thought. They are bound in servitude to Elphane, Goddess of Death and Destruction. Their main function is to guide spirits recently deceased into her domain.

'I must warn both of you that if these spirits reveal themselves to us, do not steal even a quick glance at them, as they will endeavour to absorb your life force and make you a suppliant who will owe allegiance to Elphane.'

Almost paralysed with fear, Agneish turned her back on the water and begged Taliesin and Govannin to leave this wretched place at once.

As they hurried away, the centre of the quagmire erupted with previously silent and unseen shadows who watched them depart with a deep malevolence and anger.

Unnoticed a crow left the disintegrating canopy of a timeworn tree and flew soundlessly behind them.

Shaken by what she had seen, Agneish asked in a trembling voice. 'Now where?'

'Tap your staff on the ground Govannin and see what happens.' Taliesin requested.

Obediently Govannin gave the ground a powerful rap and flames sprang out of the earth, the new trail blazing directly east.

'We must follow where it leads,' Taliesin said firmly, 'we have been given a fresh path to pursue.'

Silently the three set off, the flames springing ahead of them and then extinguishing themselves as before.

Too proud to ask for a short rest, Govannin leant heavily on his silver staff. So much walking was aggravating the pain in his crooked spine but he would not allow his disability to interfere with his plans for achieving the renowned excellence as an artisan he so desperately craved.

The dwarf's expression tightened when he realised they were still in the Swamplands and the path was going past a bog-like section of soft soil which bore an astonishing similarity to an area of land he had encountered once before. If identical, he knew it concealed isolated areas of yielding, shifting masses of loose wet sand that would swiftly and suddenly grasp anyone who stepped onto it. A hazard set by the gods.

Govannin's knowledge of plants was vast and he quickly identified the rust-coloured careering tree. When the tree sensed someone was passing by, its stout arching limbs and drooping branches would sway dangerously to one side to try and make contact with anyone walking underneath. The speckled brownish-yellow leaves of the tree touching the skin, caused fleshy tissue to feel on fire.

He recognised tall, black barked trees whose wide spreading branches produced long, upright inky-black needles and trailing streamers of black moss. The habitual action of the moss was to wind itself tightly around a passing traveller, leaving the unfortunate person gasping with pain and fighting for breath.

There was the spore-bearing, mock beggar-bush with its several twisted trunks and misshapen outstretched branches as if pleading for compassion. The spores attached themselves to the face, first making it itch, then erupt with weeping infected lesions.

Govannin was puzzled by the fact that these extremely repugnant trees which exposed individuals to injury or harm had been allowed to flourish in the Land of a Thousand Gods. Then he realised they were probably only on display for this one day, perhaps as another problem for Agneish to deal with. He must warn her about them.

The surface of the swamp was covered in free-floating brown algae, which attached itself to the trunks of partly submerged trees. Hanging from their branches were silvery-white threadlike stems which drooped into the water in long, densely-matted clusters. Govannin was intrigued, he hadn't seen this particular species of tree before. With some amusement he thought the silvery-matted stems looked similar to an old man's beard.

When he halted to identify the trees, Agneish and Taliesin had walked slowly on ahead of him but all three whirled swiftly around when they heard the powerful sound of beating wings exploding from an impenetrable mass of high, blue-black spiky bushes.

Govannin was stunned to see it was a rendon, a wading bird, thought to be extinct.

The long legs of the seven foot high wader had a single sharply hooked talon on each foot, talons which nearly brushed against Govannin's shoulders as it flew around his head in a circular motion. Its wings, covered in a leathery membrane, were about twenty five feet wide and Govannin knew the rendon's great wing surface would allow the bird to soar almost indefinitely over his hunched body.

Its huge powerful beak and featherless neck with a broad red band of skin at its base, was a clear indication to Govannin, the rendon ate flesh.

The bird's large skull, with its drab brown plumes and layer of sulphur-yellow feathery tufts covering its long body, was a terrifying spectacle as it flew over Govannin, its beak gaping and talons protruding in anticipation as it circled lower and lower.

Govannin was so immersed in watching the rendon, he was unaware that Taliesin was shouting to him, urging him to hit his staff hard on the ground in the hope the fire trail would scare the bird away.

Then echoing through the trees came a succession of strange persistent calls, calls Govannin didn't recognise but Taliesin did. They were from a zegopt, the largest bird ever known to exist in the Land of a Thousand Gods. A bird equally at home living and hunting in the treetops as on the ground.

Growing around the perimeter of the Swamplands with their roots deeply submerged, were hundred foot high poisonwood trees. Their sagging branches formed a canopy which was an ideal hiding place for any predatory creatures waiting to attack.

Then Govannin caught sight of two large birds perched high up in the crown of a poisonwood tree. He must caution Agneish against touching any sap leaking from the tree's dark-green crusty bark. It was lethal to mortals.

Hearing a scuffling sound behind him, Govannin wheeled round. The rendon was now on the ground and very close.

In the distance there was a rumble of thunder, then the sound of raindrops drumming on leaves before a solitary, raucous cry of derision, the characteristic cry of the zegopt, rang through the air.

The second zegopt merged his cries with the first, cries which had intervals of silence before increasing in volume and intensifying in pace until they resembled maniacal laughter; then the two birds burst from the trees and landed near the rendon.

The zegopts featherless red neck; black curved bill and richly coloured protuberant casques were in stark contrast to the rendon's dull growth of brown head feathers. With vivid blue and orange plumage and trailing, black and white tail feathers, the zegopts were an intimidating sight.

The two species were mortal enemies, competing and challenging brutally for the sole right to hunt prey in the Swamplands.

With the arrival of the zegopts, the rendon forgot about Govannin who gasped with horror as the two larger birds flew smoothly down and settled on the ground close to the rendon and only a short distance from himself. Their distinctive physical appearance and immense size petrified Agneish. Taliesin kept a tight hold of her as she shook from head to foot.

Taliesin felt very afraid for Govannin's safety.

The zegopts circled the rendon twice, the rendon uttering harsh, discordant shrieks as he waited for an attack. Then one of the zegopts suddenly turned round and disappeared into a nearby boggy area filled with poisonwood trees.

Taliesin shouted at Govannin to make his escape. The dwarf did as directed, taking to his heels and moving as quickly as his crooked spine would allow.

Reaching Agneish and Taliesin, Govannin tried desperately to shake off the strong feelings of revulsion and fear which were making the hairs on the back of his neck stand on end, but he was acutely aware his eager desire to leave this desolate place would not be accomplished that easily.

Taliesin's gaze searched and lingered on the canopy of poisonwood trees, but he couldn't catch sight of the missing zegopt. He was extremely conscious of the fact that if one of the enormous birds decided to attack the rendon unaided, the other could launch a swift assault on any one of them.

Suddenly, bursting out from a stretch of thick grass just a short distance away, a small flightless bird ran across their path. Startled, it took a few moments for Govannin's and Agneish's heartbeats to settle back to normal, but the nervous tension on Govannin's face was there for all to see.

Although she was trembling with fright nothing she had encountered so far was able to shake Agneish from her firm belief that Mannnnan would not let any harm come to them.

Keeping this conviction to the forefront of her mind she tried to comfort Govannin with the same thought, but she could tell he remained unconvinced, then simultaneously the three of them noticed the same nauseating smell and all three had the feeling they were being watched.

The thick grass parted again, but this time the giant predatory zegopt stood there.

It stared at them through small, glittering black eyes as it repeatedly thrashed its long, trailing tail feathers on the ground. Its jaws were open, displaying a set of long serrated teeth and Govannin knew the saliva dripping from its mouth would be infected with deadly bacteria.

Moving out from its hiding place the zegopt fixed its eyes on Agneish.

'Run,' Taliesin shouted to her. 'Run!'

Considering its bulk the huge bird was able to chase Agneish with incredible speed. The zegopt caught up with her and as its teeth buried themselves into the flesh of her leg the immediate surges of pain pulsating through her slender frame caused her to lose her balance. Wounded, she dropped to the ground.

Govannin and Taliesin raced towards Agneish, both shouting as loudly as they could to try and deflect the bird's attention.

Using his staff, the dwarf struck the ground a powerful blow and instantly a trail of flames ran alongside the zegopt.

Frightened by the fire, the zegopt reared up, screeching the same maniacal laughter they had heard before.

Crouching down, Taliesin managed to pull Agneish out of the bird's path and Govannin saw its saliva running from a deep gash in Agneish's calf. He could hear her breathing had already become gratingly harsh and laboured. Around the gash her skin felt hot and was clearly beginning to putrefy.

Gathering her up in his arms Taliesin backed away from the zegopt until he could safely put Agneish on the ground. Brandishing his dagger he stood over her as he waited to see the bird's reaction to having lost its prey, leaving Govannin free to rummage in his haversack to search for two specific types of remedies he always carried with him.

The zegopt emitted more of those curiously unsettling cries before it turned slowly towards Taliesin. The Prince of Song quickly moved some distance away from Govannin and Agneish.

Above him Taliesin heard a smooth slithering sound. Looking up he felt an overwhelming sense of panic as he saw an emerald coloured serpent twisting and winding its way down one of those black barked trees.

At its widest point the girth of the reptile had to be more than a yard wide, so Taliesin guessed it must be the type of serpent that crushed its victims to death. It was rapidly flicking its tongue as the heat-sensors on its upper lip informed the serpent its intended victims were warm blooded.

As the massive triangular shaped head of the reptile reached the ground, the rest of its body slid sinuously downwards over the uneven surface of the tree and began crawling towards the zegopt.

As slowly and as silently as he could, Taliesin warily moved backwards and away from the zegopt until he reached Govannin and Agneish's side.

The dwarf had withdrawn a small carved sandalwood box and in answer to Taliesin's enquiring look told him, that inside, was a healing recipe conceived by his grandfather. He read the label out loud.

A salve to cure most things, it contains:-

Prickly ash bark

Dried dandelion

Red clover

Dried mint leaves

Skullcap herb

Catnip

and to finish, Hawthorn berries which have been soaked in Chamomile water.

All of which have been boiled together and left to soften and thicken.

After eight weeks the salve can be spread over cuts, boils, weeping sores and open wounds.

'But first Govannin said worriedly, 'Agneish must be made ready for sleep. The healing potency of the salve is very powerful and will cause her some pain.' He delved into his haversack again, this time removing a small crystal phial.

'This is the *Tincture of Dreams*. Another of my grandfather's recipes.'
The label read;-

A pinch of Devil's claw foot

A trace of Borage

A trace of Burdock root

A spoonful of Crushed nettles

A pinch of Couch grass root

Rain-soaked Yarrow flowers

Govannin shook the phial vigorously then administered three drops of the tincture into Agneish's mouth. Her eyes flickered once, twice, then she fell into a deep sleep.

Govannin quickly opened the hinged lid of the box and liberally applied a vivid green salve to the gash in Agneish's calf, promising Taliesin it would sooth and heal without delay.

Agneish was shivering from head to foot and in an effort to keep her warm Govannin covered her with his cloak saying softly: 'The bacteria from the zegopt's saliva is capable of causing Agneish's death, but I know my grandfather has great faith in the curative properties of his recipe, so we must be patient and wait for it to take effect.'

Ten minutes passed, then gradually Agneish's laboured breathing dropped in intensity to a low husky level and she stopped shivering.

Taliesin and Govannin gazed at each other in relief, the salve had been successful.

Suddenly they heard the loud, raucous cries of a zegopt. Wild, ear-splitting cries that resounded with agony.

Moving stealthily back to where the bird had attacked Agneish, Taliesin saw the emerald serpent had coiled its massive girth around the zegopt and each time the bird tried to take a mouthful of air the constrictor squeezed its coils a little tighter. Soon the zegopt would be unable to breath.

Edging away, Taliesin backtracked to where the other zegopt and the rendon had been about to attack each other.

Used as he was to the unpredictable caprices of the gods, even he was surprised to see a blazing firebrand falling from the sky. Clouds of gaseous vapours seeping from the ground immediately ignited into a ring of flame around the two birds. In seconds they were consumed by fire.

At first he thought the firebrand had been an extravagant gesture from Aibheaog, an excitable fire-goddess whose mercurial twists of temperament made her prone to erratic behaviour. Then he noticed a white feather slowly twisting and turning as it drifted towards the ground.

Could it have been the goddess Almha?

Shrugging his shoulders he walked away.

When Agneish recovered her strength, Taliesin, softly strumming his lyre, stared hard at both Govannin and Agneish before saying quietly: 'As the goddess Almha has told you, the only approach to the Kingdom of the Gods is a footpath on the eastern side of the mountain. A difficult, dangerous undertaking, but ascending it successfully will eventually grant us the permitted access to the four Watchers.'

Govannin took a deep breath; he could hardly believe he was so near to accomplishing his goal of offering the Watchers his concept of pattern, elements and features with each individual section heavily inlaid with gold within a torque he had named *Perception*.

He was so occupied thinking about his future, he nearly missed what Taliesin said next.

'I must offer both of you a cautionary warning,' the Prince of Song said in such a serious manner that he gained their immediate attention. 'The gods will set one last momentous trial. But if you survive this final ordeal you can be sure most of these deities will offer their help in any way they can. It has been remiss of me not to mention it before, but any deity we meet along the way can only offer you the minimum amount of assistance. You must remember these trials have been set for the gods' amusement, a diversion from their day to day existence. It will be a trial without rules, the result being determined by skill, strength or chance. 'If you want their help Agneish you must play their games by exhibiting exceptional quickness of mind and imagination.'

Agneish nodded thoughtfully. She had long ago realised the reality of her situation, but deep inside her subconscious mind her inner being was glowing with a hope that was steadily progressing from possibility to actuality. It was now time to show her courage, both physical and mental and, if they approved, the gods would rid her world forever of the Norseman.

Chapter Ten

The Barbed Daegon

Once Govannin had tapped the ground soundly with his staff a rapid eruption of flames pointed towards a footpath for them to follow, a footpath which by late afternoon, led them to the foothills of the Mountain Kingdom of the Gods, a kingdom which offered complete seclusion.

Agneish, rendered speechless by the magnificence of the landscape spread out in front of them, could only stand and stare in wonder at the lush ancient forest that covered the mountain slopes.

Govannin stood quite still before inhaling a long sigh of contentment deep into his lungs as he saw the immense peak of the gods' domain towering high above the surrounding hills. The summit, wreathed in clouds of fine mists in delicate shades of purple and blue, was breath-taking and was a view he believed he'd never be given the opportunity to see.

Valleys gouged out over millions of years by the progressive erosion of gushing torrents of water, ice and wind washing away the soil on the mountain face, provided channels for the flow of three rivers, a flow that always returned to its source, the Perthro, whose name Taliesin told them later meant, 'something hidden.'

The Perthro, the longest river in the Land of a Thousand Gods began its journey at the foot of the mountain which was in the eastern region of the land, before coursing the length and breadth of the realm into the west, north and south.

The three rivers had a special meaning to the deities and were known as the Waters of Oanuava, the source from which all life flows, the Waters of Taillte, the Goddess of the Light embodied in the sun-god Lugh, and the Waters of Brigantia, Goddess of Protection of the Land because the strands of her cloak were woven with all things connected to the labyrinth of life, ensuring constancy, guidance and stability.

'Based on reliable information concerning situations we might find ourselves in,' Taliesin said briskly, 'we must first discover the hidden track through the forest that will lead us to the Perthro River. Here I'm told there will be a boat waiting at the water's edge, a boat that will transport us along an underground stream beneath the mountain. I have also been told that when the stream comes to an end, from there we'll have to find the only way out, a secret door which will open onto the footpath leading to the summit.'

Govannin was silent as he stared pensively at the steep slopes soaring high above them, slopes filled with gigantic trees, some with multiple trunks and patterned bark of light yellow stripes their branches bearing a dense covering of lavender-tinted leaves which almost concealed tiny, orange star-shaped flowers.

Others had spectacular drooping masses of silver, oval-shaped fruits, while the dipping boughs of a number of the huge trees had trumpets of fully opened, velvety saffron flowers, many of which were falling gently to the ground.

There were huge majestic trees with blue-grey leaves and soft red cones, trees with clusters of blossoms in different shades of purple, and enormous, dangling, oblong kernels. There were bushes burgeoning with glossy lime-green foliage and cascades of spiky, coral buds, further bushes spilling over with vibrant blue, cup-like flower heads as large as his face. He watched brightly coloured birds feeding from shrubbery heavy with the weight of damson-tinted berries with such a saturation of colour they appeared almost black.

Growing amongst massive red and green ferns and multi-hued grasses were stunning, tall, flame-coloured plants that looked like tongues of fire waving in the slight breeze coming off the mountain.

He listened to the calls of animals he couldn't identify echoing through the tree tops and gazed again at the steep cliffs sheltering forested valleys, thundering waterfalls and dark ravines, all serving to enhance the Kingdom of the Gods. Govannin wondered how they were going to find their way through the vastness of this seemingly impenetrable vegetation.

With understandable apprehension he hit the ground with his staff and immediately not flames, but a thin cloud of black smoke flared out of the earth.

Taliesin said thoughtfully. 'Ah, so this time we follow a trail of smoke. Safer then flames when we enter the forest.'

Govannin nodded in full agreement.

The cloud of smoke led them to a forest floor protected from the sun-god's rays by a dense canopy of trees.

Carefully they trod in and out of masses of decomposing leaf litter teeming with huge armies of trysia. These six-legged, bulky, red and black furry insects were voracious feeders, their main prey being ropods.

The trysia had large strong jaws that opened and shut sideways, making it easier for them to inject venomous fluid stored in a pocket inside their mouths directly into their victims, fluid which dissolved their prey in seconds. The trysia possessed strength far beyond what their size suggested and although they seemed to have only two eyes Govannin knew the structure of each eye was shaped from countless smaller eyes. Govannin thought they were astounding creatures.

The hairy, brown striped ropod had eight huge eyes set into four rows of two. The colour of their eyes varied in each row, some were green, others were yellow. They had eight powerful legs and their front right-side leg had three claws which would clamp onto their victim and then disembowel it in an instant. They always hunted in packs.

A war had raged between the trysia and ropods since the beginning of time.

They saw wriggling, green and black spotted marek that ate its own kind, and Govannun recognised the colossal, distinctively marled optera. The white markings on the enormous black wings of these huge insects looked like the bony head of a skull.

Smiling, Taliesin held out branches of leaves with 'drip sprouts'. The shape of the leaf held drops of rain-water enabling the three of them to drink a few mouthfuls of fresh liquid, but as they drank Taliesin's nerves were stretched to breaking point when he heard the unmistakable 'cough' of a chui.

Its woolly, midnight-blue coat allowed the chui's hunting strategy to be based on stealth and power. Weighing about half a ton and with huge, curving canine teeth which were close to twelve inches long, the chui had few enemies.

There was an edge, a sharpness in the tone of Taliesin's voice as he said: 'Time is passing quickly, we must find our way to the river without delay.'

Lowering his voice he whispered to Govannin, 'I thought I heard a chui.'

Govannin nodded discretely, he too had heard the 'cough'.

The urgency in Taliesin's voice was infectious, motivating them to force their way through the thick vegetation, their hurried movements startling small bright-red birds into taking flight as the evolving cloud of smoke continuously materialised and relentlessly moved forward. Agneish was the first to see the gleaming ribbon of water.

Shouting with delight she ran to the riverbank, Taliesin and Govannin only moments behind her.

Staring at the river, Taliesin remained engrossed in thought for some time. He was just about to speak when he heard a woman's voice calling out his name. Kicking up a tremendous cloud of dust as she ran at incredible speed towards them was Luaths Lurgann, whose name meant 'speedy foot'.

Luaths Lurgann was a warrior goddess acknowledged as the fastest runner in the Land of a Thousand Gods. She ceased running just long enough to disclose that the seeress of Moments Past and Future had sent her to deliver a warning. 'Death stands waiting for those not alert to deception and danger', she said quickly, before raising her hand in farewell and speeding away. In seconds she was out of sight.

They looked up as a carrion crow perched on a branch of a grotesquely deformed tree suddenly uttered a piercing cry before flying off in the opposite direction taken by Luaths Lurgann.

They saw a boat drifting down the river towards them.

'Powerful forces are at work here', Taliesin said softly. The deep concern verging on anxiety in his voice was picked up at once by Govannin.

Taliesin carried on talking. 'There is not much I can tell you about the Perthro River except its specific purpose is beyond ordinary understanding or explanation and its mysteries are shared only with the Watchers.

'The outer periphery of the Perthro River is the absolute domain of Caer Iboreith, the Goddess of Sleep and Dreams. If she uses her great powers to assume the shape of a swan, the goddess becomes a mystical bird whose beautiful, haunting song will lull you into a deep slumber. *This you must avoid!* The price you will pay for falling asleep will be your life!'

There was a stunned silence from Agneish and Govannin.

'The boat will take us to the entrance of the tunnel that runs beneath the mountain. The opening is called the Daegon's Mouth; why I do not know.

'As all three of us have much to gain if we safely reach the summit, I must ask if you are ready to step into the boat? The choice is yours.'

Agneish and Govannin looked questioningly at each other before slowly murmuring their agreement.

As they stepped into the boat which had halted at the edge of the riverbank, Taliesin explained a little more about the river.

'Once we have entered the Daegon's Mouth, the water flowing through the tunnel is under control of the Watchers. Here, I have been informed, you will see the walls of an underground cave inscribed with the secrets of the ancients. The meaning of this mysterious writing is known only to these same four deities.'

While Taliesin was speaking, the boat had been slowly drifting nearer to the opening of the underground tunnel.

Govannin had little to say. He was troubled by the warning sent by the seeress via Luaths Lurgann. It reminded him that by the stream of Moments Past and Future the seeress had also said. 'In this land the soul can be lost or stolen.'

Taliesin was on edge about the entrance being called the Daegon's Mouth. He *had* heard a version as to the reason, but for now preferred to keep it to himself.

So far the whole experience of travelling through this incredible land was utterly beyond Agneish's comprehension. Shaking her head vigorously from side to side in the hope of clearing her bewilderment, she suddenly noticed the water ahead appeared much more turbulent and very muddy, as if something was stirring up the sediment from the riverbed.

Taliesin observed with relief that the small boat remained fairly stable in the river's now surprisingly choppy waters and shouted out to hold onto the sides.

Carried along by the rolling undercurrents, the boat was drifting nearer and nearer to the Daegon's Mouth when a head broke through the water, a head Govannin estimated to be about six foot long.

The creature stood up high out of the water and Taliesin and Govannin realised they must be looking at the only living barbed daegon, a monstrous, primordial lizard whom, it was whispered, had guarded this entrance from the moment it had been granted life, one hundred and five million years ago.

So, Taliesin realised, what he had been told wasn't just hearsay after all.

Govannin and Agneish's eyes were wide with shock as they stared at the monster who had partially reared up in front of them like a huge menacing colossus.

'I thought the unconfirmed report that a daegon still existed was only a myth,' Govannin stuttered.

A tail lashed, a massive tail that left a visible murky trail clouding the blue surface of the river.

Its jaws fully open, revealing two rows of large, curved, serrated yellow teeth, the lizard uttered a deafening roar before lowering itself back into the water and began to move rapidly downstream towards them.

Immediately, a white swan materialised on the river and the air resounded with an unforgettable, profoundly heart-rending melody. 'Don't listen,' Taliesin urged Agneish and Govannin, 'take hold of the oars and concentrate on turning the boat back into the riverbank.'

The barbed daegon stopped moving through the water, its pursuit of them coming to a temporary halt as it listened to the mesmerising song of the Goddess of Sleep and Dreams.

'Now,' Taliesin almost screamed, ' turn the boat.'

Fortune was on their side as their combined efforts succeeded in propelling the small vessel into the side of the river.

As the three of them practically fell out of the boat onto dry land Taliesin stole a quick look at the daegon and was relieved to see it was still listening to the eerily evocative song of Caer Iboreith.

Agneish's hands were still shaking with fright as she pointed to a tall figure dressed in a loose, light-blue robe who had appeared at the water's edge.

'Who are you?' Taliesin enquired quietly.

'A traveller,' the stranger replied. His voice emitting from inside his drawn up hood was muffled. 'I am here to advise you.'

'You must ask assistance from Cebhfhionn, the Goddess of Inspiration. You will find her next to the Well of Knowledge and if she allows you to drink from the sanctified water you will instantly possess knowledge of such exceptional excellence that you will know how to slay the barbed daegon.'

Taliesin looked at the stranger with disbelief.

'Defeating the daegon is something you must do Taliesin as you will not be allowed to continue your journey until he is dead,' said the stranger.

Taliesin looked intently at the traveller; he felt he had met him before, but the pulled up hood completely shaded his face.

'Where is the Well of Knowledge?'

The stranger directed Taliesin's attention to a group of aged standing stones which appeared almost menacing to the eye as the greyness of the stones reflected only a little of the daylight trying to filter through the veil of clouds looming over them.

Taliesin stared for a moment at the tall, upright megalithic structure. When he turned round the stranger had vanished.

His instincts telling him they would be protected from harm as long as the goddess was singing, he asked Govannin and Agneish to stay where they were, a safe distance from the water's edge. Then leaving his lyre with Agneish, Taliesin walked slowly towards the standing stones.

Holding an empty pitcher in her hands, the goddess Cebhfhionn was sitting beside a well.

She stood up as Taliesin drew nearer and said in a pleased voice, 'I wondered if you would come to me.'

Her voice was warm and rich, her smile welcoming as she gazed at the Prince of Song.

Bending over the well she plunged the pitcher into the water and when it was full she offered the vessel to Taliesin.

'Drink deeply Taliesin and your imagination will be guided by the power of logical thought,' she commanded.

Taliesin swallowed the liquid and waited uneasily for the promised guidance.

A soughing wind murmuring softly over the stones carried a voice to Taliesin. 'You must find the secret hidden head of the daegon and cut it off.'

Taliesin gave Cebhfhionn an incredulous stare. 'What secret head?' he demanded, 'and what would I use to cut it off if I could find it?'

The goddess's enigmatic smile was annoying as she replied in a self-satisfied manner: 'A method has been found. Many of the watching gods have been delighted with the red-haired mortal's determination to proceed despite the hazards she has encountered. The guardian of her island will assist you with the aid of his sword Freggyragh.'

'Manannan-beg-mac-y-Lleir is here?' said Taliesin, shaking his head in annoyance at his stupidity. 'Of course,' he continued as he remembered a trace of amusement in the stranger's voice. 'He was the hooded traveller.' Manannan was apparently enjoying the game as much as the other deities.

'You must go back to the Perthro River Taliesin and assess your chances of finding the secret head of the daegon, for it is in there he hides his thought processes.'

Running back to the river Taliesin found the Goddess of Sleep and Dreams had stopped singing and Agneish and Govannin were warily watching the daegon lurking beneath the surface of the Perthro.

Picking up his lyre, Taliesin began strumming his instrument, showing little interest or care in what he played, but knowing the activity would help him to concentrate.

Without warning, the lizard exploded out of the Perthro and into their range of vision, agitatedly thrashing its powerful tail against the water as it gave vent to a series of loud, prolonged roars of rage.

From the comparative safety of the riverbank, Taliesin stared at the monster he was supposed to put to death. He observed with great care the long barbed spikes which extended along its neck, vertebrae and massive tail and made a mental note of a thick, fleshy, overhanging flap of skin at the back of its strong hunched head. He suspected this could be where the secret head was concealed.

He guessed the daegon must be about fifty foot long and about eighteen foot tall. Its head as Govannin had already speculated, about six foot in length with powerful jaws filled to capacity with jagged teeth.

It had solid, bulky back legs and two sturdy short arms with three fingered hands, each finger having long, crescent-shaped claws. Its brown and black skin covered with thin overlapping scales worked as a perfect camouflage for the lizard to blend with the mud and plant-life at the side of the river.

Taliesin looked intently at the two short horns on the daegon's spike-covered skull, at the bony bulges and furrowed ridges above its two deep-set small eyes and could identify no other place where the monster could hide a secret head, except under that flap of skin!

So that must be where he would strike the fatal blow!

After explaining to Govannin and Agneish what he had to do, Taliesin sat down on the grass near the river, making sure he kept some distance between himself and the water.

Govannin sat down beside him and watched Taliesin gazing despondently at the giant lizard as he struggled to think of a strategy and tactics that might succeed in slaying it. After a few moments Govannin began to speak. 'I have a method of attack which my race has had to use in times gone by to outwit those determined to destroy us.'

Gripping Taliesin's arm Govannin said bleakly. 'To defeat the barbed daegon is a matter of *our life and death*, so we must on no account neglect to explore even a slim possibility of victory, as you can win this battle if you are prepared.

'As your aim is to be the victor of this contest I think an unwavering confidence in your abilities to be the most significant factor.

'First, you must take the role of aggressor.

'Second, attack the daegon when he is off guard.

'Third, as the daegon's appearance is based on deception, yours must be the same.

'As you are the Prince of Song, one way could be to keep up a continuous outpouring of such breath-taking magnificent music, it would deceive it into thinking it is the song of the Goddess of Sleep and Dreams. The sound might calm the lizard and perhaps lull it to sleep.

'Fourth, that is the precise moment to cut off its head!'

The Prince of Song and the dwarf stared at each other, then Taliesin stood up. 'It might work, as I was assured I would have the use of Manannan's sword. We must remember,' he said grimly, 'for the three of us victory is not the end but merely the beginning of another journey.'

No-one noticed a white owl whispering a message to the late afternoon breeze. Almost immediately Caer Ibormeith appeared in front of them.

Although he had heard of this very special swan goddess, skilled in both magic and music, Govannin realised with surprise that as well as being extremely beautiful, she was also much taller than any of the other goddesses.

She was dressed in delicate shades of cream and white and her skin was pale and very smooth, like fine-textured alabaster. Her eyes were the deep-blue hue of the Perthro River, and her light, almost silvery, ankle-length hair glistened like newly fallen snow.

Looking at Govannin, she thanked him for the advice he had given Taliesin as she believed the vision behind his method of attack was based on brilliance and steps one, two and three were inspired; however, she believed a more favourable idea would be for *her* to shape-shift into a swan and swim slowly towards the giant lizard singing such sweet, pure music it wouldn't realise the Prince of Song was sitting on her back. This would be a greater advantage to Taliesin as it would allow her to glide smoothly alongside the lizard bringing Taliesin as close as possible to his quarry so he could carry out step four and strike the killing blow. She said, 'If Taliesin can slay the daegon, it will rest in a death slumber for three days and nights before we reinstate its secret head. We need the daegon to guard the entrance to the underground tunnel.'

She turned towards Taliesin, 'I will ensure the mortal and the dwarf will be unable to hear my song.' Taliesin smiled with relief as he gratefully thanked the goddess.

'Only two others have found a way to slay the daegon in one hundred and five million years and we are all watching with great interest to see what you can achieve.

'Now you must go to Brigit. She is waiting for you with her cauldron of ever-burning fire.'

Taliesin looked over his shoulder and saw the fire-goddess standing a little way behind him, her long, red-gold hair like a pillar of flame as it rose skyward soaring higher and higher above her head as if endeavouring to reach the heavens.

'Her life began at the first break of day,' Taliesin explained noticing Agneish's startled expression. 'Since then her hair always seems to be striving to reach the sun.'

Waiting by her cauldron Brigit was trying in vain to flatten the ripples of red and gold as Taliesin tentatively approached her. When he reached her side she gave up the attempt to persuade her hair to tumble around her shoulders.

Sighing heavily she said: 'Bring your dagger to the flames Taliesin and hold it over the energy of my fire. Don't let go of it, you will not be burned.'

Holding his dagger over the flickering light from the cauldron, Taliesin saw his treasured weapon change into smoke. He held his breath as he watched the smoke transformed into gleaming metal and in his hand he was holding Freggyragh, one of Manannan's great symbols of power.

'Bring the sword back to me when you have slain the daegon and I will return your dagger in its true form,' Brigit said briskly.

Taliesin nodded, still feeling stunned by the fact he was holding the great sea-lord's sword.

His mouth felt dry as he gazed at Manannan-beg-mac-y-Lleir's burnished weapon fashioned from the brightest gold. He knew it had strange, mysterious abilities, but what they were he had no idea.

Holding it in front of him he lunged and parried with Freggyragh as if warding off a thrust from another sword and realised at once it was much lighter to wield than it ought to be, perhaps purposely, so he could carry out his task to despatch the lizard.

The thought gave him hope.

Taliesin was not a fighter, simply a wandering Prince of Song. When Fand, Manannan's wife had commanded him to guide Agneish and Govannin through his homeland, he hadn't fully understood how hazardous the journey would be. For that reason the assistance and support they had received from other deities were both welcome and unexpected. Perhaps the three of them would safely reach the Mountain Kingdom of the Gods after all.

Taliesin re-joined Govannin and Agneish and quietly told them that although he was not a warrior and had lived by using his wits, Freggyragh had given him the courage to approach the daegon. Immediately they heard Caer Ibormeith begin to sing.

Having shape-shifted into a white swan, the goddess glided serenely through the water until she reached Taliesin standing by the edge of the riverbank. With great care he seated himself on her back.

Moving swiftly and lightly over the surface of the Perthro, the Goddess of Sleep and Dreams drew nearer to the daegon who stared balefully at her through short-sighted eyes.

Although the water was churned by violent tremors as the giant lizard whipped its tail from side to side on the flat surface of the river, it allowed the swan to approach. The goddess continued to sing.

She was now within reach of the daegon and Taliesin watched its eyes begin to close as it listened to her poignant melody.

Caer Ibormeith glided further back to a place where she realised the lizard's view of her was significantly obstructed, but cleverly positioned herself where she and Taliesin could plainly see the flap of skin at the back of its head.

Taliesin took the first step to initiate the destruction of the daegon by holding Manannan's sword firmly in his hand and climbing cautiously onto the back of its huge body. The daegon didn't feel his weight as it had fallen asleep while listening to the succession of exquisite musical refrains.

The giant lizard's wet scaly skin made it a difficult slippery ascent to the flap of skin behind its head and Taliesin had to climb slowly with frequent pauses to make sure it was still asleep.

Breathing heavily Taliesin finally reached the loose fold of skin and took a moment to wonder what it might be concealing. Gently raising it up, he disclosed a bizarre, mutant, miniature head and saw the skin covering the top of the second head was full of thick, sharp spikes. The sunken, deeply placed eyes in the miniature head flew open as the protective blanket of darkness was disturbed.

The mutant head raised itself to within a few inches of Taliesin's face and the foulness of its breath made him gasp for air.

Below him he felt movement in the daegon's bulky body and knew he must strike now!

Raising Freggyragh he slashed at the miniature head again and again until it finally stopped spurting copious amounts of hot sticky blood.

As he lifted the detached head in the air the only odour Taliesin could smell was the coppery stench of spilled vital fluid.

Immediately, whispering voices began emitting from the low-lying banks of clouds above his head.

'Taliesin has slain the barbed daegon.'

'Taliesin bloods Manannan's sword.'

Another voice loudly declared: 'From now on, Taliesin must be known as the daegon slayer.'

Tremor's shook Agneish's body as she watched Taliesin hold up the giant lizard's mutant head, while Govannin heaved a huge sigh of relief. At last they could go on their way.

Caer Ibormeith called out to Taliesin to show the daegon's head to her.

The Prince of Song clambered down the corpse of the defeated beast, elated the struggle had ended in death, but not for him.

With Taliesin on her back the swan goddess swam to the water's edge. Once they had reached the riverbank Taliesin quickly jumped onto the grass and waited for the Goddess of Sleep and Dreams to shape-sift back to herself.

With hands heavily stained with blood he handed her the head.

Smiling she said: 'Now the final part of your journey begins. The three of you have found favour with the gods and many of us will watch with interest your ascent to our mountain kingdom.'

Taliesin turned as he heard a voice calling out his name. it was Brigit asking him to return Freggyragh to her.

Walking swiftly over to the fire-goddess, he handed her Manannan's sword and as she held it over her cauldron of ever-burning fire she congratulated him on successfully defeating the river monster.

'When the transformation from sword to dagger has been accomplished,' Brigit said briskly, 'I suggest the three of you get back into the boat and proceed to the entrance known as the Daegon's Mouth: the Watchers will know you are on your way.'

Chapter Eleven

Inside the Daegon's Mouth.

The same small boat was waiting for them at the riverbank and, as they stepped apprehensively into the vessel, Agneish and Govannin looked at Taliesin for guidance.

He began speaking to them in a very calm gentle tone. 'As a Prince of Song I am considered a minor deity, lesser in importance than others of stature and because of this never before have I been invited to visit the Mountain Kingdom of the Gods.

'I am determined to view the request to escort you, Agneish, to the summit of this kingdom as a privilege and perhaps as a mark of respect from one or two of the deities of rank.'

He stopped speaking and when he began again his voice was low and his words carefully measured. 'Once inside the Daegon's Mouth, I have heard other gods say, albeit always in a subdued whisper, about a vast, cavernous underground passage and the secret waterway which flows quietly through it. Only *this* particular boat is permitted to travel along the length of the hidden channel of water.

'As we enter the tunnel we cross an invisible boundary given the name Rubicon. It simply means as we pass the boundary it is the point of no return. We have to go on!'

He drew their attention to what was undoubtedly an extremely old tree of approximately thirty foot in height with a copper-coloured shiny bark. The span of outstretched branches at its crown made the tree almost eighteen feet in width. 'It is called the Tree of Living Light. I must tell you, as soon as we cross the threshold into the underpass we will be completely isolated from the outside world.'

Agneish was filed with fear at Taliesin's words but nodded bravely to show she was ready for the journey.

The boat drifted silently through the Daegon's Mouth and immediately they were engulfed in inky blackness.

As the boat moved smoothly along the waterway, in the midst of the hushed almost tranquil silence they became aware of what seemed to be ghostly cries coming from below the tunnel.

In a quiet reverential manner, Taliesin tried to shed light on the mystery of what they had just heard. 'The cries are a strange and perplexing phenomenon not easily explained, except to tell you they emanate from a lost city.'

Agneish's face bore a dazed expression at this revelation.

'The ancient scrolls tell of another underground tunnel leading off from this cave which was once connected to a bustling subterranean city, but the scrolls also state that millions of years ago a catastrophe occurred. The tunnel collapsed and was flooded with water resulting in the city being lost forever.

'The inhabitants of the city were demi-gods, part god, part mortal, a lesser deity who had some, but not all the powers of we divine deities.

'Their abilities were influenced by the supreme strength of their immortal father or mother.

'Some had legendary skills, wit, intelligence and beauty. Some were manipulative, cunning, warlike and rebellious, but they all had one thing in common, they wanted to live with us and share our world.

'This was not considered acceptable and caused a great deal of bitter conflict between two very different social orders.

'When the demi-gods' barely concealed hostility began to endanger our world, the Watchers decided their city must be lost forever.

'There was nothing some of the more reasonable deities could do to save them, as an account of what was to happen had already been written in the Tablet of Predetermined Events.

'We know the lost city lay undisturbed for one hundred and five million years.

'Rumour has it that one day, during a ferocious tempest caused by two storm-gods having a disagreement, immense bolts of lightning struck the mountain above us, dislodging large aspects of the rock face. The outcome of this was to uncover the entrance to the lost city.

'Out of respect for the long ago inhabitants, the Watchers blocked the means of access to the lost city by closing it up again; but ever since, voices that one might say were the echoes of that long lost civilisation have resounded from the walls of this cave.

'It was at this moment in time the Watchers also decided to place the barbed daegon to guard the entrance to the passage under the mountain, but I hadn't realised the beast still existed. It was all so long ago.'

Trying to break the air of tension which had sprung up during the telling of Taliesin's story, Govannin said flippantly: 'As dwarves are not divine beings, my great grandfather used to say from the very beginning of our lives that our time is spent waiting for a spectre holding aloft a scythe which he would in due course use to sever the coiled strands of our brief expectation of life.'

Taliesin smiled, appreciating Govannin's strange attempt at humour.

Suddenly the towering roof of the cave was illuminated by a display of glistening golden drops of light, as if thousands of the brightest stars were shining at the same time.

Agneish stared around her in wonder. With the reflection of the lights glowing on the water it seemed they were floating through an infinite starlit night.

Taliesin told them: 'The illumination springs from the Trees of Living Light. The lights themselves stem from a primitive organism created by the Watchers to bestow luminosity. The organisms stand absolutely motionless side by side in the hollow trunk of the tree, 'til summoned by the sound of this boat moving through the water.'

One of the organisms dropped into the boat. Intrigued Govannin picked it up, noting its golden body of about six inches in length, its two large wings with luminous golden spots, and, out of proportion to its size, two enormous curved horns.

'Once it has begun to glow, its life span is but a single day. They use their horns to lock onto one another to maintain their balance as the beat of their wings is the source of the light,' he explained.

In the darkness, multitudes of the small creatures were lighting up the roof of the cave, their fluttering wings, as if operating to an unspoken command, were industriously discharging a brilliant radiance. As their lights flashed with a dazzling intensity they lit up a succession of upright spires of limestone.

The boat was carried along by a slow-moving current of water and as they passed more and more of the slender spires, Taliesin felt a strong premonition of danger. Uneasily he gazed around the tunnel searching for the cause of his anxiety.

Then he saw it!

As the boat began to drift past a shelf protruding from the wall of the cave, a grotesquely misshapen deity got to her feet. She was grasping a sharp-edged knife.

'Its Elphane,' Taliesin said quietly, his tone tense and concerned.

The death-goddess's skin was the colour of smoke, as if blackened by the smouldering fires constantly springing into existence in the remotest depths of the mountain.

Her eyes were too dark and her expression too secretive for Taliesin to easily understand. Then suddenly the goddess screamed a terrible mind-shattering cry as she raised her knife threateningly towards Agneish.

Uneasily Taliesin told them. 'She named her knife Oblivion.'

The terror instigated by the presence of the death-goddess and her dreadful cry caused Agneish's heart to hammer against her ribs, robbing her fleetingly of her courage.

Hurriedly, Govannin pointed towards what was now almost in front of the boat. An army of spectres had been summoned from their rest by the Watchers to protect the travellers. As always they waited silent and unseen until required and were now marching on top of the water towards Elphane.

After only one brief glimpse of the phantom army, Elphane immediately shape-shifted into a night-lizard who moved with ease over the smooth surface of the rocks. As the reptile quickly distanced itself from the boat, it turned its head just once to flick its forked tongue in Agneish's direction.

When Elphane had disappeared, the army of spectres marched out of sight to wait again silent and unseen until summoned by the Watchers.

Taliesin heaved a sigh of relief, then with a broad smile he said. 'From here I believe we enter the Realm of Dreams.'

Govannin was intrigued; he had heard his father speak in an awed manner of such a place.

A sudden silence enveloped the group as the tunnel seemed to expand. The roof became higher, the waterway broader and the walls larger, all good reasons for the raising of goose-bumps along Agneish's arms.

'I have been told we should focus on the walls, for they hold a true account of the secrets of a civilisation that existed before the passage of time faded the memories of some of the gods.' Taliesin then said with utter exasperation, 'I have also been told that once we leave this tunnel we will not remember anything we have seen. Such a disappointment, it would have made a wonderful sonnet.

'I think from now on we should travel in silence and observe.'

The tunnel then became a labyrinth of dreams in which the golden lustre of the Trees of Light seemed to shimmer in and out of their awareness as something that could not be real.

The walls portrayed a changing medley of haphazard sequences with constantly changing scenes which varied enormously in size, while remaining in focus.

Finally the walls displayed images of the decimation of a city, briefly showing the chain of events which led to the destruction of its society, as a soft, heart-rending voice narrated its collapse.

The narrator finished with the words: 'To accept without question what you have seen as the truth is your decision.'

Surrounded by the shadows of the dead, they drifted on in total silence, each one only aware of their own sadness.

Taliesin lifted his head at the sound of loud, fast-running water. 'We must be near the end of the tunnel, as that is the roar of a waterfall and look, there is the secret door which opens out onto the mountain,' he said jubilantly as he noticed a thick wooden door. He pointed to a heavily gilded gate. 'On the other side of *that* entrance is a huge corridor which leads the Watchers directly to each and every corner of all other worlds.'

Stepping out of the boat, they ran towards the wooden door and realised there was neither a handle nor a key to unlock it. In a moment of utter frustration Agneish began to thump wildly on the doorway until a voice seemingly from nowhere said gently, 'Agneish must push the door outwards and it will open.'

In moments they were standing on a flat surface of stony ground taking deep gulps of the early evening air.

Taliesin took a minute or two to check the position of a few scattered stars to make sure they *were* on the eastern side of the mountain before removing a lit lantern hanging on the doorframe, saying: 'Someone has thoughtfully provided this for our journey.' He turned and faced the footpath snaking up the slope ahead of them. 'As you know, this footpath is the only approach to the summit and I must warn you that as we near the top we must proceed with caution through the dense purple and blue mists which frequently descend upon the twists and turns of the track. We don't want to plunge over the edge.'

As if on cue, ragged patches of blue mist drifted over the broad, winding slate steps of the pathway, lightly covering masses of gold and purple flowers growing as far as the eye could see at the side of the rock-face.

There was a long silence following Taliesin's statement before Govannin said with forced cheerfulness, 'I was informed the Spectre of Death matches ceaselessly through this land searching for the unwary, so to prevent this misfortune happening to us, Agneish, we must not walk unsteadily or stumble as if helplessly inebriated on weak ale.'

Govannin's attempt at light-heartedness helped to ease the tension in Agneish's neck and shoulders.

'It is about seven miles to the summit and as the moon-lighter goddess has already removed the sun-god, we should start our ascent,' Taliesin said briskly.

Suddenly, three large silver moons appeared in the dusky evening sky followed immediately by hundreds of bright stars.

'It seems we are to be accompanied on our journey to the summit as I see many deities are watching us, some unfortunately out of boredom.'

As enormous shooting star flashed and disappeared. 'That was Sirona, Guardian of the Stars and Night sky.'

They began their ascent and, as they climbed, funnels of spinning storms crackling with lightning hung in the air. 'That must be the handiwork of either Brenos or Tannus. Both are storm-gods and both are unbelievable exhibitionists.'

Taliesin took hold of Agneish's hand and led her carefully out onto a narrow projection of rock where he asked her to call out his name, laughing loudly at Agneish's look of surprise when she heard her voice ricocheting off the mountain in a succession of echoes, the echoes continuing long after they stepped back onto the path.

As they took shelter from a rain-cloud inside a recess in the cliff-face, Govannin noticed a high curved archway. Puzzled, he turned to Taliesin for an explanation.

Grimly, the Prince of Song told him: 'Once this land began as two joined kingdoms, ours and the Otherworld. If you look down through the archway I am told you will see why we immortals are not willing to pass through it.'

Agneish stepped forward to stand beside Govannin and Taliesin and all three found themselves staring with a mixture of revulsion and fascination at the outer boundaries of the Otherworld.

Far below them the earth had ruptured, creating a gaping ravine filled with craters overflowing with streams of red-hot molten lava and where sections of the sheer sides of the mountain had become cracked and thin they could see hot lava constantly breaking through the fissures in the rocky surface, throwing out great quantities of solid rock amongst the lava, ashes and dust.

Small fragments hurled high in the air in the form of volcanic cinders were accompanied by churning clouds of luminous yellow gas and black ashes. The reek of burning sulphur nearly choked Agneish and Govannin, while Taliesin seemed immune to the stench.

As he looked down at the clouds of dust and ash, Taliesin said reflectively; 'Many of us remember a time when we heard a deafening rumble comparable to the loudest of thunderbolts the storm-gods had ever unleashed. We believe it stemmed from the Otherworld.

'We also believe this incident was initiated by the Watchers to cause the collapse of the tunnel leading to the demi-gods subterranean city and, as a result, responsible for the disappearance of an entire civilisation.'

Lowering his voice, he added. 'Many of us also believed it was necessary to be rid of this subspecies of deities forever.

'This event was followed by haloes around our moons and sun, spectacular displays of extraordinarily beautiful sunrises and sunsets, each encircled by countless iridescent colours and entirely free from the influence, guidance or control of the sun-god or the Guardians of the Stars and Night Sky. These displays continued for several years, perhaps to serve as a memorial, a tribute to the memory of the dead from the Watchers.'

Govannin remained silent as he absorbed Taliesin's account of a long-ago tragedy; his curiosity as a scholar and truth-seeker had been aroused. Then, incredibly, they saw in the red glow from a crater of fire, the tall, grotesque shape of Elphane emerging through the haze of grey dust swirling around the ravine.

Trembling with fear, Agneish stepped back from the archway.

Sirona sent another shooting star, one which flared so closely to the three standing on the mountainside that it highlighted a tall masculine figure wearing a shimmering coloured cloak standing, unknown to Agneish, directly behind her.

Elphane acknowledged the warning and strode back to where she belonged, deep inside the bowels of the earth. The tall figure disappeared.

'Come,' Taliesin said gently as he put his arm around Agneish's shaking shoulders.

In an effort to distract her he pointed to the largest of the three full moons. 'Do you see the moving shadows on the Great Moon?' Agneish nodded. 'They are all shadows of immortals who have travelled there to drink from the Fountain of Eternal Life.' She stared at him, his words made her feel she was sleepwalking through a muddled dream.

With her nerves badly frayed and feeling quite unable to make sense of anything, Agneish began to trudge up the mountain path, trying as she walked to ineffectually pull together the tattered pieces of her skirt.

With slow, tired steps the three travellers undertook the long, tedious walk along the moonlit track leading to the Mountain Kingdom of the Gods.

'Not too long now 'til we reach the summit and then we must wait until the Bringer of Light appears. Shortly after her arrival, the colours of the sun-god will glint upon the Gates of the Realm of the Morning,' Taliesin said quietly. 'When that happens we must be ready to enter and greet the deities who will be waiting to meet you.'

Govannin was just as nervous as Agneish. He too had everything to lose if he didn't impress the Watchers with his concept of *Perception*. Putting his hand inside the deep pocket of his cloak he held the torque for a moment, hoping to feel the motivating force which had driven him to create the neck-collar with the approval and blessing of his father and grandfather and from there to make this incredible journey through this strange land.

Disappointingly, he did not feel a thing.

Chapter Twelve

The Mountain Kingdom of the Gods

The further up the winding path they walked the more they became aware of an almost deafening, booming sound, and as they rounded a bend of the mountain Agneish and Govannin stopped to stare in wonder as the full panoramic view of the Mountain Kingdom of the Gods appeared.

The deafening noise was from four huge waterfalls cascading down the sides of the mountain peaks.

The waterfalls thundered over steep granite cliff-tops capped by mist-soaked forests, the mists producing multiple rainbows created by the light glistening off the spray from the sheer force of water. The roaring torrent of water from the nearest falls made the slate steps of the pathway slippery with its fine spray. Taliesin urged them to be careful.

On the mountain summit, against a background of starlight and swirling coloured clouds, towered majestic buildings of imposing symmetry. In the foreground, illuminated by an enormous silvery moon were black silhouettes of tall trees, masses of lush green foliage and a set of steps leading up to the outer walls of a kingdom governed by a thousand deities.

The eastern sun was just below the horizon when they finally reached the summit and, as Agneish quietly waited for the Bringer of Light, she felt her stomach was tied in knots; the strain of staying alert hour after hour was taking its toll and her fear and anxiety of what might happen when she met the Watchers was making her feel more uneasy and unsure of herself.

In an attempt to tidy her appearance, she was about to plait her hair when Taliesin advised her to let it flow freely over her shoulders. Agrona and Cuthubodia would be delighted to see so much crimson, to them it would resemble the spillage of blood.

Taking Taliesin's advice she left her hair loose. If they were here, the war-goddesses would see her hair gleam a warm blood-red colour when touched by the rays of the sun-god.

Govannin was fidgety and finding it impossible to stay still, so in an effort to ease their nervousness, Taliesin decided to explain what he knew about the outer walls enclosing and protecting the Kingdom of the Gods.

He told them there were two walls guarding the official centre of power. The perimeter of the outer wall was immense, about two hundred and fifty miles in length, two hundred feet high and seventy feet thick, which was wide enough for Barinthus to effortlessly drive his four-horse chariot along the top.

The inner wall was not quite as thick, but just as strong.

As the sun-god's rays were now nearly over the crest of the mountain, the trio slowly ascended the steps leading to the outer wall. Immediately three joined gateways appeared, almost phantom-like, in the wall. Govannin remembered Almha's warning about entering the kingdom only through the gateway known as the Realm of the Morning.

Taliesin and Agneish also remembered the goddesses words: *'Enter through the wrong gateway and you will cease to exist.'* Govannin shuddered as he recalled that the reason for the third gateway was unknown.

They looked anxiously at each other, each hoping someone else would think of something.

Noticing a colourless crystal cube placed outside the three gateways, Govannin wondered out loud what it could be used for. Taliesin knew and waited in silence for the arrival of the Bringer of Light.

They heard a slight noise and turning round they saw a golden-haired goddess standing at the side of the cube, all six sides now ablaze with prisms of pure light and energy which displayed the entire colour spectrum of all four worlds.

The Bringer of Light was wearing a sheer, pale-gold robe of such lightness of texture it appeared to be weightless. Around her neck was a golden pendent in the shape of the sun.

The extraordinary beauty of the goddess's face caused Govannin to sharply catch his breath. She heard and smiled gently at him before kneeling beside the crystal.

The goddess slid open the cover on top of the cube and instantly all the different shades of a sunrise flowed out of the container and soared into the sky. Pinks, reds, yellows and oranges created pathways for the sun-god to follow, the blazing stream of colours quickly dispelling the dark shadows of the night.

Govannin gave a wide smile of relief as the emerging rays of sunlight lit up the gateway to the right causing it to glint with golden fire.

'That one,' Govannin said tensely as he pointed to the gleaming shafts flickering over the linked gate.

After a moment Taliesin agreed and, taking his time, slowly turned an enormous key left in the lock.

The key also opened an entrance in the inner wall and they each took a deep breath as they absorbed the splendid grandeur laid out on the tableland of the gods' kingdom.

Agneish looked up in wonder as, what she had thought was a brilliantly coloured large bird lying on top of the gateway, stood up, allowing her to see that although it had two bright scarlet wings, it had the face, body and limbs of a beautiful young boy whose skin and hair shone with the radiance of the sun.

The eyes of the boy focused searchingly on Agneish.

With his gaze still fixed on her, he stretched his long neck and spread his broad wings revealing that the thick plumage underneath was vivid orange.

'He could be made of fire,' she said in a trembling voice.

Taliesin smiled, pleased with her intuitive observation. He explained that the boy was a Fire Elemental, brought into existence by the Watchers to become their eyes and ears inside the walls of the kingdom. The Fire Elemental suddenly soared into the air and flew away without a backward glance. 'He has gone to inform the Watchers you are now within the walls.'

As they lingered uncertainly beside the Realm of the Morning gateway, Taliesin began to speak, his voice a low murmur. 'The goddess Almha has already told you much about the Watchers; now I can tell you a little more. Long, long ago, the deities decided to select four chosen ones. These divine deities would be preferred above all others and have special qualities and powers bestowed on them, powers which would set them apart from all other gods for the rest of time.

'They were to be guardians of the portals between the four worlds. The Heavens, the Earth, our land of a Thousand Gods and the Otherworld. These deities were to be called the Watchers.

'As a suppliant you must be humble as you petition for their help, so listen carefully as I tell you about the temperaments of these four divine beings.

'The Guardian of the Earth and North sees at once into the heart of a dispute. If he believes in your cause he will endeavour to sway the other three deities into supporting you.

'The Guardian of Water and the West is a gentle, benevolent god. If you put forth your reasons for the demise of the Norseman with total honesty, he will reflect upon your appeal with unreserved compassion.

'The nature of the Guardian of Fire and the South is mercurial. He is unpredictable, impulsive and shrewd.

'The Guardian of Air and the East is learned and very skilful at evading a problem.

'As Almha has already told you, the Northern Guardian is the highest ranking deity with the second highest position being held by the Guardian of the East. They are the most powerful and advisory gods.

'The Southern Guardian observes the Gods of the Otherworld. The Watchers consider this territory of overwhelming misery as beyond description, whereas the Guardian of the West pays special attention to strange phenomenon's of nature.

'The four Watchers selected the deities who would preside over the sun, sky, weather, moon and stars. That was except for the North Star. The Guardian of the Earth is the supreme controller of this, leaving the other deities to contest and challenge for the choice of what remained.

'We have developed a very complex social order, our every expertise and ability is under the control of deities who have had the power, right or authority to choose their social standing and have become extremely protective over his or her status.

'But that is enough for the present. It is now time to enter the Place of Assembly, more usually known as the Meeting Place.'

Agneish looked down with utter dismay at her tattered, stained shift and cloak then, holding her head up high, smiled brightly at Taliesin and Govannin, turned and walked forward to meet her fate.

Chapter Thirteen

The Gods

The Place of Assembly had already reached an extraordinary level of activity, the din and commotion of a group of deities gathered closely together loudly exchanging opinions and engaging in petty bad-tempered quarrels made Agneish feel bewildered. Accompanied by Govannin and Taliesin she had to force herself to walk into the Meeting Place, the communal heart of the Mountain Kingdom.

The Meeting Place was circular in shape with forty tiers of raised seats surrounding the central area. It was the gods' social hub where they related their views involving various deities' designated powers and authority, it was also the place where reputations and rumours were discussed and friends or enemies made.

There was a sudden flurry of movement as heads turned in Agneish's direction, then the disorderly tumult died down as she became the centre of attention.

The deities began to jostle and push their way towards her.

'Welcome Agneish.'

'Bring her to me Taliesin.'

'Here first.'

'No here.'

Shaken by the disturbance she had caused, Agneish was unable to relax until she noticed many of the gods wore a welcoming smile, while others were bowing, waving or voicing enthusiastic greetings.

Taliesin wheeled round when he realised the chaotic clamour of so many deities talking at once had abruptly stopped.

Walking towards them were two goddesses, one very tall and stunningly beautiful, the shape of her face oval with high slanting cheekbones, her eyes dark with long thick lashes and her straight hair which fell almost to her knees, had the blue-black sheen of a raven's wing.

Her forehead and sides of her face were stained with coloured dyes of red, black and silver in a pattern which resembled the thinnest of spider's webs drenched in mist. A tear drop dripping with blood had been painted at the corner of her right eye and another at the corner of her full mouth. The edges of her eyelids were darkened with powdered kohl.

There was a distinctive yet intangible aura surrounding the goddess which gave the impression she was extremely dangerous, her intimidating smile seemingly to imply a threat as she disdainfully acknowledged the greetings called out to her.

She removed a crossbow and a quiver of arrows crafted from the black twisted skeleton of a blackthorn tree, (the tree known to deities as the Keeper of Dark Secrets), from around her neck and shoulders, before loosening the carved ivory fangs taken from a hound of Cernunnos's Wild Hunt which fastened her hooded scarlet cloak, and handed it to Taliesin to hold.

Agneish caught her breath in shock when she saw on the goddess's left shoulder a coiled miniature figure of a dragon-like creature, its position arranged with its head nestling against her neck. The image had been impressed onto her skin in crushed gold.

On her left hand she wore a thick leather gauntlet and a polished silver ring fashioned in the same shape as the dragon-like creature. She wore the ring on her index finger over the gauntlet. Her right hand was adorned with a gold ring set with a glowing crimson ruby. The ruby had been engraved with the outline of this fantastical dragon which surely, Agneish though, could only exist in the imagination.

A white owl flew towards Agrona and perched on the thick gauntlet on her outstretched arm, Govannin wondered if it was the goddess Almha.

Taliesin saw Agneish was fascinated by the glittering tiny shape on the goddess's shoulder, and while Agrona was speaking to one or two of the deities he whispered to her that it was a likeness of her pet wyvern, Idelonda, whose name meant Noble Serpent.

'Many centuries ago Agrona found three abandoned wyvern eggs, one shell was gold, one red, one orange and decided to find a way to hatch them. She was successful in her task and although they never grew in size to their full potential, they still retained all the magic and beauty of full grown wyverns.

'Wyverns are winged serpent-like creatures similar to dragons but unlike dragons, wyverns have two legs instead of four. They dwell in large dark caves hidden deep below the ground, but when they fly they nearly touch the stars.

'All three are Agrona's pets and the goddess has bestowed on each one a special gift. Idelonda, the golden wyvern and the only female is her favourite. She was granted wisdom.

'Ehecatl, the red wyvern, whose name means Winged Serpent, was granted compassion. Landon, the orange wyvern, whose name means Imperial Serpent, was granted strength.

'They are Agrona's protectors and would fight to the death to guard her from harm.

'Although they are much smaller than the average wyvern, when you see the three of them flying side by side it is a breath-taking spectacle watching their fiery colours shimmering in the rays of light scattered by the sun-god.

'When Agrona needs to summom Idelonda she holds her sword in front of her left eye and immediately another eye appears in the blade. The eye is yellow, large, unblinking with a vertical pupil. It is Idelonda's. then Agrona emits a long, sibilant, soft sound that only the wyvern can hear.

'Idelonda responds and flies to the goddess at once.'

Taliesin's voice was hushed as he realised Agrona was staring at Agneish.

The other goddess hobbled slightly as she progressed more slowly in their direction, her uneven manner of walking caused by a club-foot. Her stooped shoulders, tangled waist-length pure-white hair encased in a black hair-net, abnormally white skin, pale almost colourless eyes and aggressive expression made one or two of the minor deities avert their eyes. They didn't want to attract her attention.

Cathubodia's black, high-collared cloak was fastened at the neck with dagger-shaped twisted clasps glinting with the brilliant lustre of burnished jet. Impeded by her limp, she moved with difficulty across the Meeting Place, her awkward movements revealing her cloak had a bright scarlet lining.

On her right hand she wore a black pearl ring inscribed with a closed golden eye.

Taliesin bowed deferentially to both of them before turning to Agneish. 'It is with great satisfaction I can at last introduce you to Agrona and Cathubodia and as each of these war-goddesses is without equal, comparison with others is impossible,' he finished smoothly to a smattering of applause from some of the other deities.

After a moment he turned and addressed Agneish. 'As you are well aware, it is they who heard your plea for help in disposing of the Norseman and once they glimpsed your red-hair, a colour as you have been told is sacred to all war-goddesses, they decided to help you by sending Govannin and myself to persuade you to accompany us on the journey to this land.'

Agneish became oblivious to the coating of dirt on her face and her stained clothing as Agrona bent down and stroked her hair. Govannin had brushed it for at least twenty minutes earlier that morning and it was now gleaming and free from snarls.

Twining a thick strand around her finger and using it to pull Agneish closer to her, the war-goddess gazed intently at this young woman from another world, taking time to scrutinise every detail of her face.

Although she was scared out of her wits Agneish tried not to show it, knowing that only outstanding courage would be acceptable.

After a few brief seconds Agrona smiled.

Agneish found that smile terrifying.

Cathubodia also paid careful attention to Agneish's deliberately expressionless features, both goddesses apparently dismissing frayed and soiled clothes as inconsequential.

Looking at them both, Govannin reflected the difference between the war-goddesses couldn't be more extreme.

One tall, awe-inspiring, beautiful and unquestionably dangerous. The other smaller and, like himself, afflicted with a limp and perhaps, like himself, lacking in physical strength; but despite this, he knew each was as dangerous as the other.

'We have watched every step of your progress through our land,' Cathubodia said in a hoarse, gruff voice, 'and we commend you on the spirit that enabled you to face the trials we set you with fearlessness and courage.'

At the close of this declaration the deities heard a derisive snort from someone in the crowd, then an empty space materialised around the powerful thunder-god Tannus, as several deities hurriedly distanced themselves from him.

There was a telling silence from Agrona and Cathubodia.

Shocked at his behaviour Govannin stared at this formidable deity who was deliberately trying to irritate the two goddesses.

Govannin took note of Tannus's bushy eyebrows that ran in one continuous line above his eyes, always an indication to Govannin of a bad temper. The blue eyes that looked angrily out from beneath them held a cold almost menacing expression as he waited for a reaction from Agrona and Cathubodia. When none was forthcoming Tannus could no longer restrain himself.

In a loud booming voice that sought to control and dominate the assembly of deities, but in reality infuriated them, he bellowed, 'I have heard this mortal's story and it is my belief that as the moment draws closer for her to engage in battle with the Norseman, she will lack the cunning to successfully achieve his destruction. As opponents they are too ill-matched.'

'No Tannus,' Cathubodia replied harshly. 'She has Agrona and myself to assist her.'

Cathubodia was so enraged with the thunder-god's provocative remarks, the pupils of her pale eyes turned a dark red, and seconds later, a ferocious fire burst from her mouth, the flames alive and unswerving in their determination to reach Tannus.

Then a spear, the weapon most favoured by Agrona, appeared in the taller deity's hand.

Tannus was wearing two metal wristbands heavily encrusted with pieces of deep blue crystal known as the lightning stone due to the flickers of white light constantly shimmering across the surface of the gem.

Cathubodia heard the cut crystals begin to vibrate moments before they discharged jagged lightning bolts that raced towards her, the bolts succeeding in keeping the other deities at a discreet but safe distance away from Tannus.

Stepping back from the reaches of the flames, Tannus nearly collided with Segomo, a war-god legendary for his enormous strength and courage. A warrior experienced in battle, utterly devoted to war and not given to gentleness or sentimentality except in the case of Cetan, his pet blue-tailed hawk who always sat on his left shoulder. As Tannus moved quickly in the opposite direction to avoid contact, Segomo hurriedly smoothed the ruffled feathers of the bird.

Segomo's face wore his usual look of contempt when glancing at Tannus, but even this scornful expression didn't prevent Agneish from thinking she had never seen anyone so handsome.

He was extremely tall, bare-chested, with a muscular build which suggested immense physical strength.

Agneish stared at Segomo and her heart beat a little faster as she stared at his uncompromising warrior's face, slate-grey eyes, thin black moustache that hung downward at the sides of his mouth, short pointed beard and at his black, shoulder-length hair which was streaming out behind him as he strode towards Tannus. As his long strides brought him nearer to the thunder-god, the ground began to tremble, the sky darkened and lightning flashed through the skies, a declaration from Tannus that he would inflict pain upon Segomo if he didn't keep his distance.

Apart from a hammered gold collar inset with glistening black spikes and an amulet dangling from a thick gold chain in the shape of a hawk in full flight, the war-god was clothed entirely in black. Dressed in black trousers tightly tucked into black, thigh-high leather boots and black leather gauntlets, Agneish thought he looked magnificent. In his left hand he carried a shield and a spiked leather whip, while his right hand held a huge gold sword which had the descriptive name *Vanquisher* spelt in silver lettering on the hilt.

Painted in glowing colours on his left arm was an image of Cetan and Govannin was amazed to see the light-yellow eyes of the painted image swivel in the direction of Tannus and fix the thunder-god with a ferocious stare.

Taliesin explained to Govannin and Agneish that Segomo had rescued the hawk from the eastern plains of Mandor, known to the gods as the Kingdom of the Hawks. Once, long ago, the demi-gods had occupied a large area of Mandor and had trained these fierce, unpredictable birds of prey to develop their fighting qualities. When the demi-gods had ceased to exist these birds were abandoned and became even more savage.

Taliesin went on to say: 'They are some of the oldest creatures in our world and as they soar through the air they can be heard screaming out a challenge to other hawks. They are renowned for displaying bravery and courage.

'Segomo had heard about these fearless birds of prey and decided to visit the Plains of Mandor and this is where he found Cetan. Based on the reports of other gods, their trust in each other was immediate and Cetan allowed the war-god to handle him from the first day they encountered each other. Now Segomo is the only deity Cetan will permit to touch him.'

Just as Taliesin finished talking, explosive sparks erupted noisily in the air as Segomo and Tannus glared at each other, while across the Meeting Place there was a low murmur of excited conversation as the mutual hostility between these two deities was always a talking point with the other gods.

'This mortal has my support also,' Segomo said in a threatening tone, 'and that of the great sea-lord Manannan.'

'And mine.' This was said in such a gentle voice the other deities nearly missed seeing Cethlion, a gifted goddess of prophecy walk towards Agneish.

Govannin was captivated at once by Cethlion's delicate beauty. She had a grave, very formal bearing, light-blonde hair which nearly reached the ground, very fair skin and a mouth of the softest rose-coloured pink. Set in the middle of her forehead was a crescent shaped glowing moonstone, or 'midnight sun' as Cethlion preferred to call it. The moonstone was created from a solidified ray from the greatest of the three moons and gave Cethlion the power to see events which could not be perceived by her natural senses. The stone's secrets was shared by only a few. As she walked towards Agneish her sheer silver robe sparkled like a star on a frosty night.

'Welcome', the goddess said smiling at Agneish and Govannin.

The dwarf glowed with pleasure as this beautiful goddess acknowledged him.

'I have been asked to welcome you on behalf of Arianrhod who unfortunately won't be available until darkness falls. I also welcome you on behalf of Ariadne who you will meet shortly.'

Taliesin was elated. The gods seemed to be falling over each other to help Agneish and he was astute enough to know his new reputation as a daegon slayer and his role as her escort wouldn't go unnoticed and would hopefully be rewarded.

Then, holding tightly onto the ornately decorated bridle of a chestnut horse, which exactly matched the shade of her hair, the Queen of the Isle of Shadow, goddess and commander of a legion of fierce horsewomen, strode up to Agrona and Cathubodia and informed them that, if necessary, Manannan had requested that she and her horsewomen be ready to accompany the travellers back to the gates of the Land of a Thousand Gods where Enbarr would be waiting.

The war-goddesses were jubilant. So many supreme beings offering their assistance and support of the mortal's appeal.

Looking around, they took careful note of high-ranking deities who were noticeable by their absence. In their opinion this was a deliberate insult and vowed it would be taken care off when the time was right.

As it was still a long wait before the Watchers were to meet Agneish and Govannin, Cethlion told Taliesin, that Segomo was to take them to meet Ariadne, Spinner of the Universe and Time.

When he heard this Govannin experienced such a feeling of delight and wonder he actually tingled with pleasure and could only stutter his thanks before Segomo came to lead them away.

Chapter Fourteen

Ariadne

As he led them away from the Meeting Place, Segomo turned to Govannin and said, 'I am sure you will already know it was Ariadne who spun the universe in which we all exist.'

Govannin, still overwhelmed at the thought of meeting the highest ranking goddess in the land, could only mutter that it was an incredible honour.

Turning to Agneish, Segomo said in a distinctly severe manner: 'Before you meet the goddess I want you to realise just how powerful and influential she is. If you displease her she could make your world disappear in moments. Speaking for myself and many of the other deities, we would hardly notice if the earth no longer existed.

'A word of caution, we must approach her in complete silence so as not to interrupt any calculations based on probabilities she may be weaving into the universal loom. She will notice our arrival and then we must wait until she beckons us to her side.

'Come, follow me,' he said briskly as he gently stroked the feathered wings of his hawk.

The war-god marched away.

Govannin's mouth twisted in a wry smile as he tried to force his crooked body into keeping up with the long, vigorous strides of Segomo.

With the aid of his staff and Taliesin and Agneish holding tightly onto each of his arms, the dwarf followed as quickly as he could.

Segomo led them to a high plateau of land, a tableland containing a huge expanse of pitch-black water. Standing at one side of the water was a figure of commanding height dressed in a simple ankle-length tunic of the palest blue over which she wore a richly coloured purple cloak. Twisted strands of golden thread interwoven throughout her long dark hair displayed an array of brilliant precious gemstones of incomparable lustre and rainbow flashes of colour.

She heard them and turning round beckoned them towards her. The hair rose on the back of Agneish's skin when she saw the right side of Ariadne's face was formed from light and the left from shadow.

'That is because she is both night and day,' Taliesin whispered, 'there is no need to feel afraid.'

Govannin was amazed to see that Ariadne towered head and shoulders over Taliesin and Segomo. He had realised at the Place of Assembly the average height of the deities was about nine or ten feet, but the Spinner of the Universe was much taller than any he had met so far and instinctively he knew they stood before a compelling extraordinary presence.

'Welcome.' Her voice was warm and friendly. 'Agneish, I have been informed the Watchers are about to deliberate your issues with the Norseman. They are aware that many of the deities, including the guardian of your island, Manannan-beg-mac-y-Lleir are predisposed to exert their considerable influence in an effort to help you and have taken great care to assure these same deities their wishes have been closely listened to.

'So in the meantime, while we wait until they have finished their deliberations, they thought I might arouse your curiosity in the underlying forces, namely the study of matter and energy involved in creating a universe. Especially you Govannin.

'I have heard about your family's interest in apothecary and of their outstanding prowess as gold and silversmiths. I have seen the sword made for Bladud, a weapon both fascinating and magnificent. All three of you are to be congratulated.'

Govannin took a deep intake of breath. This was already much, much more than he had hoped for and *how* did this supreme goddess know his name?

Ariadne pointed to the expanse of black water. 'In a moment we will travel back to the beginning of time, past where I created your world Agneish four and a half billion years ago, to the place where over thirteen billion years earlier I created the galaxies, stars and planets that is our universe, somewhere for the gods to live and play until our existence here has run its full course. Then the Weaver of Dreams and Time will weave our last hours in this world into her tapestry. The tapestry will then begin counting out loud the hours we have left before we have to abandon the Land of a Thousand Gods forever.

'There will be more time than you might think, as in our world a day is longer than a year in your time. Now watch closely.'

Govannin and Agneish watched enthralled as Ariadne bent down and moved her hand slowly across the surface of the water. The water rippled and the goddess's voice rang out eerily from the depths of the huge black pool.

'Just as you might observe a spider spinning its web, I began spinning the universe from a primitive elemental darkness. Unfortunately, in creating that universe I produced an insatiable monster.'

'Cethlion, Prophecy Goddess and Astrologer, studies the celestial bodies and has spent countless centuries gathering information about her findings.

'As each star I formed is a speaking tablet with its own story to tell, I have created a vast interstellar compilation of events. Her continued research into these accumulated collections has led to new discoveries about all our futures.

'She has uncovered that there will be an eclipse, a night of shadows, where worlds collide and the earth will be destroyed by the death of a star!'

Agneish could only stare in horror at Ariadne. The goddess smiled sympathetically, conscious of the distress her words had caused.

'Because I have been forewarned, I create new stars every few minutes, for they will be the harbinger of a new universe.

'Far beyond our worlds, at a distance so incalculable from here it is almost incomprehensible even to me, will lie our time that has yet to come. I will have to bring into being billions of stars, millions of planets and countless moons to try and recreate what I have already achieved. In all, I created over a hundred worlds,' she told them with a distinct edge of pride in her voice, then paused momentarily before confiding that something so new, so creative, was littered with mistakes. 'For instance the first planet I brought into existence was a frozen world. Look into the pool and I will show you.'

Govannin and Agneish stared into the pitch-blackness of the pool.

The water became lighter, then clear and they could see a planet covered with frozen masses of water, an icy world scattered with debris left over from its formation.

They saw sloping glacial dunes in close proximity to geysers blasting out splintered fragments of ice and they could see clouds of icebergs floating several miles above the atmosphere.

Leaving the icy wastes behind, Ariadne pointed to a vast semi-circle of spectral colours hanging in space. The arc was tinted with shades of red, orange, yellow, green, blue, indigo and violet. A secondary arc, larger and paler appeared within the primary curve, but with the colours reversed.

'Those are the colours of the goddess Arianrhod, Keeper of the Circling Silver Wheel of Stars. At certain times she will open the entrance to her tower and saturate the darkness with her palette of phantom hues.'

Listening to Ariadne's words Govannin bit down on his lip till he drew blood. He was remembering a time when still a boy, his father had taken him out of their hidden world deep inside the purple mountain, onto the mountain-side and shown him these same colours shimmering in the night sky. Govannin had never forgotten the feeling of being free from fear and danger as he held on tightly to his father's hand. A shiver ran down his spine as he felt a strange premonition that he would never see his father again.

The goddess showed them moons tinged with orange and reddish golds, spectacular icy moons, rainbow coloured moons and a cluster of sixty moons orbiting around one planet.

Agneish's heart thumped wildly as she watched images of spinning spirals tearing across a barren landscape which the goddess told them was the future earth. Menacing dark thunder-clouds charged with lightning lit up the sky of an earth suspended in a time that hadn't yet happened, the lightning illuminating ferociously-erupting volcanoes. Then finally, a swirling storm that the goddess told them was nearly four hundred miles wide. In the middle of the gigantic storm was an unblinking eye which seemed to be staring directly at Govannin.

Ariadne smiled sadly when she noticed this strange phenomenon.

Then they witnessed the death of a star!

There was a violent explosion followed by massive shock-waves in the atmosphere surrounding the future earth as the star spiralled downwards, passing colossal glowing clouds topped by pillars of dust as it sped on its winding, twisting course.

To the fascinated Govannin it was like watching the illuminated leaves of a vellum manuscript being turned as Ariadne covered the pool with one glorious image after another.

Speaking in a low quiet voice, the goddess said: 'The pillars are the Pillars of Creation and the star travelling towards the edge of your earth is being driven forcefully by the sun-god as it is he who commands the earth's winds. The image you have just seen is of the day the earth will be torn apart!'

There was a stunned silence from Agneish and Govannin.

The sound of Segomo's hawk flapping his wings roused Taliesin into a course of action. He must do something to prevent Agneish from dwelling on Ariadne's words. After all, she couldn't yet even give a tentative calculation as to when this would happen.

He asked permission from the goddess to show the visitors the crater. She granted it immediately.

Having seen the crater on countless occasions, Segomo decided to make his farewells. Thanking Ariadne for her time, he instructed Taliesin to make his way back to the Place of Assembly when they had seen enough.

Taliesin told them, 'I am going to show you that even in our land we have to be careful about the desirability of certain deities. Just a short walk from here I am told there is a deep crater. At the foot of the crater is a lake which bears a small island; the goddess Odium has been incarcerated there for four and a half billion years. Exactly the length of time your world has existed.'

His words raised the hairs on the back of Agneish's neck.

'What has she done?'

'As yet, nothing.'

Govannin was puzzled. 'Then why imprison her?'

'A precaution. When you look down on her I will grant you both the capability to perceive she is frantically weaving tapestries of red and black. Red for blood and black for death. If she was ever released she would bring carnage, death and destruction to both our worlds for all eternity.'

He added: 'The meaning of her name is hate!'

Giving Govannin a frightened look, Agneish said she didn't care to see Odium and wanted Taliesin to take them back to the Place of Assembly.

Reluctantly, Govannin agreed with her.

Ariadne gazed pensively after them 'till they were out of sight.

Chapter Fifteen

Aerten

When they returned to the Place of Assembly they could see Cethlion pacing restlessly up and down in front of the rows of tiered seats. It was obvious she had been waiting for them to return, and the reason became clear when she whispered to Agneish that Aerten, the Goddess of Fate wished to meet her.

The shock took Taliesin's breath away.

The Goddess of Fate was permitted to speak only three times in her lifetime and Taliesin knew that long, long ago she had spoken once; but surely she had spoken again today when she had asked to meet Agneish. If she spoke today for a second time it would be at the cost of her life.

Cethlion gestured for them to follow her.

She led them across the Place of Assembly, past the inquisitive eyes of watching deities towards an enormous curved archway. In an alcove on either side of the archway was a life-sized statue of Aerten. Each statue held a double-bladed axe.

Once through the passageway underneath the arch, they followed Cethlion up a flight of stone steps which led to a bridge built over the gently flowing waters of a small stream. She walked ahead, guiding them through the thick purple mist obscuring the view, but once across they were in the midst of bright sunlight.

Their eyes were drawn straight away to a magnificent flame-coloured tree with branches heavy with unopened red blossoms. Sitting on the ground and leaning back against its thick trunk was the goddess Aerten.

Her eyes were closed and Agneish thought she must be asleep until she realised the goddess's right hand was gently stroking a double-bladed axe lying by her side.

'She sits beneath the Tree of Self Destruction,' Taliesin said very softly. 'The blossoms will open only once in its life-span as a tribute to Aerten's life and as a testament to her death, then the tree itself will die.'

Cethlion began to recount Agneish's story to Aerten, beginning with the slaughter of her family by the Norsemen and the burning of her village. How Agrona and Cathubodia had heard her anguished cries for vengeance, looked down and caught sight of Agneish's hair, a colour they both held sacred.

Cethlion knew Aerten was familiar with the war-goddesses' unpredictable, volatile natures and told how they had decided to help her as had, amongst others, the great sea-god Manannan and his wife Fand.

Aerten opened her eyes.

She stared at Agneish for a long time, then at the ultimate cost to herself spoke to Cethlion. 'In bringing this mortal here, Cethlion, you know what you have asked from me.' There was a short silence before Aerten spoke again. 'Nevertheless I will help her.

'Lately my body has diminished in strength and my sight has become impaired, but above all I am weary. It has been too long since I spent time at the Fountain of Eternal Life and now it's too late.

'I have asked to see the mortal because my thirst to inflict retribution against the Norse god Odin has never weakened. It's an old story Cethlion, one I haven't got the strength to relate, but my resolve to destroy him is as strong as ever.

'Perhaps in playing a part in this mortal's revenge, Odin will finally have to accept, *I was the most formidable.'*

The goddess lowered her head and when she lifted it a few minutes later her eyes were glittering with anticipation.

She said, 'I have decided to give you the power to use the Moon Gate.'

Hearing this, Taliesin was unable to speak, and he was filled with a sense of euphoria.

Cethlion smiled with approval at the Goddess of Fate's decision.

'Agneish will come to realise the importance of your gift Aerton,' nhe uttered.

Aerten noidded weakly, her lack of physical strength now clearly evident. 'I trust you have a plan Cethlion?'

'Yes, Arianrhod will help. She will entice the Norsemen to travel back to Mann in time to arrive on the night of a Blood Moon.'

Aerten gave a tired laugh. 'Ah, I think I see what you have in mind. The Blood Moon also known as the Hunter's Moon because it is the brightest moon of all. In which case it is up to the mortal to hunt her prey so successfully that night, that it will ensure the only colour Arianrhod blazes late into the sky will be a smouldering fiery red.'

The Goddess of Fate looked hard at Agneish. 'From this night on, the Moon Gate will be left open. The Moon Gate is a central point in which rays of moonlight meet to render a distinct image of an occurrence that will be impossible to prevent. In this case the sudden appearance of the Norsemen against the night sky. When the men from the north leave their homeland for their voyage back to Mann, their shadows will be reflected against the surface of the moon and you Agneish will be permitted to catch sight of every stage of what will be their last journey. You will see the Moon Gate as an arc of white flowing light against the darkness of the heavens, a light that always returns to its source, the moon. It was a concept conceived by the ancients and then introduced amid thousands of stars in an otherwise black sky.

'In relation to this decisive moment many deities will have helped you, but they will allow the final act of vengeance to be yours.

'You must be patient as it will be a full year before you see the Norsemen again.'

Agneish inclined her head before dropping to her knees in acknowledgement of Aerten's gift.

The goddess gave a weary smile. 'Do not be troubled regarding my fate Agneish. I offer my life as a symbolic sacrifice, a means of perhaps gaining something more desirable. The demise of Odin!'

She stared directly at Cethlion. 'When they reach Mann, the cold light of the Hunter's Moon will betray the whereabouts of the northern invaders to Agneish. You must tell Arianrhod from the moment the bright white of this moon becomes a full moon, it must turn red. When they see the sky glow with fire, the Norsemen will be filled with terror, but I want her to remember just prior to their arrival at Manannan's isle the moon must be cloaked in darkness.' Aerten stopped talking for a moment as her voice began to falter and become weaker.

The others could barely hear her when she began to speak again. 'The darkness must last for an hour with only the dimmest of illuminations from a few stars; this will give Agneish and, I assume, Agrona and Cathubodia time to prepare themselves for the confrontation between themselves and the Norsemen.'

As the goddess's head dropped back against the trunk of the tree, Cethlion held up her hand to gesture for silence. The silence became so lengthy Agneish found it difficult to breathe in case the sound disturbed Aerten's thoughts.

Raising her head, Aerten beckoned Agneish to come closer. She smiled as she held out her hands, palms upwards. In the centre of each palm was a burning flame.

'For the gift of my life I ask for three human sacrifices every three years. This will ensure success for battles yet to come. Do you agree to this request?'

Agneish was silent. How could she carry out what Aerten was asking? It was impossible.

Then eerily she heard Agrona and Cathubodia's voices

'Agree, we will respond to Aerten's request.'

As Agneish shakily agreed, the flames on Aerten's palms blew out.

The goddess feebly pointed towards her double-bladed axe.

'Place it in my hands.'

Quickly Agneish picked up the huge axe and laid it across Aerten's outstretched hands. She now seemed completely exhausted and Cethlion urged the visitors to leave at once.

Shepherding them ahead of her, Cethlion turned round as she heard the swish of wheels moving through the air.

Barinthus, charioteer to the residents of the Otherworld and, on exceptionally rare occasions, charioteer of the Watchers to transport the lifeless bodies of deities to a shadowy parallel world, had arrived.

The moment the wheels of the chariot touched the ground, the Tree of Self-Destruction burst into flames and Aerten, Goddess of Fate who had unwaveringly decided her own, died.

Govannin, who had remained silent throughout the whole encounter, turned to look back just once as they walked away and saw Barinthus was wearing the sword his father had named *Bringer of Fate*.

He thought the Goddess of Fate might have liked that.

Chapter Sixteen

The Watchers

When they returned to the Place of Assembly, a goddess, her features hidden by the wide hood attached to her cloak, was waiting to escort them to the Watchers. When she pulled back her hood, Taliesin recognised her immediately.

'Welcome Taliesin, welcome Agneish and Govannin,' she said courteously as her eyes of the same shade of sea-blue as her cloak searched Agneish's face, seeking the unique individual quality of the mortal's personality that had captivated her father.

'I am Cliodna, priestess of the five temples and daughter of Manannan-beg-mac-y-Lleir. As we await the summons from the Watchers, I have been instructed by my father to show you how the highest of our established orders have the right and power to command, decide, rule or judge how to control our kingdom.'

She gestured towards the crowd of deities gathered in the Place of Assembly where, rising behind them, the travellers caught their first glimpse of four imposing temples emerging through the shadows of hazy clouds of purple mist. The four temples encircled an immense, elevated structure that was significantly larger than the others.

Cliodna said: 'The larger building is the Temple of Serenity which you will enter presently. If you wish, Cethlion, you may leave us now. I know you have much to do.'

Nodding gratefully, Cethlion took her leave, promising she would see them again very soon.

While they had been talking, the purple mists had disappeared and Govannin realised the position of the outer four temples had been set out very carefully.

A temple with a golden roof faced east, towards where the sun-god rose in the morning.

Another faced west, seeking the rapidly diminishing rays of energy radiating from the sun-god as he descended from the heavens.

Another faced north in search of the North Star, while the fourth temple faced south and the Otherworld.

Ignoring the stares and whispers of the groups of deities, they followed Cliodna through another enormous archway at the rear of the Place of Assembly where, to lend Govannin support, Taliesin and Agneish each grasped one of his arms. They trailed behind her up a steep hillside, passing a stupendous garden with vaulted terraces raised one above the other and filled with breathtakingly beautiful flowers with heady, enticing scents. Supported by rafters, trailing across and above the lush banks of brightly coloured plants were clusters of juicy purple grapes hanging down from thick, woody vines.

They passed fountains spouting jets of perfumed water and heard the thunderous roar of a huge waterfall cascading down the mountainside. They listened to the haunting melodies of spectacularly colourful song-birds until arriving at a square entirely surrounded by high walls.

Guarded by the other four temples, in the centre of the square was the magnificent Temple of Serenity.

The sumptuous opulence of the buildings took their breath away.

The fronts of the four outer temples were embellished with the creative progress of the Spinner of the Universe.

One displayed the celestial sphere of the heavens as an infinite vastness with numerous planets, with Ariadne exhibiting the earth at its centre, then separately the others displayed the creation of the oceans, the appearance of the sun, moon and stars. Then finally the creation of living creatures and mankind.

They stood in awed silence gazing at the beauty of these glorious buildings, except for Govannin, whose artistic senses were so stimulated he was almost in tears as he whispered, 'superb, wonderful, astounding.'

Mesmerised, they followed Cliodna as she walked towards the Temple of Serenity.

Statues of war-gods and goddesses mounted on winged horses watched over the sides of the temple while dominating the frontage was a gigantic statue of Barinthus driving a chariot pulled by four black horses. A warning that the authority of the Watchers must not be challenged.

Agneish stared in astonished admiration at the succession of multi-coloured birds strutting around the majestic structure. Some had a bright plumage of yellow, blue, scarlet and green with long streamers of tail feathers, while others were yellow with a neck ruff of light orange and back feathers of green and gold. Other birds were black with saffron-coloured spots and had fine, soft crimson feathers covering their breasts. Then, beckoned urgently by Cliodna, all three travellers wordlessly accompanied her up the long flight of stairs leading to the temple.

The temple was a circular building built on two levels and, once across the threshold, they found they had entered a wide corridor. Agneish noticed straight away a winding staircase leading up to the upper floor from the left, while on the right hand side was an enormous door.

Cliodna pointed to the doorway and told them that beyond that entrance were the Halls of Judgement where the Watchers gathered for council.

'The halls,' she said, 'were actually four chambers; one for thought, one for wisdom, one for decision and one for conclusion, each one as important as the last, but the principal chamber, the one from which they could see all four worlds, was on the upper floor.'

When she said they would be summoned shortly to the Chamber of Decision, Agneish was overcome with fear. Fear she wouldn't obtain her desire for revenge which burnt like a consuming fire in her soul.

Wind chimes jingles softly and Cliodna's expression told them the Watchers had requested their presence.

Very gently she pushed open the great door and immediately in front of them were four other doors. Three were closed, one partly open. 'You may enter now. Good fortune with your petition,' said Cliodna as she walked away.

Taliesin entered the chamber first, followed by Agneish, then more slowly Govannin who was leaning heavily on his silver staff. Taliesin instantly regulated his step so he would proceed at the same pace as the dwarf whose gait was now very slow and uneven. Agneish, with legs that seemed unwilling to to bear her weight, walked unsteadily further into the room.

It was dimly lit but Agneish's senses were so alert that no detail escaped her notice and she became aware of four shadowy figures sitting in the gloom. Instantly, a Watcher waved his hand and blazing firebrands lit the huge council chamber. Govannin sniffed the air, a heated oil was emitting a warm, musky, earthy scent. He recognised it as Oil of Amber.

Facing the door were four magnificent thrones, each one carved from ivory and inlaid with sheets of gold. Set into the surface of the gold were carved ebony figures of the Watchers.

Behind the thrones a panelled wall glowed in deep, rich, regal shades of purple which changed repeatedly to a sequence of the softer more delicate shades of lilac, lavender and violet. The colours had an immediate calming effect on Agneish.

The other three walls were different. Their colours were comparable to a vivid tapestry of gleaming golds. The luminous intensity of the gold varied from honey shades to vibrant golden yellow and velvety creamy hues. Agneish felt she was looking into a distant sun as the walls seemed to be entirely filled with crystals saturated with brilliant golden lights. She thought they must be a gift from the sun-god.

Each Watcher was dressed in long, loose purple robes and all four showed characteristics of great age with shoulder-length fine white hair and silver beards.

A Watcher spoke: 'We are delighted to welcome you to our land Agneish. Your journey has been difficult and challenging and we paid attention to your progress with interest and a deepening respect.' The Watcher's smile was warm and for a moment Agneish was taken aback by his friendly greeting.

Feeling nervous in the presence of these powerful deities, at first she was unable to speak. Finally she found her voice….

'Thank you. I stand here as a humble suppliant to petition for your help.'

The Watchers noted her bleak expression, the unnatural pallor of her skin which was in stark contrast to her flame-coloured hair, while the dark circles beneath her eyes betrayed her tiredness.

'What do you hope to gain from us?' asked another Watcher, the timbre of his low voice was soothing and unexpectantly sympathetic.

Without shame or embarrassment for her pitiless words, Agneish spoke straight from her heart.

'I seek vengeance for the brutal murders of my family, justice for the slaughter of my friends and revenge for the burning of my village. I accuse the Norseman of countless crimes and I cannot accept he will go unpunished. The man who shed my father's blood must shed his own.'

The Watchers noted her eyes were devoid of emotion as she whispered. 'Since the raiders came, demons have plagued my thoughts, but now my mind is filled with but one of them. I imagine I am flaying his skin so mercilessly it is loosening from his body like bark from a tree.'

The chamber was silent as the Watchers gazed at her. She didn't look away, she had come too far to be thwarted now.

'His punishment must be death. Perhaps the Guardian of Mann would grant me the use of his magical sword for the specific purpose of cleaving the Norseman's head from his body.'

She uttered these last words harshly and loudly, barely able to prevent her body from trembling as she recalled that terrible day.

'I believe with your help in imposing his punishment, it would be a blessed retribution.'

Govannin, his face marked with pain as he tried to straighten his crooked spine, looked concerned. Had Agneish gone too far? Was it too soon to be so demanding?

Because she was staring in the Watchers' direction with blank unseeing eyes, Agneish hadn't noticed Agrona and Cathubodia had entered the chamber.

They had listened to her intense, compelling, impassioned plea and had smiled with satisfaction as they sensed the rage behind her words.

'The Guardian of the Earth stood up. 'I for one receive your petition sympathetically. Perhaps the other guardians will share their opinions.'

The Guardian of Water rose to his feet, taking a moment to give Agneish a kindly glance before speaking.

'I feel favourably inclined towards your need to punish the Norseman,' he said nodding in her direction, 'and I believe we may reach an understanding.'

Taliesin took a deep breath of relief. Two Watchers on Agneish's side, the remaining two were yet to speak.

The Guardian of the Air remained seated and when he spoke his tone was impatient, almost exasperated at being asked to deal with this young mortal's dilemma.

'I find the circumstances involving her petition are problematical, inconvenient and annoying but I accept I must also offer my support.'

His answers were deliberately brief and vague as he attempted to evade the issue.

The Guardian of Fire got to his feet and gave Agneish a piercing stare. 'It is neither practical nor wise to become involved when individuals not of our world wish to engage in battle. Above all, as guardians we must exercise good judgement in protecting our own interests.'

Pointing to the war-goddesses, he said sharply, 'I am sensitive to the fact that many influential deities support your championship of this mortal.' He was silent for a few seconds, giving Govannin a chance to gaze at this Watcher whose sharp intelligence and realistic appraisals were legendary.

The guardian spoke again. 'However it would be difficult to be in opposition to the might and power of your supporters, therefore I too cast my vote in favour of the mortal.'

The Guardian of Water, his face furrowed by strongly marked lines of compassion spoke again and was liberal with his praise for the struggles the travellers had coped with. 'Pitting your wits against ours and other deities will be the most difficult feats you will each have to face in your lifetime. I include you in this Taliesin, as we put to the test your bravery and challenged your belief you could win. How you slew the daegon will become a legend.

'The distress and suffering you endured Agneish when you thought you had met your brother on the Path of Trepidation was a severe examination of your character and gave us a basis to evaluate your courage. I believe we have had a positive result and I know we all pledge the Norseman's actions will have consequences he could never have dreamt of.'

When she heard the verdict of the Watchers, Agneish collapsed against Taliesin, the last two days had left her completely exhausted.

Agrona and Cathubodia came to her side with murmured words of congratulations and encouragement as they helped her to stand.

Govannin and Taliesin couldn't stop smiling at this turn of fortune, the future of the Norseman seemed to be sealed.

Utterly overwhelmed with gratitude, Agneish was rendered speechless as a sense of hopelessness was quickly replaced by a feeling of extreme excitement. This feeling was further compounded when the Guardian of the Earth, his face lit by a pleasant smile said. 'Come, all of you will follow us to the upper chamber of the Temple of Serenity.'

As they climbed the winding staircase leading to the upper chamber all Agneish could hear above the pounding of her heart was the flapping of the Watcher's sandals against the highly polished surface of the white crystalline stairs. The Guardian of the Earth smiled when he heard Agneish gasp in wonder when she saw a spectrum of colours flickering through the steps.

'He told her: 'Because of this phenomenon, the phantom crystals are called the Frozen Fires of Eternity. We believe they are spiritual lights that protects us from unknown realms.'

At the sides of some of the crystalline steps were various sizes and colours of the ice-like glittering gemstone. The guardian pointed to a mass of black shimmering shards embedded in a solid piece of its crystal matrix. 'Those exquisite shards are called The Blades of Truthfulness.'

Pointing to another he said. 'That dark-blue crystal is called the Stone of Celestial Power.

Look deep into its core and you will see it has captured the centre of a tempest.' As Agneish gazed intently into the dark stone, she saw reflected in its facets, raging winds, turbulent waters, churning clouds and brilliant flashes of white light.

He paused by a large, glowing red stone. 'Look into the depths of this gemstone and you will see threads of smoke leaping from the inextinguishable flames of a fire deity.'

Halting by a multi-faceted deep-green crystal, the guardian said. 'This is Cethlion's favourite. She recognises its mysterious quality and that it is a stone not yet fully understood. For now it remains one of natures secrets and is known as the Stone of Anticipation. But come, Cethlion will be joining us very soon.'

The interior of the upper chamber took Agneish's breath away. Never could she have imagined anything that looked like this.

'It must measure about 180 feet on each side.' Govannin spoke in an almost indistinct voice, not wanting to attract the attention of the Watchers as he stared around the vast square room. The ceiling was high and domed, the floor laid with white, almost translucent, smooth gleaming tiles and the walls constructed from pale, fine-grained sandstone.

Carved columns of pastel-pink rose quartz, quarried from along the Perthro River millions of years ago by the demi-gods, lined the walls of this illustrious chamber, a chamber where the Watchers could see and guard the portals between all four worlds.

On the northern side of the chamber, they followed the Watchers up another few steps which led to a spacious gallery. Here, a circular, flat glossy wall had been erected next to a milky-white, flawless chalcedony statue of Ariadne.

The Watchers halted near the circular wall.

Speaking very softly the Guardian of the West told them this was a whispering wall where voices from the past told their stories to those who could hear them. As he said this, they heard a low murmuring sound which resounded in the same way as a blend of many voices.

They listened attentively as the guardian told them that in primordial times the ancient gods had created a Star-Stone, a Stone of Prophecy and added it to the whispering wall, but not before bestowing its powers upon Cethlion.

They heard a rustling noise, like leaves blowing in a slight wind and suddenly Cethlion was standing by Agneish's side.

The goddess was now wearing a midnight-blue, floor-length robe embroidered with constellations of stars. Sewn with fine silver thread, they glinted through the softly draped folds of her robe.

Smiling gently at Agneish, Cethlion said. 'The wall has already whispered to me. The force that controls events is fate and yours has already been woven into the infinite moments of time.'

The Watchers nodded in agreement with Cethlion's words.

The goddess turned towards the wall. 'With the assistance of the Star-Stone I will endeavour to foretell yours and the Norseman's destiny.'

Cethlion touched a large, gleaming, black round stone placed in the middle of the whispering wall and immediately the outline of the stone changed into the silhouette of a star.

Agneish's mouth went dry and she found it difficult to breath as she waited to see what would happen next.

Taliesin and Govannin stood close behind her, but remained silent, both intimidated by the presence of the Watchers.

A face appeared in the Star-Stone, a face without eyes. Then the Star-Stone detached itself from the wall and hovered in the air above their heads, shining and crackling with energy.

Agneish saw the gaze of all the deities were focused on the floating star as a beam of light surged through its centre, creating a whirlpool of intense pressure which divided into two rays gliding across the star's surface.

The rays became eyes which opened and stared around the gallery until they found Agneish.

Looking into the eyes of the black star, Agneish felt the strongest urge to cry. Strangely, she felt they might be healing tears which would cleanse the hate from her soul; but then she heard a controlled chilly voice whispering to her from the wall. It told her not to look into the centre of the star but to remember her father, mother, brother and friends all slain by the Norseman and his brutal crew. There was a terrible edginess to the voice which instantly brought her to her senses.

Hurriedly she turned away from the stone.

The deities smiled at each other. Again Agneish had shown her inner strength.

Cethlion spoke quietly. 'In this gallery momentous decisions are made. You can perhaps understand an hour in the future cannot be stolen as it is not yet there to steal. But if we use the unfocused key to unlock time, the future can be adjusted so that a preferred influence is applied at the desired moment.

'At the cost of her life, the goddess Aerten pledged to help you by allowing you to use the Moon Gate, the only entrance through which a stream of moonbeams can release their light upon the earth. The moonlight will be the Norsemen's enemy. Arianrhod, High-Priestess of the Moon and Weaver of Celestial Time and Fate has also pledged her help. Her weaving implements are the full moon and the colours of the Aurora Borealis.

'Arianrhod will send their leader disturbing dreams, dreams that will promise him all his heart desires if he will journey from Norway on the 20th of September on course for Mann; dreams so favourable he will be lulled into making an error of judgement despite protests from his crew, all seasoned travellers who know the voyage is an undertaking of six weeks. This will take them to the end of October when a Blood Moon will be hanging in the sky. The raiders consider it extremely ill-fated to cross the seas when a Blood Moon will be waiting at the end of the voyage.

'Arianrhod will also entice the Norseman to leave his homeland when nightfall arrives early, by throwing open the doors of her castle and flooding the hours of darkness with colour. He will see this as a good omen. As I have calculated it will take the Norsemen 42 days to reach the coastline of Mann, she will continue to do this until the 31st of October.

'We will work together to ensure there are two Full Moons during this month.

'On the first day of October there will be a Full Harvest Moon and it will be bigger and brighter than any that have gone before. We will suspend it very low in the sky enabling the Norsemen to travel from Norway with more light than on any previous journey.

'The second Full Moon, a Blood Moon, will appear on the Feast of the Dead, the last day of October. This is when I promised Aerten the moon will turn red and the sky will glow with fire.

'Agneish, Aerten told you the second time the men from the North approach your island will not be until a full year has passed. They will not reach their homeland for another few weeks by then it will be too late to return to Mann, the weather conditions will be against them. You must have patience, a year will pass quickly.'

Cethlion turned to the Watchers and asked respectfully if her proposals met with their approval, then bowed her head as she waited for their reply, an acknowledgement that if the Watchers decision was unfavourable there wouldn't be any possibility of further discussion.

The Guardian of the Earth spoke for the other three. 'All excellent proposals Cethlion. Agrona and Cathubodia, do you agree?'

As they inclined their heads to confirm their agreement Agneish felt the light touch of Agrona's fingers as she stroked, then lifted, a thick strand of her hair. Agrona's eyes glistened as she said very softly: 'When the Norseman takes his last breath I know the scarlet of your hair will match exactly the colour of his blood as it spurts from his body.'

Cathubodia's voice bristled with such venom it raised the hairs on the back of Agneish's neck as she uttered. 'Never fear, we will be keeping a close watch for your Day of Retribution.' She went on to say: 'As we leave you with Cethlion, we bestow upon you our blessings and, as a token of our appreciation, Agrona and myself would like to present the Watchers with a small gift, one which we hope will evoke favourable memories of this extraordinary day.'

Agrona held out her hand, revealing a tiny, crimson-speckled egg.

Bending down, she placed it on an ornate amber table situated beneath a flaming firebrand, the light cast from the firebrand onto the amber resin suddenly produced a brilliant source of illumination which made everyone blink, the colour reminding Govannin of the golden hue of sunflowers.

They all heard a distinct breaking sound and fine cracks began to appear in the crimson egg-shell. The shell shattered and a miniature figure of a golden wyvern emerged from its centre.

The war-goddesses smiled. Cathubodia whispered to the wyvern and the diminutive creature instantly grew to twenty times its original size.

Agrona picked it up from the table and set it down on the gleaming tiled floor where to everyone's amusement they saw twelve fiery, glowing rubies were inset along the length of its body. One on its head, two for its eyes, the others positioned along its back and tail, producing a dazzling, luminous glow.

From its mouth the wyvern discharged one flaring flash of fire before transforming into a bejewelled figurine of solid gold.

The goddesses bowed to the Watchers and Cethlion and then they disappeared.

Govannin had been waiting nervously for just the right moment to ask permission for an audience with the Watchers. He instinctively felt the right moment was now!

Taliesin stood in stunned silence as Govannin hesitantly told the Watchers about his dream of being renowned as the finest goldsmith and artisan in his own right, not simply because of his family name. His voice wavered and he stumbled over his words as awkwardly and falteringly he managed to convey a little information about the torque he had created and named *Perception*.

The Guardian of the North intuitively grasped some of what Govannin was struggling to put into words and watched with heightened curiosity as the dwarf placed his hand inside the seemingly bottomless pocket on the inside of his cloak and withdrew a round, generously-sized golden casket.

The eyes of the four guardians were riveted on the casket as they noticed the engraved, intertwined ribbons of gold on its extended sides and the golden neck collar etched on the hinged top.

Slowly Govannin opened the casket and removed an object loosely wrapped in a shimmering silk cloth shot through with golden threads. Unwrapping it carefully he revealed to the waiting deities, *Perception*.

The Guardian of the North beckoned Govannin to follow him and the other Watchers to the Chamber of Thought, at the same time asking Cethlion to take Agneish and Taliesin to the Place of Assembly where Govannin would join them when they had observed what he was offering.

Govannin placed the torque back in his pocket, then leaning heavily on his staff he staggered slightly as agonisingly he twisted his crooked spine trying to keep pace with the Watchers. At last he was standing outside the door of the Chamber of Thought.

'Come, sit here,' the Guardian of the West said gently, noticing the expression of pain on Govannin's face. He offered Govannin a drinking vessel carved from a deep-purple amethyst crystal. The crystal had a fine mist of violet flames spurting out of the top which quickly vaporised. 'Drink,' the guardian urged. 'The moisture left in the vessel from the mist has now strengthened into a solution of potent energy. It will refresh you.'

Gratefully Govannin thanked him, then sat down, knowing what he said in the next few minutes was crucial to his own petition.

Govannin held the metal collar high in the air, giving the Watchers just a moment to glance at it as he said. 'Let me present the style of neck ring favoured by many Celtic tribes, Agneish of course belongs to one of them.

Their possessions of geometric Celtic art combined with inlaid enamelled work is the irrefutable symbol of position and power amongst the highest members of these tribes, a style I thought perfect to demonstrate the quality of imagination required to represent my own individuality. I hope you will agree.'

The Watchers looked at three long lengths of burnished gold, each about six inches in width which had been grouped into ropes and twisted around each other. Intriguingly, the end of each torque had been cast into two separate shapes. The right side was shaped as a full moon and the left, a star. He told them both sides would perfectly interlock if they wished to use the torque as a method of deliberating, meditating or thinking.

Etched on the right side, next to the full moon, was an ancient Celtic sun symbol, the triskele. It had three legs united at the thigh with a face at the centre of its complex design.

'Gold,' Govannin said reverently as he looked at the torque, 'the most powerful of colours and associated with the radiance of the sun-god. But first, let me draw your attention to both the inside and outside of the collar.' The Watchers saw the inner part of the gold band was embossed with geometric patterns, while the outer surface was decorated with a path of astronomical spirals which gave the graceful round curve of the torque a sense of movement through time. Exactly what Govannin had intended.

He knew the heavenly symbols would bring a continuous mystery to the neck ring which was unique, meticulously detailed and perfectly circular.

'From the beginning of my concept of *Perception* I knew I had to permeate it with the faculty of memory, images that could be stored in the centre of the triskele which would be the seat of thought and recollection. To put it another way, the torque would have a soul!'

Govannin stopped talking but the Watchers faces remained impassive. Govannin continued, his voice rising a little as he tried to convince the deities of the desirability of his creation.

'I named it *Perception* because I gave it the ability to perceive, detect and interpret information by means of the sensory receptors at each end. The moon and the star.'

The four guardians leant forward, their interest now fully aroused by Govannin's explanation of how the design of the torque was in itself a channel of further knowledge.

'The challenge to create this torque was formidable, but now, today, I would like to offer its capacity for awareness to the discerning minds of four supreme deities.' Govannin paused for a moment as thoughts kept spinning and tumbling through his mind as he tried to put into words his belief in the powers of *Perception*.

Hesitantly he continued: 'I have implanted into the torque a special feature that will individually be of use to each of you when you place it around your neck.

'To the Guardian of the North, *Perception* will grant you a penetrating vision that will enable you to form images beyond the four known worlds and to be able to see in your mind's eye travel weary malignant spirits as they journey from one unspecified place to another.

'To the Guardian of the East, a clear perception of a situation. For you, an additional ability to understand as you will gain the total experiences of *all* the senses at the same time.

'To the Guardian of the West, the gift of extraordinary perception, enabling you to perceive any sudden catastrophic changes in the earth's surface and thus prevent harm befalling its season of renewal. Forewarned, you may be able to avert the tragic destruction of this planet.

'To the Southern Guardian, it will give you a perception of a bodily existence, something that has no physical reality and something you may not be able to see. Perhaps a formless creature from the Otherworld whose presence foretells of sinister developments that will threaten your kingdom.

'The enduring concept of *Perception* will be its representation of your individual positions and power, continuing power.' Dramatically Govannin emphasised these last few words.

The Watchers were silent, all four deeply preoccupied with their own thoughts as Govannin, sensing the futility of further speech, refrained from any further added discussion.

Eventually the Guardian of the North spoke. 'What you have created Govannin has inspired awe and admiration for your command of skills that perhaps even surpass those of your grandfather.' He smiled broadly as the other guardians noisily agreed.

After a minute, which seemed endless to Govannin, the Watcher spoke again. 'If your ingenuity and skill has instilled into the collar an intellect displaying specific functions for each of us, the value or, should I say the significance to us, would be beyond measure.

'However, obviously we cannot reach a judgement before evidence is available based on observable phenomena or facts. Do you all concur?'

Elation such as he had never known before surged through Govannin when he heard the excited assent from the other three guardians. He knew he had captured their imaginations and he knew he was just a step away from the attainment of fame for posterity.

Perception would fulfil all expectations and he would be hailed as a genius.

A tremendous feeling of happiness was spreading through his body, so near was he to accomplishing his dream.

He presented the twisted coils of gold to the Guardian of the North, bowed and asked their permission to leave the chamber.

They waved him away, each Watcher eager now to test for himself the different sensations embedded in the sensory receptors of the torque. Powers which made the collar a masterpiece!

Chapter Seventeen

Govannin

Ignoring the bombardment of questions from scores of gossiping deities, Cethlion waited with Agneish and Taliesin at the Place of Assembly for the emergence of Govannin from the Temple of Serenity. Taliesin, as usual, passing the time strumming quietly on his lyre.

When he finally appeared Govannin was struggling to stem the flow of tears cascading down his cheeks. When his emotions were under control he was able to tell them he had succeeded in his quest, as all four Watchers had been convinced by the desirability of *Perception*.

Agneish couldn't stop hugging him, she knew how much his search for recognition as a skilled artisan meant to Govannin.

Cethlion gave them a few moments before urging them to embark on their journey down the mountain path, reminding them that before the first light of the following morning they must listen for the sound of the Time Messenger as at that moment *it would be the day after tomorrow.*

At once this remark had a sobering effect on Govannin and Agneish. Thanking Cethlion for her help and support, the travellers began to make their way down the rock-strewn path, but with their sense of good fortune so strong and compelling they kept bursting into spontaneous laughter, the sound booming back at them as it echoed off the sides of the mountain.

Govannin, his face wearing a contented smile, was tightly clutching a roll of parchment, a decree from the Watchers declaring his new status as their principal artisan and creator of extraordinary objects.

No one noticed the silent onlooker hidden by the shadow of a stone ledge.

Suddenly they felt rather than heard a presence behind them. 'Someone is here.' Agneish's anxious voice sounded like a broken whisper.

Fear drained the colour from her face as she whirled round and caught sight of Cernunnos.

His dark scowl, threatening expression and the broad knotted veins throbbing in his forehead, lent a pervading sense of menace to his tone as he spoke to Agneish. 'I will not be cheated. You have been an elusive quarry but you will ride from here as a fatality of the Wild Hunt and enter with me the Halls of the Otherworld.'

Agneish's terrified screams rang through the air as, directly in front of her, she caught sight of a severed skeleton hand holding a huge key.

'The key to the dark region of the Otherworld,' Taliesin said, his voice filled with alarm.

Govannin closed, then immediately reopened his eyes as the air filled with Agneish's screams. In those few split seconds her cries seemed to have an ominous importance, as if a fateful encounter was to take place with a particular consequence to himself. Then he saw Cernunnos was holding a small tyranni bird in his hand.

Colonies of these small, venomous, black and grey birds lived in the gloomy crevices of the Otherworld and one drop of their venom brought numbness, paralysis and death.

At a whispered command from the Lord of the Wild Hunt, the bird flew straight towards Agneish.

Govannin stepped in front of her, his outstretched arms flailing about helplessly as he tried to beat it away.

Irritated at Govannin's attempt to block its progress the tyranny bird flew at Govannin's throat.

They all heard a slight scraping sound as its claws scratched across Govannin's skin leaving a narrow cut in his neck. A lethal secretion of venom seeped quickly from its sharp curved nails into the wound.

Govannin's head flopped forward as he fell to his knees before collapsing slowly onto the ground.

As he gasped his last breath, the dwarf's clenched fingers opened and slowly released his precious document, the slight breeze on the mountain lifting it high into the air before wafting it gently over the side.

Agneish ran towards Govannin when she heard the sound of his falling body, but Taliesin was quicker and Agneish wept uncontrollably as she watched the Prince of Song hold Govannin's limp body in his arms before lowering him gently onto the earth.

The sound of her weeping deafened her to the raucous caw of a crow as a swollen mass of thunderclouds crackling with lightning swirled overhead. A moment later Agrona and Cathubodia appeared on the pathway.

A thankful smile appeared on Taliesin's face at the arrival of the war-goddesses.

Agrona threw back her cloak revealing her right shoulder, and Agneish had to bite her lip hard to prevent herself from shrieking with terror. Clearly outlined on the tall goddess's arm was a detailed design of a skull whose empty eye-sockets seemed to stare into the core of Cernunnos's soul. Its black rotting teeth were firmly clenched onto two sharp pointed daggers, objects that would cause agony, torment or death. Shockingly, Agneish could distinctly hear the sound of knives being sharpened. Then behind Cathubodia's stooped shoulders Taliesin saw a nightmarish procession of phantoms who had each refused to be incarcerated in the hidden depths of the Otherworld, moving stealthily towards Agneish. They were followed by a cart drawn by two black horses. In the driver's seat was an emaciated figure with large, bony hands. If the Lord of the Hunt commanded it, the driver collected the dead.

Standing in the back of the cart was a tall spectre dressed in a dark-grey hooded robe.

The cart stopped and the spectre threw back his hood revealing the fleshless face of a skeleton. Agneish's eyes were filled with horror as she watched the spectre bend and pick up a long handled scythe with a curved blade.

Keeping his voice very low, Taliesin said. 'That is the Severer of Souls and Record Keeper of the Dead. I believe you have a similar spectre in your world you call the Grim Reaper.'

Agneish could only nod. At that moment she was incapable of speaking as although the severer's lips were bloodless and his eye sockets sunken and empty, she detected a grimace which could have passed for a smile.

These visual representations of death goaded Agrona into a verbal confrontation with the Lord of the Hunt.

'Keeper of the Dead, Cernunnos, that is the only fitting occupation for you,' she said with such scorn and derision in her tone, it made Taliesin wince.

Shadows were moving furtively behind Cernunnos and Agneish could see the skeleton of a child grasping his leg and then a cadaver holding the bloated body of a young woman in his arms. The young woman couldn't have been dead very long as there were faded yellow flowers in her lifeless hair.

But then, terrifyingly, came the shock of seeing the corpse's eyes, now covered with an opaque film, flood with tears.

Cathubodia glanced at the moving shadows with contempt. 'We are aware that those who inhabit the Otherworld are without mercy or pity,' Cathubodia snarled, 'but you will find Agrona and myself have been tested and found not wanting in those particular characteristics ourselves, so be warned!'

Cernunnos's insolent smile mocked the war-goddesses, but the Watchers high up on the upper floor of the Temple of Serenity had also seen the death of Govannin and were hurrying to the Chamber of Conclusion, seeking an object of great beauty and inestimable value.

It was a richly decorated, papyrus writing tablet with two individual carved leaves hinged securely together. The tablet contained an ever-changing list of the living and the dead. Govannin's name was illuminated amongst the dead, Agneish's was not!

Hanging above the tablet was a pair of interlocking alabaster boards with a waxed surface for writing. Swiftly the Guardian of the North began to write. When he'd finished he spoke of his conclusions to the other Watchers.

'Cernunnos strikes in the manner of a hawk, primarily as an instrument of certain death. However, for this death he must be punished.

'But first we must pay tribute to Govannin's courage and invincible spirit. I suggest we place him amongst stars which have lit a billion nights, possibly in the Northern Crown where his spirit will be under the protection of Arianrhod. I believe her ever-changing display of colours will delight his creative mind.'

The Watchers agreed at once.

'His will be a world without end,' said the Guardian of Fire.

'From there he will be able to see the splendour of the Land of a Thousand Gods,' the Guardian of Water said approvingly.

'And who would not wish for that?' The Guardian of Air said with satisfaction. This was to him a suitable conclusion to Govannin's misfortune.

There was no more to be said.

Chapter Eighteen

Banishment

The mournful sigh of the wind sweeping across the side of the mountain carried the stern voice of the Guardian of the North to those standing on the rocky pathway.

'Cernunnos, you must be disciplined for the death of the dwarf and the severity of your punishment must be in keeping with your unacceptable conduct.

'By general consent we will cast you out from our society for a period of time yet to be determined. The imposing of such a penalty leaves us with a heavy heart but you must be held accountable.

'You have openly expressed your intention of forcibly taking this young mortal to your world and we advise you to desist from this threat. We warn you now to beware of our wrath if any harm should befall her.'

The barely controlled hostility vibrating through the air between the three powerful deities waiting on the path was unmistakable as Agrona and Cathubodia struggled to contain their deep-seated antagonism towards Cernunnos as they waited for the Watchers to give their ruling on his fate.

The Guardian of the North spoke again: 'You do not merit your status as Lord of the Wild Hunt and we all agree you must leave here at once.

'You will not be permitted a purpose and you must wander alone, avoided by others except during the hours of darkness which is the habitat of shades. These dark shadows of the night will follow you wherever you go and you will not be able to drive them away.

'You have shown no mercy and none shall be shown to you.'

As he said this, Cathubodia pointed towards a dense cloud bank moving quickly through the sky in their direction. The clouds were separating with a violent tearing sound as if a concealed power was ripping them apart.

'The Doorway of Death is now visible but Agneish shall not enter it,' the Guardian of Fire's voice said forcefully.

Agneish's stomach churned with fear as she heard an uneasy burst of laughter from Cernunnos followed by a bellow of rage.

'You forget who I am,' he growled threateningly. 'Not only Lord of the Wild Hunt and Guardian of the Ancient Forests, but a god of a world beyond this one, the Otherworld.'

He pointed at Agneish. 'I demand she rides across the skies with me.'

As he said this, the sound of baying hounds filled the air. With an abrupt gesture Cernunnos silenced them and a stillness descended over the mountain path as the mournful sigh of the wind dropped to a soft murmur.

Slivers of moonlight were beginning to appear in the heavens as the Moonlighter lit the three large silvery moons, making clearly visible to all the enormous size of Cernunnos as he moved away from the cliff-edge.

His eyes blazed with fury as he stared with intense enmity at the war-goddesses. Then came the eerie sounds of fluttering wings, rustling leaves and thudding hooves as unseen creatures left their forest dwellings to join their master.

Taliesin looked at Cernunnos with awe mixed with apprehension. He knew this deity was a being that had existed before all other gods and images of him had decorated the caves and hillsides of primitive man. He also knew Cernunnos had a sinister, deceitful nature and had been known to display a loss of self-control verging on madness to those who threatened him or his domain.

There was a brief silence until Cernunnos could no longer contain his rage and his fury erupted in ferocious, explosive anger.

'You have dared to challenge my status, power and position amongst the gods but I will ignore this provocation if you give me the mortal. Be warned, I will not spend my life in obscurity far from the centre of my world and until the end of time I *will* ride out on the eve of the four great Celtic Fire Festivals. The next one is Samhain and I will lead the Wild Hunt across the heavens as always. Do not get in my way or I will release a host of lost souls to wander from corner to corner of your realm forever and I promise you they will bring many nameless and strange diseases to the Land of a Thousand Gods.'

Hearing this threat from Cernunnos the Watchers suddenly came into view, materialising as four colossal heads looming through the light-purple haze which had begun to drift over the mountain.

The Lord of the Wild Hunt stared defiantly up at them.

'To prevent the plague of lost souls and the diseases I will ensure they bring, I demand the mortal is offered to me as a sacrifice.'

Agneish's face was the colour of parchment as she waited for the Watchers' reply.

The Guardian of the North spoke. 'We learnt long ago a deity can be overbearingly arrogant, take the example of the demi-gods, but on this occasion I am describing you Cernunnos. Your demands show your distain for the wishes of others, others with a comparable exalted status as yourself. You would do well not to offend them.'

Cernunnos stepped forward. His swagger, scornful smile and expression of contempt spoke volumes about his volatile nature.

His eyes narrowed when he heard the harsh, shrill caw of a crow. He knew it was the Morrigan. Even appearing as one aspect of the trinity she was a formidable deity, a fitting contender to challenge his own terrifying powers.

The crow settled briefly on his shoulder before taking flight and soaring swiftly into the air. When it alighted on the ground the bird rapidly shape-shifted into the Queen of the Otherworld.

'The destructive forces of your nature Cernunnos have brought you to this and now you must reap the seeds you have sown,' she said coldly.

Thick veins pulsated wildly at the temples of the Lord of the Hunt as he stared threateningly at the Morrigan.

'I will be your inseparable companion Cernunnos, a spectre who will pursue you throughout every part of the Otherworld 'till we reach the final resting place of all the dead you have transported there and I shall whisper to them to awaken.'

Her voice, low and soft sounded more menacing than if she'd shouted with rage.

Agneish's lips were white with terror as an Air Elemental's hand appeared in the sky with jagged lightning pouring from its finger tips, a signal to Agrona and Cathubodia to take their place beside the Morrigan.

Agrona pointed to the prone figure lying on the pathway. On Govannin's cheek was a round, frozen teardrop and each deity could clearly see it contained an image of *Perception*. It was Govannin's last thought.

Cathubodia placed her hand over the frozen tear and looked compassionately at Agneish. 'I give my pledge it will never leave his cheek. The image of *Perception* will remain with him for eternity.'

The Queen of the Otherworld had shape-shifted back into the guise of a crow in preparation for carrying Govannin's soul safely in her black wings through the Doorway of Death.

When he saw the crow the Guardian of the North's voice resounded loudly through the purple mist. 'No, the dwarf will travel to his last destination along the secret footpath amongst the clouds.'

Taliesin took a deep intake of breath, this was a magnificent gesture from the Watchers which fully demonstrated their respect for Govannin.

When the Northern Guardian had finished speaking the moonlight revealed a spectacular staircase formed from brilliant white starlight.

At once Taliesin removed the golden lyre from around his neck and began to play. The silvery notes of his voice accompanying the soft, low sound of his gentle music brought floods of tears to Agneish's eyes as she watched Govannin's dead body stand up, then begin to climb the staircase.

'The starlight flight of steps will take him from the beginning to the end of the secret footpath amongst the clouds. The end of the path is where he will spend eternity.' Cathubodia told Agneish.

As Govannin climbed the staircase Taliesin noticed at once that not only had his limping gait disappeared, but the largest moon appeared to be glowing with fire.

'We deities honour the fire which sometimes burns in the moon during the darkness. It tells of a true spirit making its way to the heavens,' he whispered to Agneish.

Cathubodia had sent Air Elementals in the form of cloud dragons to guard Govannin as he climbed the stairs and as his shadow drifted across the three moons Taliesin said consolingly. 'He will soon cross the threshold of a realm beyond his wildest dreams and take his place among the stars.'

None standing on the mountain path could see Govannin passing a goddess spinning moonbows. The luminosity and radiance of these lunar rainbows would highlight every step of his journey.

The goddess stopped spinning for a moment to give him a sympathetic smile before returning to her work.

Govannin climbed on.

There was an expression of deep sadness in Taliesin's eyes as he said quietly. 'We must depart now Agneish, we cannot be late for the Time Messenger.'

'Taliesin is right,' Agrona affirmed swiftly, 'but you must take Govannin's staff with you, you might need it.'

As Taliesin bent to pick up the silver staff they all heard a curious sound. It was the staircase of starlight reverberating with the echoes of Govannin's final footsteps.

With tears streaming down her face Agneish walked slowly away without once looking back.

The skin tightened around Cernunnos's eyes as he watched her leave.

'Do not attempt to follow her,' Agrona warned.

The war-goddesses and the Lord of the Wild Hunt glared at each other, their anger and hostility now so palpable it was almost a solid, physical presence.

'You revel in your role as Lord of the Wild Hunt Cernunnos, and one day you may be allowed to resume that status, but not if you are a continuous source of danger to the mortal. You must let her go,' Cathubodia said fiercely.'

Unexpectantly, Cernunnos disappeared from sight; then came the loud sound of flapping wings as an enormous black-plumed bird flew over their heads. The bird's head was a featherless, bony skull.

Cernunnos had shape-shifted into part-bird, part-skeleton hoping no-one would recognise him disguised in this hideous body. He would withdraw from the Land of a Thousand Gods until the Watchers recalled him. His egotism and arrogance would not let him be known by anything other than Lord of the Wild Hunt, Guardian of the Ancient Forests and a principal god of the Otherworld.

He would bide his time and endure.

Cathubodia said very softly. 'Without mercy or pity are those who live solely to inhabit the region of the Otherworld. I hope we don't see you again Cernunnos for a very, very long time.'

Chapter Nineteen

The Time Messenger

As they made their way along the twisting downward path, Agneish's eyes were wide with fear. She was experiencing an intense overwhelming terror that Cernunnos would appear and force her to travel with him to the Otherworld. Taliesin knew this wouldn't happen. He realised that for now, the Lord of the Wild Hunt had ceased to exist.

Heavy-footed, Agneish walked along with slow, tired steps, unable to think about anything but Govannin.

'You must walk faster Agneish,' Taliesin demanded, 'or we are going to be late. We must not miss the Time Messenger heralding in the new day. The instant we hear his song we must move quickly. Remember, when the first light appears above the eastern horizon tomorrow that is all the time we have been allotted to spend here.

'If we are early, the Morrigan will be waiting to open the gates so we can leave, but if we are late you will be confined in this land forever. Providing all is well, Enbarr will be outside them, ready to take us back to Mann.'

Taliesin's words awoke the realisation of the danger she was in, and after that, the need to hurry drove her to make a greater effort.

Finally they reached the locked wooden door leading into the underground tunnel. Agneish, completely drained of strength and energy, was tiredly wondering how she was going to force herself to make the long journey back to the locked gates of the Land of a Thousand Gods. It was then Taliesin told her the Watchers had provided another way for them to descend from the mountain plateau.

Pointing ahead of her, he said. 'In that direction lies the horizon we seek, but first tap the ground with Govannin's staff.'

Agneish complied and immediately at the edge of the mountain side a narrow, steeply downward-sloping bridge appeared. Protected by a roof with enclosed sides and an attached hand rail, the bridge provided a passageway to the mountain's foothills. Once they reached the bottom Taliesin had been assured by Cethlion they would find the route which would lead them to the Time Messenger.

Shivering in the cold night air Agneish stepped onto the bridge and for a brief moment looked down into the deep ravine hundreds of feet below. Taliesin, noticing her frightened expression, said briskly: 'Using Govannin's staff as before, we will locate the first light of the sun-god, but we must make haste.'

After a long, much slower descent than Taliesin would have wished they finally reached the foot of the mountain.

Agneish banged the ground with the staff and a trail of flames blazed forwards in an easterly direction. Stumbling along the dark track with only the thin flames to guide them both, she was shocked when suddenly the flames went out.

But the relief was evident in Taliesin's voice as he said. 'This is where we wait for the messenger.'

They settled down to wait and although they talked far into the night, both were listening carefully for the first notes of the song bird. Then in the shadowy gloom, they heard the Time Messenger's mesmerising song.

They didn't linger to hear his rising crescendo of high and low notes as Taliesin urgently tapped the silver staff on the solid surface of the earth. Immediately a lit path lay ahead for them to follow. It led them to the Gates of a Thousand Gods just as the first light of day began to appear over the horizon.

The old crone wrapped in a cape of crow's feathers was waiting by the gateway.

As she opened the gates she gave Agneish a sympathetic glance and said gently. 'For your friend it is not the end. It will comfort you to know he will be under the watchful eyes of the Guardians for all time.'

Agneish could only manage to whisper, 'thank you,' to the Morrigan as with a loud bang the gates closed firmly behind herself and Taliesin.

Outside the gates there was no other sound except the lapping of waves against the golden bridge. The smell of salt reminded her unbearably of home and for the first time in days she had time to think about Catat. She reached into the pocket of her tunic and was reassured by the feel of the small phial Govannin had given her to awaken him.

Then they heard the thud of hooves upon the soft sand and Enbarr stood before them.

Taliesin first making sure his lyre was securely fastened around his neck, jumped onto his back, then bent down and pulled Agneish up in front of him.

'Go,' Taliesin said softly to the white horse, 'return to Mann.'

Enbarr began to run towards the bridge, his long, shiny mane streaming out behind in a smooth flowing line as he mounted the raised crossing, cantered along its length, then plunging into the sea.

As Manannan's horse rode through the spirals of coloured mist springing up ahead of them, for the second time Agneish found the surrounding silence both peaceful and strange, then, exactly where the sky and earth appeared to meet, she saw the outline of Mann shimmering in the distance.

Heavy waves were breaking over the rocky beach at Port Grenaugh as Enbarr galloped onto its pebbly shore then raced unerringly towards Santon.

As they reached the outskirts of what remained of the village, the stench of burning was still strong enough to make Agneish's hands shake as she dismounted from Enbarr's back.

Her eyes widened with surprise when she saw Taliesin had stayed astride the Guardian of Mann's horse.

'I must return with Enbarr to the Land of a Thousand Gods Agneish, leaving you to take control of your own life,' he told her.

'A year will pass quickly as you have much to do and a great deal to think about. Never assume you are on your own, many of the deities will be watching over you, not least the Great Sea-Lord, Manannan.

'Do not forget to inspect the moonbeams flooding through the Moon Gates for images of the Norsemen as they travel back to this island during the months of September and October next year. They *will* come, Cethlion and Arianrhod will make certain of that.'

Taliesin smiled at her as he said. 'One day I will compose a magnificent verse about you and the Viking leader, and travel up and down my land singing about your victorious crusade against him.'

Taliesin's blue eyes looked steadily into hers as he said very softly. 'Walk away and take care.'

Too distressed to argue with him, without another word Agneish walked uncertainly into the village. She looked round just once, but Enbarr and Taliesin had vanished.

Agneish had never felt so alone in her life as she did at that moment and had to force herself to take each breath slowly as she searched for Catat.

She found him exactly where she and Govannin had left him.

Untroubled by any dreams or nightmares, he seemed to be fast asleep. Relieved, she withdrew the phial Govannin had given her to wake him and opened it underneath his nose as the dwarf had instructed.

Catat awoke instantly.

With tears streaming down her face Agneish couldn't stop hugging him. It was just the two of them now, they would take care of each other.

There was no light chirping sound of birdsong from trees on the hills behind the village as Agneish shuddering violently, smelt the stench of decomposing corpses and walked past bodies thick with blow flies. In her mind she could hear the screams of these men, women and children as they pleaded for their lives.

Everywhere was covered with ashes as she plodded wearily through the charred remains of the settlement. Standing outside her father's house she found his axe stained with the blood of Vikings as Engus had desperately fought for his life.

Picking up the axe and calling to Catat to follow her, Agneish hurried towards the *keeill*. Pushing open its thick wooden door she found the interior looked exactly as it had on the day of the raid, only the smell of rotting fruit and vegetables lying on the floor was different.

Agneish put down her father's axe, pulled away the filmy cobwebs hanging from the *keeill's* timber beams, sat on one of the long benches and laid her head in her hands.

Eventually, worn out and drained of any remaining energy, she drew her legs up onto the bench and quickly fell into a troubled sleep. Catat curled up beside her.

When she awoke darkness had closed in and Agneish decided to stay where she was until morning.

As she lay on the bench listening to the hoot of a hunting owl, the clicking sounds of insects and rustling noises from small rodents running through the underbrush, all sounds of the night she was familiar with, the need to survive gradually overcame her sense of despair.

The next day dawned with clear blue skies and with it an awareness of her predetermined destiny stole into her heart. When she met the Norseman at the appointed hour set by the gods, she was as far as possible firmly resolved to be mistress of her own fate.

Going outside she unfastened the tight thick braid of her hair and let it blow freely around her head, smiling when she heard the songbirds morning chorus, which gave her a feeling of optimism after their silence of the day before.

She made a decision and gripping Engus's heavy axe tightly in her hand, Agneish, trailed closely by Catat, walked away from the village. She needed a new start, a time to think, she couldn't do it here.

Chapter Twenty

One Year Later

As dark shadows gathered at nightfall on the first of October 799, the sky gradually filled with the brightest Harvest Moon Agneish had ever seen. As promised, Arianrhod, Celtic Moon Goddess and Weaver of Celestial Time and Fate had thrown open the doors of her castle, the Aurora Borealis and flooded the sky with colour.

Sitting with Catat on the water-worn boulders at the edge of the shoreline at Port Grenaugh, Agneish gazed at the sky with breathless wonder.

She watched as leaping, fluttering ribbons of dazzlingly bright colours lit up the night sky, saturating the heavens with iridescent hues of green, yellow and orange.

She held her breath in awe as the colours altered to red, blue and violet which twisted and turned in narrow streamers of tinted amethyst shades before changing into an enormous, spinning green ring of light which gradually disappeared from the display.

Then began a faint glow of soft mellow tones which slowly formed an arc with a full spectrum of vivid colours.

She watched soaring waves of rippling coloured lights merge from greens to reds to vibrant orange, which then tore a haphazard trail across the dark-blue sky. Suddenly, through a gap in the waves of coloured light, Agneish saw the Moon Gate was discharging an unbroken stream of brilliant moon-beams. She stood up and concentrated her gaze on the moon, then, incredibly, she caught glimpses of the Norsemen's images flickering over its surface like the pale flame of a will-o-the-wisp she had often seen glinting over the marshlands at night. She took a few deep gulps of air to steady her breathing.

They were coming!

As the fiery colours of the Aurora Borealis stretched across the sky, Agneish, shaken at catching sight of the Norsemen, walked back to the *keeill* with Catat close to her heels.

A year ago when she had strode away from the charred ruins of her village, Agneish had vowed never to return, but after spending one night in the open air she had quickly realised this wasn't the way to survive the coming winter, but just thinking about returning to the burnt-out settlement had sent shudders down her spine. Instead she had returned to the *keeill*, sat on one of the benches and reflected on what she needed to do.

Closing her eyes she had thought for a long time about her childhood, her parents, her brother and her friends, then pondered about the pledge she had made to stay alive until the Norsemen came again. She made a decision, she would have to return to the village.

When she returned she took her time thoroughly searching through scattered articles of clothing and managed to salvage a few useful garments and bits and pieces of bedding.

She found a functional tripod, a cauldron only slightly distorted from the heat of burning houses, a small number of wooden cups and bowls, a wooden chest with a broken leg, (she could prop it up with a stone) and was overjoyed when she found a bone comb which was still in one piece.

Now Agneish had a few clothes to wear and some domestic items, but nowhere to sleep; then she realised she could do worse than to make the *keeill* her home. She and Catat moved in that day.

She laid a stone fire-ring on the hard stone floor, they would be warm at least, and once she had checked the plots for usable vegetables, they would possibly have something hot to eat and drink.

Isolated from any human companionship, but with a determination and tenacity which would enable her to withstand the hardships of the coming year, Agneish concentrated all her thoughts on survival.

She loosened and dug over soil on a small section near the Crogga River, upstream and away from the remains of the village and its tainted water and at a far enough distance so she wasn't continuously reminded of the massacre. She found and planted seeds and her vegetables flourished.

She ate crabs, mussels, cockles and any fish she managed to spear, and now and again she succeeded in snaring a rabbit.

Catat would eat anything Agneish put down in front of him, but for both of them it would be a difficult twelve months.

As the weeks progressed and the winter gales howled around the three hills, the blustery winds shrieked through the damaged roof, making the chapel bitterly cold. Without sufficient warmth Agneish's hands and feet were often raw and bleeding.

Then came the snow, just a light covering at first, then falls heavy enough to cause snow-drifts, making it impossible to forage for food.

She was able to melt the snow on the fire-ring so they always had fresh water and by adding a few hoarded, withered vegetables they were able to survive on a weak watery soup.

It was during this cold period that Agneish first noticed the crows.

Soft white flakes had been falling all day but unlike the past few weeks they weren't sticking to the ground. Finally the layers of snow began to thaw.

The burning of her village had left the area of Santon a desolate, lonely place, but Agneish did not seek companionship from farther afield. She discovered the only way to bear the hardship she faced each day was to become emotionally detached from her surroundings and live a solitary, active life. Almost every moment of her day was occupied with hard demanding work and the dark, friendless nights were dominated by planning the destruction of the Viking leader; but on this particular night Agneish was finding her lonely existence almost unbearable and had stepped outside the *keeill* with Catat, as always close to her heels.

Staring up at the January moon through the leafless branches of a tramman tree growing in the centre of the burial grounds, the hairs suddenly stood up on the back of her neck as she clearly saw silhouetted in the moonlight, three motionless crows resting on the topmost branches.

Then the air was filled with the sound of their beating wings as they soared skyward away from the *keeill*. From that moment Agneish felt less lonely; instinctively she knew the crows were the Morrigan trilogy, who had come to reassure her the gods had not abandoned her.

She did not see them again until march. In the Celtic calendar the March moon was known as the Moon of Winds and early one windy evening, as Agneish sat on the headland watching a grey seal bobbing up and down a little further out to sea, she saw three crows fly slowly across the bay then disappear behind the clouds; but long after they had become lost to sight their image was reflected on the surface of the water.

She sat there for a while longer, looking at the dull clouds moving across the vast expanse of the Irish Sea. Suddenly excitement and elation such as she had never known before surged through her body as she recognised fully for the first time there was only another six months to endure before the Norsemen would be persuaded by Arianrhod to leave Norway and travel to Mann.

With the help of the gods, she prayed they would be defeated.

Chapter Twenty One

Odin

In the hall of Valhalla, the spiritual home of Nordic warriors gloriously slain in battle, the greatest of all the Norse gods, Odin, waited for the return of his two ravens, Hugin, whose natural ability was thought and Munin, whose special aptitude was memory.

The ravens were sent out each day at dawn to gather information and would return at dusk to whisper to Odin everything they had learnt during the daylight hours. This was how Odin first heard about the mortal Agneish's plea for vengeance against Ulfr, a Norseman whose adventurous spirit had given him a frequent familiarity with danger and the boldness to deal with new, often hazardous ventures.

His ravens whispered how the Norseman was thoroughly experienced in battle, the co-owner of five *snekkes* and leader of one hundred and twenty five raiders. The type of man who could one day find his soul resting in Valhalla.

The ravens whispered on.

Odin heard how the mortal was protected by Agrona, Cathubodia and the Morrigan, war-goddesses for whom he had the greatest respect.

He heard how Cethlion and Arianrhod had also publicly endorsed their support and were now putting into play their reprisals against the Norsemen's slaughter of the mortal's family and the burning of her village.

He was informed about the protective role of the Watchers and how Aerten, the Goddess of Fate had given her life to support the young earthly being's relentless request for retribution.

Odin remained silent for a few moments at this disclosure; he and Aerten had been bitter enemies for so long it was difficult to imagine a world without her ferocious hatred.

Finally he was told about the high-ranking, powerful Celtic sea-god Manannan and his wife Fand's involvement with Agneish.

Stroking his bedraggled grey beard, Odin sat in his high-backed chair turning over in his mind the course of action he would take. He could not allow Celtic deities to put Norsemen to death; he must act quickly to remove any threat to their safety.

It was a challenge he could not resist.

Although he was the Principal Norse God of War, Odin was also a God of Wisdom and Magic and long, long ago he had sacrificed one of his eyes for the opportunity to drink from Mimir, the Fountain of Wisdom. It was an exchange he had never regretted.

Wearing an old, wide, shapeless hat and black cloak, Odin strode up and down in his Great Hall before eventually deciding to summon the spirit of a mystic. When she appeared, the pallor of her physical appearance confirmed she had been marked by death and no longer existed.

Odin, his one eye fixed inflexibly on the mystic, demanded to know Ulfr's future.

The mystic had no intention of answering Odin's question. In her previous life he had deeply offended her and she decided to settle an old score and refuse to answer his query; after all, what harm could he do to her now? With a coolness in her voice that enraged him, she taunted him with her refusal before disappearing from the hall.

Perched on his shoulder the two ravens remained silent until Odin made a decision and called for *Sleipnir*, his eight-legged grey stallion to be brought to him. Reminiscent of Manannan's horse Enbarr, *Sleipnir* could travel over land, sea and through the air.

He shouted for Thor, his eldest son, to follow him and bring *Mjollnir*, Thor's hammer which caused lightning to rip apart the sky.

Together, these two mighty Norse gods could surely protect five *snekkes* and their sailors from harm.

Chapter Twenty Two

Rafnir

Yawning sleepily as she heard the first notes of the morning chorus Agneish knew that as she slept she had experienced a deeply unsettling dream.

She had dreamt she had returned to the Path of Trepidation and was fleeing into the forest to avoid Cernunnos and the Wild Hunt when she saw, grazing quietly in a wooded clearing, a white hart, the mystical deer held sacred by the gods.

An eerie silence settled over the forest as the deer lifted its head and sniffed the cool morning air as it inhaled Agneish's faint scent before turning and staring curiously at her. His white coat was gleaming so brightly in the first rays of morning sunlight, Agneish felt there was something so unnervingly beautiful about him she felt close to tears.

Then her dream began fading quickly into an unreliable memory she could not quite recall, but not before she heard Govannin's voice warning her she must be strong. The sound of his voice comforted her.

Tidying her hair which was hanging in uncombed tangles about her face, she left the *keeill* with Catat padding quietly at her heels.

She wandered slowly past green, silent hills and walked unhurriedly through fields of long, yellow-green grass until she reached the promontory fort at Port Grenaugh.

The sky was blue and cloudless as she shaded her eyes and gazed far out to sea. The horizon was clear, unobstructed, for now, from a display of red sails and longships. However, during the hours of darkness, the constant beams of light through the Moon Gate had allowed Agneish to see how close the Norsemen were to the island.

She was sure they would come today!

Agneish sat on the seaward side of the fort looking down at the breaking waves and listened to the plaintive, melancholy calls of curlews; the shrill cries of black and white oyster catchers; and watched dozens of gannets plummeting into the rolling swell of the sea.

Having been lost for a while in her own thoughts, she suddenly realised the early morning sky had become extremely dark and flocks of sea-birds were flying inshore, surely a sign a storm was on its way.

Butterflies hovering over the coastal scrub darted away in another direction as she and Catat made their way carefully down the twisting path from the fort onto the beach.

Agneish looked up at the darkening sky with the certain foreknowledge that something momentous was about to happen in the next few hours. The entire previous twelve months had been leading up to this day, this one day when she would exact her revenge on the Norseman who had murdered her father.

She walked the length of the beach, oblivious to the fact she was kicking her way through layers of grey shale as she watched the incoming storm churning the waves over the rocky shoreline. A high tide accompanied by a high wind flowed into the mouth of the bay with tremendous force, leaving thick masses of kelp which had surged in with the tide wedged into rocks where the seaweed had been caught floating across the rise and fall of the sea.

There was no sound other than the crash of white-capped waves breaking onto the shore as Agneish beckoned Catat to follow her as she began to make her way back to the keeill.

....

The storm had subsided as Agneish, wearing a torn, bright green cloak salvaged from the ruins of a roundhouse, returned with Catat to the bay.

Keeping a constant watch for a glimpse of red sails, she paced restlessly up and down the shoreline when Catat's growl, rumbling deep and threatening made her spin round. Standing just a few feet away were Agrona and Cathubodia.

The war-goddesses laughed, evidently appreciating with some humour Catat's attempt at protecting Agneish.

Hobbling towards him Cathubodia held up her hand and murmured something in a language Agneish was unfamiliar with, but Catat seemed to grasp the inflections in her tone meant he had to be quiet. He sat down, his distress evident as his body trembled with fear, then he bounded to his feet, his footfalls muffled by the sand as he padded away.

He did not go too far, although, obviously, disturbed by the presence of the two goddesses, he remained close enough to Agneish to defend her if needed.

Agneish had almost forgotten how beautiful and intimidating Agrona was as the goddess reached out as she had done the first time they met, to touch her red-hair.

Agrona smiled, and as before a teardrop dripping with blood was visible at the corner of her eye.

After a brief moment Cathubodia spoke. 'An old friend of mine, a kitsune, informed me the Norse god Odin has sent for assistance to help him defeat Agrona and myself on this extraordinary night, which will be forever set apart from all others.'

She explained the kitsune, a fox-like creature with velvety, creamy golden fur and nine tails, had caught sight of Odin's ravens flying along an ancient route to the icy stronghold of Niflheim, the most northerly region of the Nine Nordic Worlds. It was an underworld of ice, fog, mists, darkness and unbearable cold and home of countless Frost Giants, moulded from the melting icy waters of this inhospitable world.

It took a kitsune a thousand years to grow all of its nine tails and once it had them it was endowed with magical special skills.

It gained the capability to see and hear anything happening in any of the known worlds, had infinite wisdom and could, at will, shape-shift into human form. It was also an absolute source of reliable information.

The kitsune had quickly sought out Cathubodia and told her what it had seen. Cathubodia had immediately closed her eyes and in a moment a third closed eye materialised then opened in the middle of her forehead.

This secret eye, nearly always hidden from others and known to only a few, was unique. It was the war-goddesses 'Eye of Knowledge.'

Cathubodia had concentrated all her energies into following Hugin and Munin with eyesight without equal. Her exceptional mind and extraordinary mental powers now worked together as one and she had been able to observe clear, powerful images as she followed the ravens far beyond the field of her usual vision.

The long freezing winters of Niflheim left a permanent snow cover which persistent winds constantly whipped up to create the illusion of continuous snowfall, but Cathubodia's concentration had never wavered as she engaged in watching the ravens fly over the icy slopes of glaciers carved and shaped from bitterly cold currents of air. But the ravens were not what she was looking for,….then she saw it, an exhalation of vapour! She caught her breath when in the distance she saw a Frost Giant descending from a huge glacier.

The ravens had been sent to find Rafnir, a dwarf who once had so displeased Odin he had transformed him into a Frost Giant and banished him to the snowy wilderness of the frozen north. As a further punishment he had given Rafnir breath that was hot steaming vapour, which meant the dwarf always had to be extremely wary he did not thaw part of his altered shape.

Cathubodia had stared at the gigantic figure of the transformed Rafnir who could now exhibit such extraordinary strength and power that even amongst the fearless Celtic warrior gods he was spoken about in hushed tones. Then she had gazed at the giant's glistening, icy-blue brittle slivers of hair, beard and eyebrows, all heavily covered in snow and at his long pointed fingers made from ice needles. His eyes were almost colourless except for a tinge of the glacial blue found on the surface of snow-capped mountains.

Wearing a white fur cloak, boots and leggings, the giant carried a long shaft with a spear-head made from a solid shard of ice.

There had been one heart-stopping moment when the giant having looked up and seen the ravens in flight, seemed to sense he was being watched. Halting, he stared hard at the bleak landscape around him before shrugging his shoulders and carrying on with his journey, the shrug creating a miniature snowstorm as he dislodged the mantle of snow covering his fur cloak.

Hugin and Munin had also seen the vapour and landed instantly on a frozen rime-frosted slope in front of Rafnir.

Rafnir remained silent as he listened to the ravens advising him of Odin's urgent demand that he travel immediately to the shores of Mann where the Norse god would be waiting.

The dwarf who had become a giant made from frost, felt intense hatred towards everyone. An emotion which had increased in intensity until the greatest desire he possessed was to inflict suffering and harm on others to such an extent that he aroused fear and unease amongst the Norse gods. Only Odin could control him and Rafnir knew Odin had made a demand he couldn't refuse.

The ravens went on to say, Odin would provide him with a horse for his journey to Mann.

The giant nodded and, instantly, a horse made entirely from ice appeared in front of him.

It was enormous and glazed with an icy film which glimmered in a rainbow of iridescent shades of light frosty blues and the palest of purples. Melting water droplets ran down its snow-covered face and its watery eyes held the faintest tint of silvery-white.

Cathubodia watched the giant leap effortlessly onto the back of the ice-horse which smoothly began to gallop at full speed through the numbing cold of the thick, freezing atmosphere above Niflheim.

Cathubodia's 'Eye of Knowledge' closed, then disappeared. She had seen enough.

…………………………………………………………………………

Cathubodia spoke again. 'You have nothing to fear Agneish, Agrona and myself are more than a match for Odin, indeed we are eagerly looking forward to the contest as outwitting him will be a source of great amusement to us both.'

Overhead, the raucous cries of three crows circling the beach made them look up. 'So it begins,' Agrona said with such an air of menace in her voice that Agneish felt a strong desire to flee.

'We must leave. The battle lines have been drawn and a contest of wits and superior abilities will continue long into the night.' As the loud harsh cries of the crows filled the air, the goddesses seemed to evaporate as if they had simply ceased to exist.

Agneish raced back to the headland, her gaze scanning the horizon, then her eyes narrowed as far out to sea she glimpsed the billowing sails of longships. *This* is what had disturbed the Morrigan!

Catat whimpered softly as he nuzzled her hand, seeking reassurance as he sensed her anger.

Patting his head, Agneish said. 'The longships are here Calat.' She was silent for a moment before whispering. 'The shadow of death hangs over us all this night. I have asked the gods to spare us.'

Chapter Twenty Three

The Fire-Spitter and the Glashtyn

As the longships drew ever closer to Mann there was still enough daylight for Ulfr to notice that its green hills were shrouded in a thick mist, almost as if the island had been completely covered with a hazy magical cloak. He smiled at the thought. It was just the kind of strange tale his wife liked to hear.

When he had returned to Norway, he and Geirr had taken many months to build and furnish a longhouse for Ragnhilda that had more than surpassed his own exacting requirements.

Ulfr knew he had a good head for business and when Ragnhilda's father saw the longhouse and heard Ulfr's plans for adding to his fleet of ships and of his desire to trade along distant remote coastlines, to buy and sell any commodity that would fetch a profit, he had given his consent to the wedding.

They had been wed barely a week when the dreams began, dreams filled with a seductive voice that had whispered to him night after night. The voice was low, beguiling and promised much. His rightful destiny!

He would have a kingdom to rule, wealth and good fortune if only he would return to the island of Mann.

After only a short period of time he found himself incapable of resisting the overpowering appeal of both the voice and its promises. The voice repeatedly urged Ulfr to leave Norway for Mann on the 20th of September and furthermore, in order to obtain that which had been pledged to him, he must arrive at the shores of Mann on the 31st of October when a Blood Moon would be waiting. Even though he was in a deep sleep, Ulfr flinched. With such a moon on the horizon the voyage could be singled out for a terrible fate.

But even forewarned about the boding evil of a pending Blood Moon, Ulfr and Geirr left for Mann on the 20th of September. He had been married for two months.

···

The setting sun, its glow dimmed by countless shadows of birds returning home to roost, had been quickly replaced by the light of a full Harvest Moon which just prior to their arrival at Mann had been masked with total darkness. As Agneish stood on the headland with Catat she saw the first *snekke* sail into sight, the wolf's head at its prow clearly visible as it rounded the cove at Port Grenaugh. When she saw the tall figure standing at the front of the ship, she felt a rush of intense fury as she recognised the man who had murdered her father.

When all five *snekkes* were lying at anchor outside the bay, the second full moon of the month appeared in the sky, a Blood Moon only a few short hours away from achieving complete fullness.

A tense silence had fallen upon the Norsemen at the appearance of this malevolent moon, many casting guarded glances at Ulfr and Geirr.

They had been persuaded by the brothers to make this voyage, even though they had been warned they would arrive at their journey's end when this ill-omened moon would be in the sky, through promises of enough prime land for each of them to farm and build his own longhouse.

A few veteran sailors had refused to accompany them, declaring it would be madness to attempt a voyage when a Blood Moon would surely be in attendance. *They all knew this particular moon was also known as the Hunter's Moon, as prey, human or animal, could easily be tracked under its exceptionally luminous light. If the conditions surrounding the voyage went beyond the sailors' control, the brightness of the Blood Moon could condemn those who sailed to be marked for certain death. A factor Cethlion and Arianrhod knew would contribute to the Norsemen's demise.*

The Blood Moon was now so red it seemed to blaze with fire and lay so low in the sky it seemed to the superstitious seamen it was sitting on top of the sea. At each side of the moon, a horse appeared to be standing, one white, one black.

As the moonlight gleamed upon the two horses, Agneish gasped with shock as she recognised Enbarr, then her jaw dropped when she realised the image cast on the surface of the water by the black horse was formed by the masquerade of darkness. It was Enbarr's inseparable companion. His shadow!

She looked past the five *snekkes* to a point beyond them where Agrona and Cathubodia seemed to have released every force of nature upon the Irish Sea.

The sky was filled with jagged lightning bolts which struck the water with such ferocity they created a gigantic swirl of white water. As the waves rose and fell with increasing acceleration, the circling spiral movement of water developed into a twisting vortex of encircling winds. All the ferocious, wild, destructive might of the universe seemed to have combined to meet at this exact moment, with explosive cracks of thunder, lightning strikes and spinning storms. But for the time being they did not alter direction towards the *snekkes*.

On sighting the tempest raging further out to sea Ulfr gave an loud uneasy laugh that offered little or no reassurance to the worried crew.

A crow flew close to and only slightly above the height of the ships. Its outspread wings and open curved beak did not strike fear into the Norsemen's hearts, after all it was only a solitary crow. What did make them afraid was the malignant look in its eyes. Improbably it seemed to be threatening them.

Two other crows joined the first, the three circling the longships over and over again. A wave of fear spread amongst the crew when the birds, illuminated by brilliant flashes of lightning, flew in a twisting path over the *snekkes*. With their deep-rooted superstitious beliefs, it appeared to the sailors the crows had summoned the flashes of light which snaked across the path of first one longship, then another.

Ulfr's stomach tensed as the crows' caws resounded through the air; then he felt an awareness of approaching disaster as he heard a dog howling at the Blood Moon.

Glancing up at the headland, Ulfr saw stepping out of the shadows, a young woman wearing a bright green cloak. Walking at her side was a large brown dog. Ulfr saw her long red hair caught by the wind and lifted high above her head. As the moonlight lit up Agneish's face which strongly resembled her mother's, a frown of almost puzzled recognition creased the Norseman's features.

Far off to Agneish's left, nine flickering lights began to blaze a trail through the night sky.

From her vantage point she saw a wide moving body of white mist creep stealthily over the sea towards the *snekkes*, a white veil which completely hid colossal deposits of ice being placed on its surface. The war-goddesses had decided to freeze the sea surrounding the longships.

The goddesses watched with amusement as the wildly churning waves teeming with enormous pieces of ice crashed into the sides of the ships. The freezing sea-water breaking over the longships quickly accumulated as rime on the open interior of the vessels, the added weight causing them to sit lower in the water, increasing the chances of flooding.

The Norsemen stared at the powerful bursts of white foam surging around their ships which, as it split and tore, revealed jagged pieces of floating ice beneath the waterline. Mesmerised they looked further out to sea where a huge solid wall of water had changed direction and turned towards them.

The atmosphere in the *snekkes* was charged with tension as the men looked to Ulfr and Geirr to secure them a safe passageway into the cove.

Ulfr knew of only one way, he must ask Thor to protect them.

Kneeling on the wooden boards of his ship and repeatedly turning in his fingers the small silver replica of Thor's hammer hanging around his neck, Ulfr implored Thor to help them. Moments later, when he saw an immense flash of lightning lighting up the sky and bursting into flame, he knew the Norse god had heard him.

....

As Rafnir drew closer to Mann the islanders looked up as they felt a vibration in the air which was bending even the strongest of their trees, as if under the force of the fiercest of winds. Then it stopped and the air became still as the Frost Giant hovered over the rock-strewn cliff tops of Port Grenaugh where Hugin and Munin were waiting to tell him of Odin's demands.

Odin and Thor had seen the Norsemen struggling with the ice accumulating on their ships and the ravens quickly relayed what Odin wanted him to do.

If successful, Odin would restore him to his former self.

This was all Ratnir needed to hear. Instantly he set off to do Odin's bidding.

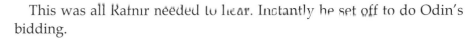

Several miles above the sea a massed group of clouds became suspended over the longships.

Cathubodia and Agrona had been expecting them.

For some time they had looked skyward waiting for the appearance of the Frost Giant, and when the dense grey clouds came into view they watched the thick bank of vapour grow thinner, patchier. Then a horse and rider emerged from an opening in its centre.

The heavy moisture from the clouds clinging to the body of the ice-horse made it glisten a watery, glittering white and so great was its size it elicited awe even from the war-goddesses.

As seagulls wheeled above the waves smashing against the ships, on the headland Agneish shook with fear as she saw the terrible vision of a giant horse and rider hovering menacingly in the air.

Agrona stared at the Frost Giant and decided what they must do.

'We must gather together spirits renowned for their evil disposition,' she said with a tinkling laugh.

'I know of one,' Cathubodia said immediately. 'We must sent for Caorthannach the fire-spitter, but who will fetch her?'

'The water horse,' Agrona replied instantly.

Caorthannach was a demon feared by the Celts as she was known as the mother of the devil and a prolific spitter of fire.

Agrona turned to face the shoreline, her gaze forcing the wind to push the raging waves higher and higher until, blown by the same wind, every white crest dissolved into foam. Breakers flowed over one another until, with a deep mournful sound, the foaming water became dozens of leaping shapes that seemed to be riding on the swell of the sea. The shapes separated then dispersed until only one was left, one that manifested into a grey horse. Agrona had invoked the *glashtyn*.

The colt waited by the waterline for the war-goddesses to come to him. Quickly Agrona whispered what she wanted him to do.

Agneish began to tremble when she saw the *glashtyn*. Every islander had heard of the water horse who haunted the rivers and streams and rejoiced in drowning anyone foolish enough to climb onto his back. She had been told he would gallop at full speed with his hapless victim clinging onto his mane before plunging into the deepest part of a nearby river where he would wait with malicious pleasure until his rider had drowned. She knew the *glashtyn* was the malevolent essence of a dead soul.

The colt listened to Agrona, then reared up once before turning and charging into the sea. In moments he returned, leaping out of the water with Caorthannach sitting astride his back. He had submerged far below the surface of the Irish Sea to the sweltering heat of Caorthannach's underwater cave. She was reluctant to leave at first until the *glashtyn* informed Caorthannach who had sent for her. The fire-spitter knew better than to disobey the war-goddesses' summons.

The goddesses stared at Caorthannach. Strangely the three had never met before. Her hair seemed to be formed from a multitude of various Crustacean claws and her skin was an intense deep-yellow. The fire-spitter's eyes remained downcast as she listened to the war-goddesses' request. When they had finished speaking she raised them and wide tongues of flame leapt from their centre.

She did not engage in a discussion with the goddesses, just nodded once, then kicked her heels into the sides of the *glashtyn* and horse and rider sped off to ride the wind.

Taking time to assess the danger to the Norsemen and noting how low the ships were now sitting in the water, Rafnir made a decision.

Jumping off his horse he landed upright on the high wall of water that was now very close to the longships. The tremors from his weight as he alighted caused a tidal wave in the open Irish Sea that lasted for three days.

The ice-horse remained in the air.

With his feet firmly planted on the water-wall which now substantially lower with the immensity of his size, Rafnir leaned over the longships and slowly exhaled his heated breath.

His hot breath scorched the exterior of the wooden ships, melting the thin coatings of ice. The terrified sailors gasped as they saw large chunks break off and float away, while pools of melted ice-crystals covering the surface of the sea vaporised and disappeared like smoke.

The *glashtyn* and fire spitter were now alongside Rafnir.

With one contemptuous look, Rafnir dismissed the stooped figure of Caorthannach as someone lacking importance. That scornful glance made her even more dangerous, if that was possible.

Illumined by the moon, three crows flew above the horizon where sea and sky met.

Caorthannach stretched out her right hand and one of the crows wheeled downwards and settled on her left shoulder. Then, from the fire-spitter's right eye, an arc of fire leapt towards the Frost Giant. The fiery curve of bright-red flames twisted and turned high in the night-sky before plummeting down and splitting into gold and orange arcs which quickly transformed into the rich glowing shades of a Fire Elemental.

Avidly watching the spectacle from the shoreline, Agrona said in a subdued voice to Cathubodia; 'The Fire Elemental was once a god who so displeased the Watchers, this was his penance for time without end. To be constantly devoured by a voracious, pitiless enemy. Fire!'

A scorching mass of gold and orange flames appeared over the top of Rafnir, flames from which emerged the face of the fire-spitter. She now had a colossal head with red eyes that burned with a brilliant light before they ignited and discharged a sulphur-yellow firestorm directly onto Rafnir's frozen body. Her open mouth spat hot glowing embers into the air which embedded themselves into the ice-horse.

The Frost Giant and ice-horse began to melt.

Caorthannach kept on spitting an avalanche of red blazing embers while her eyes began to emit a torrent of erupting sparks.

Rafnir's bellows of rage ricocheted through the heavens as he realised he was melting, bellows which rapidly grew fainter and fainter.

The fire-spitter smiled, then without a word to the war-goddesses ordered the *glashtyn* to carry her back to her underwater cave.

....

The dripping mists above the *snekkes* which had been the ice-horse and the melting blocks of ice which had been the Frost Giant deposited a hanging panel of water into the turbulent sea, sending the *snekkes* crashing against each other and then against the line of jagged rocks protruding above the surface of the rapidly rising sea outside Port Grenaugh Bay.

Riding on the back of the eight legged horse, *Sleipnir*, Odin and Thot had reached the headland and Odin, as shrewd as ever, despatched an ocean giant of enormous strength and size to stride along the high surges of waves to trample them back to their normal dimensions.

As Agneish stared at the five *snekkes* being tossed about on the rolling swell of the waves, she heard Catat whine softly, then fall silent, but she felt strong agonised shudders race through his body as he leant against her legs.

Striving to find a reason for his unease, Agneish listened intently for any unfamiliar sound but heard nothing but the rush of the waves and her own breathing.

Then every instinct she possessed alerted her. She *knew* someone was there!

Shivering with fright she turned around and saw the Severer of Souls.

The ghostly figure, an inseparable companion of the shades of the world, stood alongside Agneish on the soft grass of the headland. The macabre spectre of death in a hooded, floor-length, dark-grey robe which swirled around his skeletal bones, pushed back the hood which overshadowed his features, revealing his hollow-eyed, bloodless face. Terrified out of her wits, Agneish felt her heart was going to stop beating when she saw fragments of skin were clinging to the sunken cavities which had once been his eyes. Although they were now sightless, Agneish knew they saw everything.

Shocked and afraid Agneish and Catat ran away from the unearthly spirit that haunted the living.

The spectre gave a fleshless smile and, as she ran, Agneish heard him call out a name, but it was carried away on the wind.

Chapter Twenty Four

Idelonda

When she saw the fire-spitter leave, Agrona held her sword in front of her left eye and immediately one of Idelonda's large yellow eyes was mirrored in the blade. The blade began to bend as Agrona emitted a strange, sibilant whistling sound that only the wyvern could hear. Through the reflection in the broad flat surface of the weapon Idelonda saw Agrona beckoning to her and responded instantly to the goddess's call.

Giving the Severer of Souls time to leave the cliffs, Agneish and Catat had crept back to the headland, the one place which gave her an unparalleled vantage point over the sea and sky. Startled, she looked up when she heard a loud rushing movement overhead. It was the sound of Idelonda's wings as she flew through the blustery coastline skies.

The wyvern alighted on the shingled beach in Port Grenaugh cove where Agrona was waiting to embrace her.

Illumed by blue and silver flares discharging from Thor's hammer, Agneish gasped in shock when she saw the goddess hugging a winged, dragon-like creature with scales of burnished gold. She recognised it at once as the miniature image she had seen impressed on Agrona's shoulder in the Land of a Thousand Gods.

Idelonda was about fifteen feet long with a wing span approximately the length of its reptilian body and long tail. Each of the three curved talons on both of its legs gleamed with the rich metallic lustre of the same metal.

Over Idelonda's head Agrona placed a bridle of the softest leather to which was attached long lengths of golden chains that the goddess used to control the power and direction of the wyvern's flight. Then Agrona arranged a harness of gold chains that fitted and looped securely around Idelonda's body.

The wyvern knelt on the sand, a position that allowed Agrona to climb onto her back, then the pair soared far above the ground towards the promontory fort at Cronk ny Merriu.

As Idelonda flew over the craggy cliff tops, Agneish could clearly see her glittering golden wings, pointed ears, yellow eyes and nostrils that breathed fire. Sitting astride Idelonda's back Agrona looked down and raised her hand in acknowledgement of Agneish's presence.

Across from Agneish on the right side headland, Odin sat on the eight legged *Sleipnir*, holding his javelin, *Gungir*, firmly in his hand. Standing close to the edge of the cliffs, Thor stood next to him and was beside himself with fury when he saw Agrona turn the wyvern around and fly straight towards them.

Odin threw *Gungir* directly at Agrona.

It missed the war-goddess but she immediately knew what it was and who had thrown it. She also knew the lob of Odin's javelin had served to instigate a war and she smiled in anticipation of the approaching battles between herself, her Celtic sisters and the Norse gods before uttering a chilling laugh. The prospect of danger always stimulated her.

Idelonda turned her head in Agrona's direction. The sound of her laughter seemed to disturb her. Neither noticed nine flickering lights in the night sky becoming brighter as they drew nearer to Mann, but *Sleipnir* reared up when he saw them, alerting Odin and Thor that the contest would now accelerate rapidly. They needed to issue their challenge.

Armed with his sword, shield and hammer, in a frenzy of rage Thor released explosions of lightning from *Mjollnir* in a display of energy that arced and twisted high into the night sky.

Standing at the cliff edge Thor plunged his sword he called *Ragnarok*, which meant 'The end of all things,' deep into the ground and as his long, reddish-yellow hair flowed out behind him as it was grasped by the wind, his body became illuminated by a blue glow, the richness and intensity of the colour emblazoning his silhouette far across the skyline before vanishing into the night. Vivid hues of indigo, gold and purple began to stream across the heavens as he knelt behind *Ragnarok*, both arms leaning on its hilt. Vast, leaping flames of red and gold sprang from his sword setting alight the sky and leaving a continuous trail of colour straddling the stars.

As Idelonda soared over the steep cliffs, Agrona looked down and smiled when she saw a cadaver wearing a frayed dark cloak. He was standing on the beach outside a small crevice in the cliffside, out from which flew the large mass of bats who frequently accompanied him. Once in the open air they took wing to the left, veering sharply away from Odin and Thor.

She had recognised the cadaver as the Severer of Souls, who was also accepted by the gods as the Record Keeper of the Dead. He was the consigned scribe who entered in his everlasting book the names of those destined each day for the Otherworld. Hanging from a long chain around the skeleton's neck was a huge Celtic cross on which she had previously seen engraved. *'Eternal time is promised to those embraced by the Gods of Death.'*

Steering Idolanda to alight on the right headland, Agrona immediately dismounted, her eyes scanning every inch of the rugged terrain for a glimpse of the Norse gods. She had just seen Thor's hammer unleash rapid flares of violet rays and knew they were very near.

The moment Thor had seen Idolanda flying above him with Agrona on her back, he reached up the heavens to pull down to the earth a continuous stream of brilliant bursts of lightning.

As he sat astride *Sleipnir*, Odin heard the wyvern roar out a challenge and, always astute and at all times blessed with a shrewd judgement, he instantly sent for the kaimira.

It only took moments for it to materialise.

The kaimara was a huge, monstrous, truly demonic creature, its appearance part human, part massive bird of prey. In reality, it was a bizarre mutant with projecting fangs and sharp hooked talons.

Its head was human, hideous and covered in bushy, matted brown hair and the glint in its tiny, light-orange eyes displayed both cunning and cruelty. It was standing upright, its stance clearly revealing three, long blue talons on both of its feet and hissing continuously at the end of its long, thick feathered tail was a serpent's head.

The kaimira's human head had five, sharp needle-like spikes growing from its crown, perfect for impaling an enemy. Its body and legs had a dense layer of reddish-brown feathers and although it had two wings they were quite small in comparison to the size of its body, which meant the mutant could only fly a short distance.

As it listened to Idelonda's roars the kaimira's face distorted with rage. Swinging its head from side to side and constantly flicking its long, greenish tongue, it began to move stealthily towards the sound. The mutant was short-sighted, but with a favourable wind the fearsome predator could detect the smell of any living creature.

Sniffing the air, the kaimira detected Idelonda's odour and taking flight was able to land near the golden wyvern.

It rushed towards Idelonda, talons outstretched and long, feathered tail curving upwards over its body, its tail then drooping downwards to hang over its human head.

Hissing aggressively at the end of the tail, the serpent's head sought a site to deposit its deadly venom.

The lightning Thor had pulled to the ground lay there deceitfully inactive, while above, jagged lines of light shooting from cloud to cloud together with the radiance from the Harvest and Blood Moon lit up the whole sky.

The mutant attacked without restraint or pity, its sole aim to inflict pain and suffering, to wound and eventually kill.

Overhead, the thunder and crashing of Thor's storm lent a strange and eerie atmosphere to the pitched battle being fought by a wild barbaric beast and the courageous golden wyvern.

Then Thor activated the lightning lying on the ground!

Spectacular, powerful strobes of high intensity beams of light flashed towards Idelonda, beams which continually struck and weakened her.

The golden wyvern crumpled to the ground and as her strength diminished, struggled bravely to regain her balance. The physical effort this required brought her to the point of exhaustion as she laboured helplessly to move her legs and wings.

Lacking support from Cathubodia who still had not reappeared, Agrona was helpless to deflect the terrifying multitude of lightning discharges away from Idelonda.

Then three crows joined the war-goddess in defending the vulnerable wyvern, flying round and around the kaimira's head as they tried repeatedly to strike at its eyes.

Then Agneish saw two small wyverns, one red, one orange, flying through the thunder clouds generated by Thor. There was a single sharp crash of thunder as they landed near Idelonda and focused their attention on the kaimira. They surrounded the mutant, their open jaws discharging roaring, blistering fire as they snapped and bit at its legs.

Watching from the headland, Agneish had to briefly close her eyes. The dazzling colours in the night sky glinting from the reflective surfaces of the wyverns scales and the vividness of their fiery breath was too intense for her to bear.

Terrified, Catat whimpered almost soundlessly, hiding his face against her skirt as Agneish brushed a trembling hand over her eyes when she looked at the confrontation being played out near the edge of the opposite headland.

Deprived of strength and unable to help herself, Idelonda lay on the ground almost on the point of death when Agrona finally managed to repel countless lightning bolts heading straight for the wyvern. The war-goddess took a sharp intake of breath as she looked up and saw a snow-white bird flying overhead. It was the caladrius who was averting her eyes away from Idelonda. The bird was notorious throughout the Celtic world for refusing to look at anyone who was dying.

Agrona shook her head in anger. She would not let anything happen to her beloved pet.

The crows' beaks were now wet with blood as they pecked at the eyes of the kaimira as it twisted and turned, trying to flee from Ehecatl and Landon and the full strength of gale force winds.

Agrona had stolen the winds from the north, south, east and west then released them to blow at their maximum capacity across the clifftops, harrying the mutant until he was forced to run towards the sheer drop of the rock-face.

The quivering tongue in the serpent's head persistently tried to strike at the crows as the mutant, disorientated and in pain, uttered a shrill scream as it swayed unsteadily back and forth before falling into the high breaking waves at the bottom of the cliffs.

There was one swirl of white water and the kaimira disappeared.

Thunderbolts released from *Mjollnir* shook the ground as Odin sitting motionless on *Sleipnir* thought about his next strategy.

The wily old Norse god looked skywards and saw the flickering lights were now considerably nearer. He did not have much time!

The instant he realised this, Odin caught sight of a blue, luminous, ghostly fire leaping up and down on all of the five ship's masts, shedding enough light for Odin and the Norsemen to see gliding above them the mystical suzaku bird whose plumage was created entirely from the smouldering fires of a sleeping crater in the southern region of the Land of a Thousand Gods, a vicinity of fire and flames.

The bird soared high in the air and its feathers of orange, red, yellow and deepest crimson glowed so brightly Odin understood the war-goddesses were going to wage warfare with a bombardment of fire.

The suzaku bird soared higher and higher before plummeting downwards towards Ulfr's *snekke*.

Ulfr was a brutal, violent man, but he was at all times a brave one, except during the next few moments when he became filled with such a steady escalating sense of terror he was afraid to turn his head away from the intent gaze of the suzaku bird.

The bird vanished from the Norsemen's sight, leaving behind an image of itself shimmering in the darkness.

On the headland Odin saw the stooped figure of Cathubodia appear at the side of Idelonda and quickly bend over the exhausted wyvern. The war-goddess closed her eyes and the secret eye opened in her forehead.

Her penetrating vision moved rapidly along Idelonda's injured body, detecting views of her wildly beating heart and the deep wounds inflicted by Thor's lightning, the golden wyvern could be saved.

Long, long ago Cathubodia had been trained in the healing arts by using her extraordinary third eye as an instrument as sharp and incisive as the stroke of a dagger in cutting out impaired fleshy tissue and restoring damaged muscles and nerve endings to their original sound condition.

Once repaired, Idelonda's heart settled back into its normal rhythm and the golden wyvern was once more able to stand erect, making low contented sounds as she looked at the two goddesses crowding around to stroke her.

Several moments passed before Agrona and Cathubodia, standing a few feet apart, turned to face the clifftops. They were staring at the upright figure of Thor who was looking down into the crashing sea below.

Tendrils of green glinting smoke began to flow from Agrona's right hand, at the same time as tendrils of the same coloured smoke began to flow from Cathubodia's left and little by little the streamers of green aimed at Thor began to diminish his strength. As the multiple mists of green began to wrap themselves around him, tugging and pulling until he was brought to his knees, Thor wildly tried to cut through the smoke with *Ragnarok* but his efforts had no effect as the goddesses invoked their curse.

His body became insubstantial and began to waver and flicker, a sight that made Odin roar with fury. Grasping his javelin firmly in his hand Odin threw it into the heart of the smoke. Immediately Thor began to stabilise into a recognisable solid shape.

Dark shadows on the clifftops were now bathed in a vivid reddish glow as the moonlight revealed Ehecatl's and Landon's bodies flickering like slow burning fires, one red, one orange as they touched Idelonda gently with their out stretched wings. In moments the three wyverns were rising high into the clouds. Agrona watched them flying in between Thor's charges of silver and purple eruptions of lightning, when from the corner of her eye she saw something moving.

Sent by Odin, five cloaked, silent figures were striding towards the war-goddesses. An air of pervading menace emanating from the figures was unmistakable and their eyes which were devoid of pupils, shone with a sinister, colourless light.

In retaliation Cathubodia summoned a fire-worshipper to challenge them.

First came intense heat, then smoke, before a fire-worshipper emerged through an arc of crackling yellow flames. With one smooth, graceful movement he flowed over the ground like liquid gold before, in a single fluid motion, he assumed a definite form.

His hair, which twisted around his head in curling lengths of blazing flares, threatened to ignite his deep-crimson robe which glowed with dancing shadows reminiscent of firelight leaping against a wall.

With his hands clasped tightly in front of him he stood quietly in front of Odin's figures, staring at them with unblinking eyes. Then, suddenly, he moved forward and struck the figures with a light tap of his fingers and immediately a liquid began to ooze from behind his long, curved fingernails. The liquid ignited and in seconds this particular challenge from Odin was over as the figures were devoured by a choking orange inferno. In an instant they were reduced to ashes.

The fire-worshipper wore a veiled smile of satisfaction as he trickled their ashes through his fingers before re-entering the bright-yellow crackling flames.

Cathubodia and Agrona smiled at each other. So far they were keeping a step ahead of Odin and Thor.

Chapter Twenty Five

The Sea-Serpent

The Norsemen had fallen into a shocked silence after witnessing the wounded kaimira plummeting into the churning sea, then they were further shocked by the tense shouts of a sailor as he pointed towards the presence of three tall shapes wearing black feathered cloaks standing on the surface of the water.

Agneish's heartbeat was erratic and her breathing ragged as she stared down at the three cloaked figures, then she screamed in absolute terror as a gigantic wolfhound galloped soundlessly past her. The hound had a single massive head which bore two identical faces. It was being ridden by the Record Keeper of the Dead.

At first the dark outlines of the shapes silhouetted in the bright moonlight remained motionless, then they began to drift slowly towards the *snekkes*.

The Vikings were courageous men but each one uttered a low moan of fear as the shapes beckoned to Ulfr.

Ulfr's face drained of colour when he saw, rising to the top of the water, a gigantic tablet, the brilliant light from a shooting star illuminating the open leaves of wooden pages bearing the names of Norsemen who would die that night. He caught his breath in horror when one of the silhouettes whispered, 'Can you hear that sound Norseman? It is reverberations ringing through the air as the Record Keeper of the Dead rides towards you.'

Cries of terror from the men on Geirr's *snekke* alerted Ulfr to the sudden appearance of a collection of misshapen skulls covering the deck of his brother's ship. Overwhelmed with fear, the terror-stricken sailors began to tremble as they watched the skulls regain soft oozing flesh, then in utter disbelief they recognised their own faces. Then Geirr heard a sharp prolonged sound which seemed like an exclamation of derision arising from the water.

Gazing down he saw something reflected just below its shadowy surface which filled him with dread. It was a face, but a face like no other he had seen before. It was enormous, grotesque and he knew it had to be a primeval sea-creature.

Its skin glowed a pale-green and protruding over its lower lip were two, long, razor-sharp teeth.

Suddenly Geirr recalled a story about a reclusive sea-monster, half man, half serpent who shunned the light of day and lived in the murky subterranean regions of the sea. He had also heard the monster had a disquieting reputation for being unpredictable and unrelentingly ferocious. Then very quickly the creature came up from underneath the *snekke* and as it rose out of the sea the stench of rotting fish from its breath was overpowering.

Speechless, Geirr and his crew stared at the sea-monster's long black hair covered with masses of thick green algae and trailing seaweed. They stared at its silvery-green eyes, pointed ears and forked tongue flicking in and out of its mouth.

It rose higher out of the water until its head reached the top of the *snekke's* mast and the Norsemen realised that while its bulky body above the waist was human with two colossal arms, below its waist was a long, scaled, serpentine tail.

At the same moment that Odin realised Manannan must have summoned the sea-monster from its home in the vast depths of the sea, the creature, with a savage hiss, coiled its tail around Geirr and pulled him into the choppy waters.

The Norsemen were rooted to the deck of the ship as the creature seemed to drag Geirr with almost deliberate slowness along the swell of salt water before tugging him below the waves.

Two things occurred when the monster submerged.

The sea-serpent had created in its wake a huge whirlpool which sucked Geirr's *snekke* and the frantically shouting seamen below the surface level of the sea, causing a tidal wave that broke over the hull of the four remaining ships and flooding them with water The *snekkes* pitched and swirled on top of the gigantic swell as Ulfr stared in stunned disbelief at the stretch of sea where his brother and ship had disappeared. Lifting his head and gazing at the heavens, he searched for any sign his gods were with him.

Then Ulfr felt the *snekkes* shudder as Thor first donned his magical belt of strength then threw *Mjollnir* at the enormous wave, his hammer dispersing it instantly into a small trickle.

His gods *were* with him!

A Celtic sea-goddess holding an enormous fishing net reared up in front of Ulfr's *snekke* causing Ulfr to shout in a combination of pain and misery when he saw the net held the drowned body of his brother.

With eyes completely lacking emotion, the sea-goddess smiled at him before sinking beneath the cold darkness of the sea with her prize.

As he looked at the Kingdom of Mann, now so near, that had been promised to him in the midst of his disturbing dreams, Ulfr shook his head wildly from side to side, trying to block out the whispers that had resounded through his thoughts when he was tired and his mind heavy with sleep. Whispers that had promised him the island now within his sight, but instead had brought about the death of his brother.

As he stared at the island, an army of Water Elementals became visible and he realised they were guarding Port Grenaugh's shoreline. Watching their massive heads with mouths spewing foam as they rose and fell with the waves pouring over rocks lying on the periphery of the cove, left him with a strange foreboding that on this day he would cease to exist.

Chapter Twenty Six

The Valkyries

Hearing the terrified cries for help from the sailors as they were swept overboard from the decks of Geirr's *snekke*, Agneish could not feel pity for them.

Their remorseless brutality to her family and people from her village, their atrocities and the blood they had shed, left her entirely indifferent to their sufferings.

A blaze of light followed by a single sharp crash of thunder made her look towards the sky where she saw the gigantic figure of a man with eyes that flashed lightning, throwing an enormous hammer through the air. A succession of flashes of intense brilliance burst in a continuous stream from the hammer which lit up the clouds massed around him with an eerily beautiful tapestry of deep purples, blues and silver.

The exquisite beauty of the lights in the clouds made a powerful impact on Agneish's senses. She was to remember them all her life.

As Thor glared down at the expanse of water where Geirr's longship had sank, his attention was drawn to nine lights glinting against the dark background of the sky. The Norse god knew it was the Valkyries arriving to pick up the dead.

Then Agneish saw Fand. The Irish sea-goddess was sitting astride Enbarr who was hovering just above the seas swirling around the *snekkes*. Manannan's wife bent forward and whispered in Enbarr's ear.

Ulfr became aware of Fand just moments before the haunting call of curlews alerted him to the sight of a horse galloping across the night sky. To his disbelief it seemed to be holding something in its mouth and, incredible as it seemed, the horse appeared to be made from shadows. Behind him he heard the frightened low voices of his crew as they pointed to 'the horse made from the night.'

Enbarr's dark image had been brought to life by Fand.

The shadow horse reached the headland and stepped lightly onto the rocky cliff peppered with clumps of tall sea-grass. The glow of the Hunter's Moon shining through Arianrhod's palette of coloured lights allowed Ulfr to see the woman in the green cloak reach out towards the phantom image. The horse lowered its head and a second later she was holding aloft a heavy sword.

On the verge of leaving, the shadow horse paused for a moment. In a split second it made a decision and began to dance on the lightning strobes flashing in the sky. His movements extinguishing a chain of intense displays of white jagged light hurled by Thor.

Agneish's eyes held a look of panic as she realised the possible close proximity of Manannan, a deity powerful enough to influence events throughout the remainder of the confrontation between the Norse and Celtic gods.

The expression of fear on her face became more and more noticeable as she waited for a sign from Manannan to command the lightning exploding across the heavens to strike Freggyragh. Instinctively, she knew this would happen.

Agneish lowered the sword. Her hands were now shaking so badly she could hardly hold it above her head.

Wind-tossed seas smashed against steep cliffs as the tempest raised by the Norse and Celtic deities raged across the heavens until Agneish found the courage to call out Manannan's name as again she raised his sword.

Manannan had been listening for her cry for help and immediately threw a bolt of lightning in the shape of an arrow. The arrow struck its target, Freggyragh, and as the discharge of energy from the arrow travelled safely down the length of its hilt without harming Agneish, she knew the Protector of Mann would keep her safe from harm.

The sword's ornate hilt was decorated with the most powerful of sun symbols, the triskele, and, as on Govannin's torque, the three legs of the triskele were united at the thigh. But this time, instead of a face at its centre, the middle of the triskele was emblazoned with the Three Legs of Mann in the most potent of colours, gold, a colour reputed to provide both protection and courage and to ward off sorcerers capable of harmful intent.

As hundreds of lightning flashes unleashed from Freggyragh tore through one storm cloud after another, Agneish heard mocking peals of laughter that sent shivers down her spine. She knew it was the war-goddesses declaring their contempt for Odin and Thor.

It was time to exact her revenge.

Catat, his ears pricked and his body tense with fear, uttered a low growl of protest as Agneish commanded him to 'stay'.

Reluctantly he obeyed as she walked away from him and stood at the edge of the headland.

As the coloured fires from Arianrhod's palette lingered across her face, again Agneish held Manannan's sword above her head, holding it firmly until the blade was charged with the energy from a lightning bolt set free by Agrona.

Instantly Fregyragh was spun out of her hand and sent whirling towards Ulfr's *snekke*, then, unbelievably, Agneish saw a mass lacking a specific shape rise up from the pitch-blackness of the sea. It was the lost ones, spectres of drowned Norse sailors sent by Odin to form a chain from the edge of the shore to Ulfr's *snekke*, holding out grasping hands to snatch Manannan's sword before it reached his longship. But the sword had already sped past them.

Holding Freggyragh, Agrona appeared at Ulfr's side. The three crows that the sailors had seen circling the ships earlier, joined her. One sat silently on her shoulder, another on her wrist. The third emitted long, hoarse raucous caws.

The war-goddess smiled at Ulfr, a strange smile that made him tremble with fear as she stroked the glistening black feathers of the crow resting on her wrist. Agrona bent towards the crow and softly gave the command. 'Now!'

Immediately the crow changed into an old hag with an air of malevolent intent. It had become the savage war loving goddess, Macha!

Quickly Odin hurled his javelin in Ulfr's direction aiming for his heart. His intention was to kill the Norseman before Macha did, but he was too late. Macha was already holding up Ulfr's dripping head.

Standing on the headland, Agneish's nerves were so on edge she was unable for a moment to understand what she was seeing, then in utter triumph she screamed out her father's name.

The flickering lights were now directly over the four remaining *snekkes* as the spectres of the Norse sailors silently withdrew back into the murky darkness from where they had emerged.

When Macha cut off Ulfr's head, Cathubodia had been standing alongside the Severer of Souls who was busily entering the names in his Book of Many pages of those destined this night for the Otherworld. She decided it was the moment to play out the final stages of this conflict.

Closing her eyes she allowed her third eye to open and turned her gaze to the howling, violent tempest she and Agrona had created further out to sea. Its menacing strength waiting like a sleeping giant to be activated by the war-goddesses.

Through the power of her mind she used the force of the winds to drive numerous spinning storms towards the longships. The wind-driven waves accompanied by a ferocious thunderstorm surged towards the bow of the ships, the waves now many feet above normal sea level.

In moments the air was filled with terrified screams as ghostly apparitions of Santon's dead villagers surrounded the Norsemen as they were swept overboard into the swollen waves.

As Cathubodia observed the longships spin round and around in the fierce winds, she watched, with a complete lack of interest, the Norsemen's possessions swirl along the surface of the water before they, the Norsemen and the four longships sank beneath the sea.

....

Odin saw the nine flickering lights flashing in the night-sky were now hovering over the expanse of water where the Norsemen had disappeared, the surface of the sea now flat and still as if the storm had never taken place.

The brilliance of Arianrhod's incandescent colours revealed the lights were the sparkling armour of nine helmeted Valkyries riding their winged horses. These beautiful blonde, blue-eyed Nordic female warriors armed with spears had been commanded by Odin to ride a particular path through the skies which led directly to Mann. Their task, to gather dead Norsemen from the sea.

Cawing their raucous cries, the three crows flew amongst Odin's female deities, allowing the Valkyries to display their superb riding skills as the birds constant high-pitched caws unsettled their horses. Then the crows swooped downwards, circling beneath the riders as the Valkyries were joined by Odin on the eight legged *Sleipnir*.

As they bent over the side of their horses to gather the drowned sailors, Thor's thunder rampaged across the heavens as a tribute to the winged, riderless black stallion moving soundlessly through the air towards them. The stallion would wait until the Valkyries selected a rider for him, then they would both lead the procession of the dead to Niflheim. As none of the dead sailors had fallen in battle, Odin could not permit them to join him in his Great Hall of Valhalla which had been created to receive and honour the souls of warriors killed in combat.

The souls of the crew of the longships would have to join the others spending eternity in the 'House of Mists', the cold, dark underworld of Niflheim.

Agneish, hesitantly followed by Catat, ran down the path leading from the headland to Port Grenaugh beach. Ordering Catat to lie down, she waded into the sea to watch Odin's female soldiers collecting the corpses. After the Valkyries had completed their grim task they rode slowly through the night sky towards Niflheim and Agneish was stunned to see the sky light up with hundreds of stars. A mark of respect from Odin for the untimely death of so many Nordic men.

The four deserted *snekkes* had risen from the sea and were riding close to the shore. The one nearest to the beach had its anchor wedged in the sand. It belonged to the longship with the carved figurehead of a wolf.

The last blazing arc of lightning fired by Thor's hammer illuminated Agneish as she stared at Ulfr's empty *snekke*. Behind her on the shoreline Enbarr galloped past with Fand on his back without leaving a trace of hoof prints in the wet sand.

Agneish would never see either of them again.

Chapter Twenty Seven

The Conclusion

Odin and Thor strode impatiently up and down the clifftops, mindful of the fact that one of the Celtic goddesses would come to them, to pronounce the dispute for the lives of the crew of the five *snekkes* had been resolved in the Celtic deities favour.

Odin was wise enough to know that as well as being gracious in defeat, he must keep his hot-tempered son under control.

They heard the sound of beating wings, then the golden wyvern loomed over the headland. In moments she landed smoothly with Agrona seated on her back.

The war-goddess slowly dismounted and the Norse deities saw she was carrying Ulfr's head.

She placed the head on the ground in front of Odin and the wily old god remained silent as Agrona looked fiercely at Thor and, with a voice dripping with venom, warned him they would cross swords again very soon for his part in the near death of her beloved Idelonda.

The two deities, not totally dissimilar in nature, locked glances.

Seeing his son's face become distorted with fury, Odin well practised in the art of deceit, gave a sly laugh and assured Agrona, that as these particular Norsemen's lives held no significance for him, there would not be any repercussions from either himself or his son for their deaths.

Agrona did not believe him, but, for now, the contest had been brought to an end.

Without another word she mounted Idelonda and the golden wyvern soared high into the clouds leaving Thor to vent his rage upon his father.

As Agneish left the water and returned to the beach, the deep-purple night sky was still crowded with the stars Odin had summoned earlier. She turned and looked cautiously behind her as a slight breeze flapped the sails of the deserted longships.

As Catat bounded towards her she heard the soft rustle of fabrics gliding smoothly along the pebbles. Catat halted in his tracks, his ears down, tail tucked between his legs as he recognised Agrona and Cathubodia.

Pushing back the hood of her scarlet cloak Agrona smiled warmly at Agneish. Cathubodia, her long white hair this time unconfined by a hair net, held out a partially closed hand. In it she held a ring formed in the shape of a golden wyvern holding between its wings a smooth, perfectly spherical, glistening silver pearl.

'Take this ring Agneish and if ever there are joyless, dark times which make you doubt you journeyed to our land and these last few hours ever happened, gaze reflectively at the pearl,' she instructed.

Agneish gently stroked the pearl's silky surface with an overwhelming feeling of wonderment and delight. She said quietly, 'It will be as if I am wearing the moon on my finger.'

'Both Cathubodia and myself are particularly gratified with your observation, as we deities believe pearls are formed from moonlight,' Agrona responded, 'but now it is time for us to return home. You demanded vengeance for the Norseman's monstrous crimes and retribution has been granted to you; as from this moment he walks among the dead,' adding, 'when we leave, Agneish, we must ask you not to look at us, just kneel and wait.'

The goddesses and the mortal gazed intently at each other. For a brief span of time their two very different worlds had merged together and neither had been found wanting.

'Kneel,' Agrona repeated, the tone of her voice sounding almost affectionate.

Agneish knelt in the sand, her head lowered as she waited for something momentous to happen.

The winds had calmed and there was a stillness, an absence of sound as Agneish experienced a gradual sense of freedom.

After a momentary interval of time she was bathed in three separate circles of glowing, brilliant light radiating from the three legs of the triskele on Manannan's sword.

Reverberating around the headlands she heard three softly spoken words. 'Be at peace.'

Epilogue

Agneish, her long red hair now faded and grey and her body bent and frail, stood on Port Grenaugh beach and, as always, the smell of salt air, the splashing sound of waves crashing over nearby rocks and simply just being able to quietly gaze at the ebb and flow of the sea brought her a sense of contentment.

Shading her eyes with her hand she turned around to look behind her at the sun setting on the other side of Santon's hills, watching its splendour slowly descend until there was barely a thin fragment of its golden-red rays visible. As the sun slipped below the skyline, in front of her only the total blackness of the Irish Sea remained.

She sat down and leaning back against a rock, fell into a troubled sleep.

For the first time in many years Agneish's dreams were of Cernunnos. Since his banishment other deities had caught only a fleeting glimpse of this most ancient of gods as he rested in the bleak shadows of his separate world. In her dream she saw his sinister figure turn slowly round to look intently at her, then with a sidelong glance full of malicious intent he beckoned her to draw closer.

Abruptly waking up she realised she must have been asleep for a long time as the sky was flaunting a full Hunter's Moon.

Unexpectantly she recalled a memory from long ago and moments later she held a shaking hand over her mouth as she saw the dark silhouettes of five longships rounding the bay, the leading ship bearing the figurehead of a wolf.

Except for the soft sigh of a gentle breeze everything was silent as the ghost ships drifted slowly past, but within the whisper of the breeze she heard music. Agneish knew instantly it was Taliesin.

He was sitting on a large boulder staring out to sea at the *snekkes* when Agneish heard the evocative, haunting notes of his voice ring through the air. The clear, rich tones arousing a sense of sadness as they immediately made her remember Govannin.

Taliesin plucked at his lyre, the soft, rippling music conveying a bewitching symphony of the sea as he invoked the sound of wind and water in flawless harmony. His music suggested the cries of seabirds, the direction of a light wind, waves breaking on the shore and the splash of gently lapping water, all of which she found profoundly moving.

Then suddenly the music changed, became wild, harsh, lacking harmony and the discordant notes became a confused mingling of reverberations that agitated the sea. Then chillingly the heavy swell of the waves carried along with them a loud, unnerving clamour. It was the screams of drowning Norsemen pleading for help.

She stopped thinking about the screams as Taliesin turned towards her and smiled.

He said softly, 'It seems but a fleeting moment since we were both fellow travellers on the footpath which decreed our fate. I wrote a sonnet about you Agneish and sang it throughout the length and breadth of my land. The gods requested to hear it again and again in celebration of the favourable outcome of our hazardous experiences.'

For a few moments she was young again as she remembered the epic journey across the Land of a Thousand Gods.

A bank of clouds cast their shadow across the moon. The Prince of Song stood up, smiled gently at her, then disappeared through the clouds.

Agneish began to feel exceptionally tired, then, startled, she stared up to the heavens as the gods released the brilliant radiance from a thousand stars into the night sky.

As her eyes closed, the last sounds Agneish would ever hear was the gentle murmur of the Irish Sea and the call of curlews. A smile lit her face as she thought she felt Catat's wet nose nuzzling into her hand.

Glossary

Manannan-beg-mac-y-Lleir, the Guardian of Mann

Fand, Manannan's wife. The fairy Irish sea-goddess known as the Pearl of Beauty

Enbarr, Manannan's mystical horse

benaaishnee, a female fortune teller

cailleach groarnagh, the old woman of spells

chibbyr, Manx holy well

glashtyn, malevolent Manx water horse

keeill, Manx chapel

seanachadh, a teller of tales

wyvern, mythological creature similar to a dragon, but smaller

Odin, the greatest of all the Norse gods and principal god of war

Thor, Odin's son and Norse god of thunder and sea-farers

Mjollnir, Thor's magical hammer

Sleipnir, Odin's eight-legged horse

Ragnarok, Thor's magical sword

snekkes, Norse war-ships

thralls, Norse word for slaves